DEVIL'S BREAD

A DCI REECE THRILLER

LIAM HANSON

CP

Published by CRIME PRINTS

An Imprint of Liam Hanson Media

ISBN-13 : 979-8398304817

For Faye, Connor, and Alyx

Current books in the series:

————————————————————

DEVIL'S BREAD

Chapter 1

SNOWDONIA, NORTH WALES

MALI INGRAM SPRINKLED A pinch of dried tobacco flakes on a wafer-thin cigarette paper like she was adding salt to a plate of chips. Not yet satisfied, she added a few more and slung her legs under the table of the picnic bench, enjoying the warmth of the afternoon sunshine on her face and bare arms.

She wasn't trying to tan, and knew from twenty-something years of experience that any attempts to do so were completely futile. From pasty white; to bright red; then itch and peel; and back to white again, was how it went most summers.

'You'll have heard management put me on another poor conduct warning?' she said, wetting the edge of the paper with the tip of her tongue. She folded it over and rolled out a new smoke with the expertise of someone well practised in the art. 'They're singling me out for some rough treatment to keep the rest of you quiet.'

'And why would they do that?' Rhydian asked. 'What reason is there?'

'Because I don't take any of their shit and they don't like people who stick up for themselves.'

'Maybe you *should* take their shit from time to time. Play the game—that's all it is—just a game. Then you might stay out of trouble for a while.'

She caught his eye and held it for an uncomfortably long time. 'Or maybe I shouldn't. Definitely, I shouldn't. And neither should any of you, for that matter.'

He looked away, having heard it all before. 'It's your call, I guess.'

'You're bloody right, it is. Someone has to stick up for the little guys in life.'

'And that someone always has to be you, does it?'

'Look – all I'm saying is: you don't have to let their sort walk all over you just because they think they've got the power to.'

Rhydian pulled the ring on a can of Coke. 'You do when they pay your wages. That's exactly the type of power I take notice of.'

There was a small green tin on the table between them; its lid removed and a half-dozen completed cigarettes lined up and waiting to be smoked. Wedged between Mali's knees was an open pouch of tobacco that looked like it might spill with every jerky movement she made. 'They can kiss my arse before I bow down and kiss theirs.'

Rhydian gulped a good mouthful of the Coke and stifled a burp behind a clenched fist. 'Excuse me,' he said with a shudder that involved most of his upper body. 'Suit yourself.'

Mali bent under the table to scratch her shin. Rhydian was still staring at her when she reappeared. 'What now?'

'How have you been since ...?' his voice trailed off and he lowered his head. 'Since you know ...'

'Jesus, you're not still going on about that, are you? I told you at the time, it was nothing. *Nothing* – do you hear me?'

'It could have been serious. You were this close to having a major accident,' he said, measuring the distance between a finger and thumb.

'We've been through this already. The wind blew grit in my eyes. I couldn't see what I was doing, so I took a moment to settle myself again. Everything was perfect after that.'

'Only because there was a second instructor up there with you. If he hadn't taken over at that moment, then who knows what might have happened?'

Mali put the cigarette tin away in her rucksack and tightened its toggle like she was throttling the life out of someone. 'You know that's bullshit.' Opposite and across the lawn was the mirrored glass of the climbing centre's reception area. She couldn't tell if anyone was watching from the other side of it, but suspected they might have been. 'Did that lot put you up to this?'

'The concerns are all mine,' Rhydian said, tapping his chest. 'I'd never be able to live with myself if something happened up there and

I'd done nothing to prevent it when I had the chance.' He finished the rest of his Coke and tossed the empty can into a nearby bin, sending a scouting party of wasps into a frenzy. 'I haven't told them what happened.'

'But you're going to? I can tell by the tone of your voice.'

'That depends on what your GP has to say?' He groaned when she didn't answer. 'You haven't been to see one, have you?'

'I don't need a doctor every time I get something in my eye.'

'You do when I tell you to go see one.'

'Pulling rank on me now. Is that what you're doing?' She gave the mirrored glass another look of defiance. 'Shifting sides and readying yourself for the next management opportunity that comes along?'

Rhydian stared into the distance and barely shook his head. 'Go see your doctor. If only to keep me happy.'

'All right. All right. I'll ring them first thing in the morning.' Mali reached for his hand and winked. 'Happy now you've bullied me into it?'

'I'll be a damn sight happier once you've been and we know what's what.'

'You realise it's easier to get an audience with the dead? It'll be weeks before I'm given an appointment.' She searched each of her pockets in turn. Then rummaged through the contents of the rucksack. 'Where's my lighter? I had it with me a minute ago.'

'Why would I have it? I don't smoke.'

'I didn't ask if you had it. *"Have you seen it?"* is what I said.'

Rhydian pointed to a yellowed patch of grass next to the winding gravel path, and only a short distance from where the wasps were still flying noisy circuits of the open-topped bin. 'There it is.'

Mali got up to fetch it and returned to her seat, venting lungfuls of smoke through a pierced nose. When she tried to speak, Rhydian cut her off almost immediately.

'You keep staring at those people over there?' He twisted the upper half of his body to show who he meant. 'Any reason why?'

Mali lowered her voice. 'That's Bridget Payne—Member of the Senedd in Cardiff.'

Rhydian took another look. 'I wouldn't have recognised her without the clothes and makeup.'

'Neither did I before I read her name on the booking forms.'

'I'm sensing from the tone of your voice that you don't think much of her?'

'I've only just met the woman,' Mali said, taking a long drag on what little was left of the cigarette. She turned her head away and exhaled downwind. 'But I'll tell you this much: she and that bearded guy are up to a heap of no good, and the poor husband has no clue what's going on.'

Chapter 2

CARDIFF, THREE YEARS LATER

Bridget Payne heard the rattle of the letterbox from where she was at the kitchen table. It couldn't be mail. Not on a Sunday morning. A flyer for a local business, perhaps. Or a charity bag for the collection of unwanted clothing. It would go straight in the bin, whatever it was. She couldn't abide such things. Curious, she tightened the tie of her silk dressing gown and went to see for herself.

There was a single white envelope lying on the mat. It carried the postmark of the Wrexham sorting office in North Wales. When she opened the front door, all she saw was the back of a courier driver climbing into his van on the other side of the tall, wrought-iron gates.

A special delivery.

On a Sunday.

Intriguing.

She ran a painted thumbnail along the flimsy seal and raised the torn flap. With the open letter in her hand, she returned to the kitchen, reading the typed threat in full:

> ***You killed your husband and blamed it on me.***
> ***I'm coming to tell the world what you did.***
> ***Your career is over.***
> ***Sleep tight, Bridget, while you still can.***

Payne lowered herself onto a chair, deep in thought.

At first, she was shocked.

Then she was angry.

Next, she made a call, using a phone that was in no way connected to her or any of her businesses.

Chapter 3

DCI Brân Reece was enjoying his Sunday off. As lead detective for the Regional Murder Squad in a big city, down time came along infrequently. Ahead of him was a tough week. Emotionally, even if nothing more taxing cropped up at work.

The coming weekend represented the second anniversary of his wife's death. Anwen had been stabbed and killed in a bag-snatch gone horribly wrong while the couple were on their honeymoon in Rome.

Reece blamed himself for what had happened to her. For not being at her side when the thieving scooter riders had taken her life.

He'd scattered her ashes—and at a later date, those of her father, Idris—on the summit of nearby Pen y Fan, in the Brecon Beacons

National Park. It was a suitable homage to their love of the mountains and surrounding area.

Reece made the pilgrimage to the summit many times a year. In all weathers and states of health. Mostly alone. Sometimes in the company of his loyal best friend Yanto. But anniversaries of such terrible events were always more difficult to get through. They forced the survivor to relive the awful moment, second by second, frame by frame.

For Reece, it was no different.

He'd spent two years trying to erase the sights and sounds of it from his memory. Two years of beating himself up for allowing it to happen in the first place. His love for Anwen had known no bounds, and there wasn't a day that passed when he didn't sit alone with his memories of better times.

Sunday morning began like most days of the week. He rose with a five o'clock alarm after snatching no more than three or four hours sleep from the greedy clutches of the Sandman.

Redlar was busy dreaming between his feet, his head draped across his master's left shin. There was plenty of twitching and whimpering going on as he no doubt chased birds across open fields. Given where they lived, he hadn't yet set eyes on a cat. He still had that to look forward to.

How Reece envied him the trouble-free innocence of youth. The detective's own dreams were usually filled with endless dark shadows and faceless demons. Or images of Anwen, down on her knees and clutching her abdomen in a puddle of expanding blood while screaming his name.

The Huntaway puppy came alive in an instant and followed him over to the window, pressing itself against his legs, reminding him it was there to be fussed and loved.

It was wet outside. Heavy orbs of rain clung to the window before succumbing to the ever-present laws of physics. Mist hung on the mountains like it always did at that time of year. It wouldn't be many more weeks before a dusting of snow joined it.

They made a brief pit stop in the bathroom, Redlar watching him the whole time. 'I suppose I watch you do your business,' Reece said with a chuckle. 'It's only fair you do the same, I guess.'

Redlar agreed with a series of loud barks.

'Boy, you're getting big.' The dog had more than trebled in size since he'd found him abandoned at the side of the road in Llandaff, but hadn't yet fully grown into its paws. Yanto teased he had a horse in disguise and Reece was beginning to think that might be true.

They went downstairs, Reece dressed in several layers of top-end outdoor clothing. Only fools dared to taunt the Beacons during the savage colder months, and usually just the once. He'd been born and bred there. Knew never to underestimate it, no matter how beautifully it presented itself.

He went through a short routine of stretches in the living room, Redlar bouncing around and pawing at him the whole time. 'You're not making this easy for me,' he said, giving up on it as he did most days.

The chill morning air bit like a frightened snake when he stepped into it. A minor inconvenience for an activity that would set him up nicely for whatever challenges the day had in store. He was at one with nature. Running with the whispers of the wind. Crying with the pitter-patter of rain. Redlar bounding along at his side.

They followed the bobbing puddle of white light thrown by Reece's head torch. Redlar carried his own on a thick neoprene collar. Winding gravel tracks and potholes came and went. Replaced by mountain streams and open crevasses in the land. Then they climbed steep slopes and pushed through forests of trees. How could anyone go through an entire lifetime and not experience such a wondrous thing?

Breakfast was sausages and eggs, with lashings of brown sauce. Ceirios—Yanto's wife—had kindly brought them over from their farm the previous day. The man himself had been too busy mending a hole in a stretch of fencing, which he remained convinced was the work of weekend warriors pushing through on a shortcut to the mountains beyond.

"*I'll nail one to a post, if I catch them,*" he'd promised. "*That'll put the rest of the bastards off.*"

Reece hadn't doubted him. Yanto's temper was legendary among locals. Those coming from further afield would do well not to get on the wrong side of it.

Getting a newspaper to catch up on the previous day's sport involved a short trip to the village and a drive through the spectacular

National Park. The Land Cruiser managed it with ease, though its bulk made parking difficult when he got there.

The afternoon and evening were spent watching rugby on the television, and playing acoustic guitar in an armchair. It was *the* guitar. The one Anwen had bought for him on their fateful trip to Rome. The one he'd been playing in the shop while she was dying in the street.

He couldn't change any part of that now. It was simply impossible.

He put the guitar away, the lights out, and climbed the winding stone stairs like a condemned man walking towards a waiting noose. Redlar nudged him, letting him know he'd always be there during moments like these.

Another day was almost over.

Tomorrow, he'd get up and do it all again.

Chapter 4

DETECTIVE SERGEANT ELAN JENKINS winced in sync with the all too familiar sound of an alloy wheel scraping against a concrete kerb. It was yet another battle scar for her little Fiat 500 to carry. She'd driven the vehicle for only a couple of months; her previous one written off when a crazed murder suspect sent her skidding uncontrollably off the carriageway and into a ditch. She'd spent several hours strapped in and hanging upside down before anyone found her. Even the thought of what might have happened on another night gave her the jitters whenever she travelled that particular stretch of road.

'That's not right,' she said, turning off the engine and releasing her seat belt in quick succession. 'Not right at all.' The front door to her mother's house was wide open, the interior lights on, the downstairs curtains drawn fully apart. She broke into a trot as she went up the path, not waiting to lock the car. 'Mam,' she called, hopping across the threshold step and into the cold hallway. 'Are you in?'

The only answer came from a muffled conversation between two television characters, neither of whom was talking to her.

She poked her head through the living room doorway. In the kitchen, she checked what little she could glimpse of the dark garden. Then went out onto the patio to be absolutely sure. Margaret wasn't pegging out washing. Nor was she staining the fence in the pouring rain. That bizarre episode was something they'd both laughed off the day after it happened.

At the bottom of the stairs, mild panic replaced her initial apprehension. 'Are you in the bathroom?' That was it. Margaret must have gone up to use the loo. But why the open front door? Had it not caught on the catch after her mother paid the paperboy, and then blown open again in the wind?

There were so many questions, but as yet, no answers.

She stopped briefly to get her breath on the landing, then checked each room with the methodical efficiency of a dawn police raid.

Margaret wasn't upstairs.

Downstairs, neither.

And definitely not in the garden, staining furniture.

So where was she? Next door perhaps? Jenkins doubted it. Mostly because just about everyone Margaret had once known was now either dead and buried, or moved away to be nearer family. The neighbourhood had long since filled with a younger generation who were far less driven by the community spirit existing when she was growing up.

There was no answer at the first property. A shrug of the shoulders and a weak apology from the owner on the other side. Jenkins stood on the doorstep, looking left and right along the street. She went left, towards a couple of small shops near the junction at the far end of the road. Margaret could well have gone to pick up something for her tea.

'Have you been out here a while?' Jenkins asked a woman vaping on her front lawn. There were two, maybe three, kids arguing inside – at least one of them sobbing uncontrollably. The woman appeared numb to it all. A casualty of a very long day. 'Did you see Mrs Jenkins go by? She's the old lady at number seventeen.'

'Who?'

'She lives a few doors along in that direction.' There was little more than a vacant shake of the head in response. 'Thanks for your help,' Jenkins said with as much sincerity as she could manage.

There was a patrol car parked on the corner, its flashing blue lights illuminating most things close by. Three people were standing next to it. Two of them wearing yellow, hi-viz jackets.

'*Mam!*' Jenkins crossed the road with minimal regard for her own safety. 'It's okay,' she called to the nearest uniform. 'That's my mother you've got there.'

Margaret was in full conversation with the second officer, wearing a nylon nightie and nothing on her feet. The fuzzy glow of the overhead street lighting gave her the appearance of a ghostly apparition. There was a small gathering of people nearby.

'Put that phone down,' Jenkins warned one of the local youths. 'Show some respect.' The youngster laughed and continued to film the event. 'Sort him out,' Jenkins told the nearest uniform.

'And you are?' the officer asked.

'DS Jenkins. Cardiff Bay.'

'Police?'

'Isn't that what it usually means?' She put a hand to her face and spoke from behind a fan of fingers. 'I'm sorry. I'm having a bit of a moment right now.'

'You know this woman?'

Jenkins took off her jacket and draped it over Margaret's shoulders. 'What have you been doing?'

'She was in the corner shop,' the officer explained. 'Trying to pay for tea bags and a pack of smoky bacon, using pieces of torn up newspaper.'

'They were money-off vouchers,' Margaret protested. 'I'm not completely stupid.'

'Where's your purse, Mam?'

Margaret patted herself down. 'In my coat pocket.'

'And where's your coat?'

'I gave it to you before we came out.'

'Let her sit in the back of the car,' Jenkins said, steering her mother towards it. 'Her feet are turning blue.'

When the uniform opened the door, Margaret backed away, waving her arms. 'I'm not getting in there. I know what you're doing. Help. *Help!*'

The youth with the phone called up the street to someone pulling wheelies on a bicycle. 'You've gotta come and see this. Granny's off her tits on something.'

Jenkins rounded the rear of the patrol car. 'Why don't you fuck off before I ram that phone up your arse!'

'You can't touch me,' the youngster goaded. He bent over and wagged his rear end at her. 'I'll have you done for ass-ault!'

Jenkins leaped onto the pavement and grabbed for the phone, knocking it to the floor. She swung a leg and kicked it along the gutter. 'Don't say I didn't give you plenty of warning.'

'You've scratched the screen!'

'You're lucky I didn't stamp all over it.'

'I want her arrested,' the youth told the nearest officer. 'I've got witnesses to everything that just happened.'

Jenkins went after him. 'Let me smack you in the gob first. Make it worth my while.' She turned to the watching uniforms. 'Are you two brain dead? Sort this out before I start on the pair of you.' She took Margaret by the arm. 'Let's get you home.'

Margaret didn't resist. 'I'm cold.'

Jenkins slipped off her shoes. 'Put these on. It's not far.'

'They're too tight. I'm going to fall.'

'We'll take them off again once I get you home.' She sought the youth among others in the crowd. 'Give one of those two your contact details and I'll pay for a new screen.'

Chapter 5

JENKINS PUT A MUG of hot chocolate in front of her mother and joined her at the kitchen table. There was an important conversation to be had, but such things were becoming increasingly likely to provoke the worst of arguments between them. Margaret had always been a mild-mannered and easygoing woman. Now, not so much. The slightest event could set her off and have her saying the most awful things in retaliation.

'Are you hungry?' Jenkins asked. It was a harmless opener. Tame by her usual detective standards and unlikely to draw out anything useful on its own. 'I could do us both something to eat. Or do you fancy a nice piece of fish and bread and butter from the chippy?'

'Had my dinner before I went to work,' Margaret said without a shred of doubt. 'Gammon, new potatoes, peas, and parsley sauce.'

'Shopping,' Jenkins corrected. 'Not work. You went shopping this evening. At the end of the road.'

'On my way home from work,' Margaret insisted. 'We needed frozen peas and a bottle of milk. The one I had in the fridge had turned sour.'

Jenkins moved her chair closer to the table and took a sip from her mug. '*I* brought the milk round this morning—a fresh one—before I went into work.'

Margaret nodded. 'And I made you breakfast before you left again. Your favourite: scrambled eggs on toast, with a dollop of brown sauce.'

That had been her late father's favourite, not hers. She'd managed coffee only, and even that had made her late. She'd read somewhere that playing along with a person's inconsistent memories was considered ethically questionable. But also read that it was wrong to always challenge and correct. 'Dad liked scrambled eggs, didn't he?'

'Yes, but he always had to add a pinch of spice to them,' Margaret said with a smile that lingered. 'He could never eat them plain out of the pan, like the rest of us.'

'That's right. Paprika and lots of pepper.' Jenkins squeezed her mother's hand. The memory was so vivid that she could almost see her father sitting opposite, a knife and fork clutched tightly in both hands while he waited.

Margaret's face crumpled. 'I couldn't eat them like that myself. But your father loved them that way.'

'Me neither,' Jenkins agreed. 'That's why most mornings I only have coffee for breakfast. Like today.'

'You wouldn't let me make you anything,' Margaret said. 'I remember now. You were running late.'

'And you also remember you don't go to work anymore?'

Margaret cocked her head to one side. 'Don't I?'

'You're retired now and help at the church when you can.' That wouldn't be an option for very much longer.

'The vicar loves my jam sponge.'

'Me too. I only wish you'd make it more often.'

'I don't have time. Not with work getting in the way.'

'You were here all day, Mam. Here in the house.'

'Except for when I pegged the washing on the line.'

It hadn't long stopped raining, and the clothesline had been empty on Jenkins's arrival. Here she was at last, the fingers of her free hand crossed beneath the cover of the table top. 'Do you remember leaving the front door open when you went to the shops this evening?'

'Because you were here. I'd have shut it if I'd been on my own.'

'You were already gone when I arrived.'

'Then it must have been your father who left it open. Did you ask him?'

Jenkins's grip on her mother's hand loosened. She closed her eyes and swallowed. 'Dad's not with us anymore. You know that, don't you?'

Margaret stared right through her. 'He *was* earlier. We had our tea together.'

'Mam—'

'Did you check upstairs?' Margaret tried to stand. 'I'll go call him.'

Jenkins had her sit down again. Mam—'

'You think I'm going mad?'

'I didn't say that.'

Margaret pulled away. 'That's what you've been telling people. Don't think I don't know.'

'I never would.'

'You told that floozy.'

'Cara's my partner?'

Margaret blew a raspberry. 'Is that what you call them these days?'

Jenkins went limp in her chair. 'I really don't know what to say.'

'I bet the floozy does.'

'Stop calling her that.'

'She put you up to this.'

'That's not fair. It's also not true.'

'What you're both doing is a cruel, cruel thing.'

Jenkins got to her feet, unable to get a word in now she'd set her mother off.

'You're after the house. Going to put us both in care so you and the *floozy* can move in here together.'

'Stop it.' Jenkins was close to tears and just about running on empty. 'I'm trying to do what's right for you. That's all I want. All I've ever wanted.'

'Your poor old father would turn in his grave if he knew what was going on here.' Half of her was glad Margaret had suddenly remembered her husband's passing. The other half was in total shock that her own mother could think her capable of such awful things. 'And a police officer too,' Margaret continued. 'You should be ashamed of what you've become, Elan. I never thought I'd see the day when my own daughter turned against me.'

She reached and lay her arm across Margaret's shoulders. 'Mam—'

'Fuck off.'

'Please don't swear. It's not like you.'

Margaret twisted violently, knocking over her mug of hot chocolate. 'You've burned me, you silly cow.'

'Let me see your hand.'

'Get away.'

'Let me *see*.' The pad of flesh between the finger and thumb was already turning red. 'Put it under the cold water tap.'

'I'll report you for this. You see if I don't.'

Jenkins ran the water. 'The sooner we get the heat out of it, the better.'

'You'll lose your job. And there'll be no house from me.' Margaret threw her head back and laughed wildly. 'What will you and the floozy do then?'

Jenkins soaked a tea towel. 'I don't care about that right now. Give me your hand before it gets any worse.'

Margaret struggled to get away. 'You wait until your father gets in, young lady. You're in so much trouble.'

Chapter 6

DALE LYNCH LIMPED OUT of the drop-in centre, clutching his side, and braced himself for another night's rough-sleeping on the cold city streets. Almost nine months of homelessness were taking its toll on his young body and mind. If he could only get through the long winter months, then spring and summer might make things more bearable. That made him sound like he was a squirrel. But squirrels normally had more food than he did.

He'd suffered with a pig of a cough for two or three weeks, and the relentless hacking was doing little to fix his fractured ribs. Douglas Hames's thugs had beaten him up for trespassing on the waterfront development site. But their threats didn't scare him, even if they did scare Cory Daniels. Some mate he was turning out to be. Scared of his own shadow, that one.

The decision Lynch was struggling to make while under the influence of at least one bottle of cheap vodka was where to bed down for the night ahead. The possibilities were almost endless for the open-minded. But not usually in a good way.

Would it be the underpass of one of the city's many bridges? Sharing it with smack heads, pervs, and people who only stopped off there to take a piss on the way home from the pub.

Or should he try the cramped crawlway beneath a rat-infested storage unit in the docks? He'd been there. Done that. And on more occasions than he'd care to remember.

Then there were the industrial bins parked behind the restaurants along the stretch of Mermaid Quay. The huge lids did a sterling job of keeping the rain off, even during the heaviest of downpours. They were just about perfect if a person could bear to sleep on a bed of rotting food. For the most part, the worst of the smell disappeared after a while. And if Lady Luck dealt a kind hand, then there was sometimes something still edible to be found among the waste produce.

There were several multi-storey car parks to choose from. Those kept out the rain, but sucked the wind right through them. A person could literally freeze to death in one of those.

'*Shimple*,' Lynch decided with a drunken slur. 'I'm going back over there. I'll show them.' His attempts at identifying the true direction of the waterfront development were severely hampered by his inability to see where it was. But first, he needed a few sheets of cardboard to act as a mattress and quilt.

The main thoroughfare of Mermaid Quay was busy, as usual, with all manner of people passing through. Some were stopping to enjoy a slap-up meal before catching a show at the nearby Millennium Centre. How he envied them for what they would consider being normal life. A day's work followed by an hour or two playing with the kids. Then a hot shower and change into something fitting of the occasion. Splash out on a taxi to top it all off.

It was the lifestyle of successful footballers and movie stars, as far as Dale Lynch was concerned. So removed was it from his own pitiful existence that it was almost impossible for him to comprehend.

He staggered behind one of the busy restaurants, bumping against things on the way. There was a door open in the side wall, a man in chef's clothing smoking beneath a light that buzzed like an electric razor. There was music, the work-sounds of a busy kitchen, and the laughter of the clientele at the front of house.

Lynch kicked a toe into the ground and grabbed at the upright of a lamppost. Not an angry gesture by any means. 'Happiness,' he muttered in a melancholy whisper. 'I knew him a long time ago.'

Chef nodded and didn't tell him to get lost. A positive for sure, and not something that happened most days. He nodded back, more hopeful of getting what he'd come looking for. The short walk from the drop-in centre had sobered him up enough to get most of the words out with some semblance of coherence. 'I'm after cardboard,' he said, going no closer without an invitation to do so. Another kicking was something he didn't need.

Chef squinted through a cloud of rising smoke, and after the longest of pauses, gestured silently. He hadn't understood. English unlikely to be his first language.

Lynch pointed to a folded wedge of cardboard pushed behind a large wheelie bin. 'Like that over there.' It was almost perfect for his needs. He hugged his shoulders and shut his eyes in an attempt to make the other man catch on.

Chef's expression changed suddenly. He raised a hand and took his foot off the wall to stamp out his cigarette. When he went inside, Lynch wondered if it was to round up a mob. Two beatings in as many weeks. But when he returned, he was carrying a white paper bag and a bottle of something alcoholic.

Lynch gladly accepted, sticking his face into the bag, inhaling the aroma of roasted duck. There was even a small pot of orange sauce in there. And cooking sherry to wash it all down with.

Chef flapped a hand in an *out-of-here-before-you-get-me-in-trouble* sort of gesture.

'That's me sorted,' Lynch said, staggering away without taking much notice of the bearded man leaning against the railings.

Tonight, he'd eat like a king. Beneath the stars. In the finest of cardboard beds. And if anyone had stopped to warn him that by morning, he'd be dead, he'd have no reason to believe them.

Chapter 7

REECE FEASTED ON A breakfast of egg McMuffin and sweet coffee, watching the rubber wiper blades create a fan-shaped smudge on the Land Cruiser's windscreen. When they squeaked, he turned them off and checked the sky, reluctant to believe it had finally stopped drizzling.

It had. Though another downpour didn't look too far off.

He repositioned his phone between shoulder and chin, wiping his hands on the paper napkin that came with the meal. 'Jenkins was supposed to meet me here. Where is she?'

'I texted her,' said Detective Constable Ffion Morgan. 'Told her where you'd be and that she should go straight over and not come to the station first.'

'The two of you didn't speak at all?'

'Not exactly,' Morgan said. 'Hers went to voicemail after only a few rings. But I did leave a message to go with the text.'

Reece tossed the scrunched napkin onto the passenger seat and massaged his eyeballs with his knuckles. It was already gearing up to be one of those deeply annoying days when nobody did what they were supposed to. 'And did she reply?' he asked.

'Not as yet.' There was a prolonged silence, then: 'You don't think she's upside down in a ditch again, do you? I didn't think of that before now.'

'She's more likely to have slept in, if recent weeks are anything to go by,' Reece said, smoothing a crease in the thigh of his trousers. When he stopped patting it, the material went back to how it previously was. 'It's getting to be a habit with her. Do you know what's up? Problems at home, maybe?'

'Nothing she's mentioned to me. Not that I remember.'

'It can't continue like this.' He left it at that.

Morgan had no choice but to agree. 'I'll try her one more time and get back to you.'

Reece licked his finger and dabbed at the crease. It worked no better than the smoothing attempt. 'I'll go take a look myself.' Ending the call, he finished the rest of the McMuffin in one mouthful and stepped out onto the tarmac.

The assembled crowd wasted no time in having a go at him as he approached.

'Enjoy your breakfast?' someone called.

'Checking Facebook, were you?' asked another.

'What do you know so far, Chief Inspector?'

Reece was no stranger to the owner of the gravelly voice. 'Maggie,' he said in a lack-lustre greeting. 'What is it with reporters and crime scenes? You're like flies drawn to shit.'

'Ever so eloquent.' Maggie Kavanagh lit a new cigarette off one that had burned down to within a few millimetres of its lip-stick-stained filter. 'We should give you a column in the Herald.'

'That'll be the day.'

'Seriously though,' she said, shoving a recording device in his face. 'What's going on here? Murder, I'm thinking, given your arrival.'

He didn't stop to chat. 'Sounds like you already know more than I do.'

There was a white tent pitched on a patch of damp gravel and grass just off the road. Next to the overhang of a concrete bus shelter. The tent was struggling to stay put in a wind that bullied it relentlessly. Someone had added a few extra weights at one corner to stop it from lifting and blowing away. A measure that was, so far, working as planned.

Reece skirted a solitary fire appliance, its engine rattling, the crew packing up to leave. There was a first-responder paramedic present, as well as an EMS ambulance. Parked side-on, and blocking both ends of the road, were high performance police cars. Every vehicle present had its blue lights flashing. 'What a way to start a Tuesday morning,' he said to the back of someone crouched next to scorch marks on the ground.

The woman lowered her camera at the sound of his voice, but remained in a squatting position. 'You're telling me. Roll on the weekend, is what I say.'

He signed his name and rank without response, donned appropriate PPE, and entered the tent taunted by vivid flashbacks of Rome. He fought against them and pushed through.

Doctor Cara Frost—Home Office Forensic Pathologist—looked up from what she was doing and rolled her eyes. 'That's all I need.'

'Morning to you too,' Reece said, approaching the body. The smell of burnt flesh was overpowering, and left him grateful for not ordering bacon to go with the egg McMuffin. 'What can you tell me?'

The victim was as black as anthracite coal. There was a slight bow in its back, arms drawn into a pugilistic pose, held there by muscle tendons that had shortened in the searing heat. Its lips were retracted to reveal sooted teeth. The eyelids and underlying structures were no longer present. Although the legs had suffered the same tendon shortening, the feet were fairly well preserved.

'What's that wrapped around the ankles?' he asked, getting down to Frost's level.

'Plastic bag ties is my best guess. Melted into the underlying tissue.'

'Bound before he was burned?'

'I'd say that's likely,' Frost said. 'I'll know more once I've completed the post-mortem examination.'

Reece had seen enough and came away. 'When can I expect your report?'

Frost grabbed hold of an imaginary crystal ball and '*Ummed,*' theatrically.

'That's the best you have?' he asked, waiting by the exit flap of the tent.

She put her things away in a metal case. It was more of a *tossed them in*, than it was a careful packing of her belongings. 'At the moment, yes.'

He followed her out into the damp morning air. 'Where's Jenkins?'

Frost made a show of looking every which way before shaking her head. 'Isn't she here yet?'

'I wouldn't be asking if she was.'

'Elan stayed at her mother's last night, if you really must know.'

Reece picked up on an undercurrent of discontent. 'Did the two of you argue?'

Frost came to a sudden stop, the case swinging ahead of her before she got better control of it. She turned on her heels, the gravel surface crunching beneath them. 'What business is that of yours?'

She was pissing him off, and counting five back to zero was doing nothing to improve things. 'It's my business when it results in one of my officers being absent from work.'

'Take it up with your employee, not me,' she said, relieving herself of the last items of PPE.

Reece watched her march towards her car. 'And that's it?' he called after her.

She neither slowed her pace nor turned to face him. 'For now, yes.'

'And?'

'And what?' When she shut the boot of her car, it was with an unnecessary level of force. 'If it's the post-mortem you mean, then we've already had that conversation.'

A male CSI leaned closer and whispered in Reece's ear: 'Imagine having to go home to her every evening.'

The detective said nothing. He'd have been happy to go home to just about anyone.

Chapter 8

JENKINS PARKED AT THE far end of the police station compound and scanned the entire area more than once before daring to venture out of her car. There was no one about that she recognised, other than a couple of female PCSOs she'd once given a brief tour of the Murder Squad Incident Room. Neither woman appeared to have remembered her. Both were engaged in reliving something on their phones that was quite obviously hilarious. To them, at least.

Jenkins was late again, and now had to get to her desk without being seen and bollocked by anyone of a senior rank.

Reece's Land Cruiser was parked only five spaces away from her Fiat, taking up enough room for two smaller vehicles. She checked his office window and saw no sign of him watching, as he often did.

She made a break for it, running across the open compound, round the corner, and straight up the steps at the front of the building. Then through the sliding door and into the foyer while the desk sergeant had his back turned. Not wanting to be spotted while waiting for the lift to arrive, she entered the stairwell and groaned in anticipation of the climb ahead. Rarely did she do the stairs anywhere, and was reminded of that fact by a heavy build up of lactate acid in her calves and thighs. 'How does the boss do this every day?' she gasped. 'And without needing to. He must be mad.'

Opening the stairwell door on her floor, she checked the landing in both directions before making a sudden break for the incident room at the far end. It was near-enough empty of people when she got there. She flopped into her seat and raised the lid of her laptop, wiping sweat from her brow with the cuff of her coat sleeve. She'd made it into work unseen by anyone who mattered.

That's what she thought.

Ffion Morgan appeared in the doorway from the landing, a mug of coffee held in one hand, a piece of toast missing a ragged semi-circle in the other. She came to a stop, nodded, and grinned. 'Look what the cat's dragged in. A heavy night on the tiles, by the looks of it.' She came closer. 'Come on, then – I want to hear every sordid detail of whatever went on.'

Jenkins gave her only the briefest regard and entered her username and password in the required boxes. 'Unlikely, don't you think? What with me being completely teetotal.' She waited for the laptop to finish booting up. There were rumours circulating the station of new devices on order, but until they arrived, a person usually had enough time to go boil the kettle and get back again before the *Home* screen appeared. If the public only knew how much of an officer's day was wasted on such mundane things, there would be an outcry of protest.

Morgan looked like she might leave again, but didn't. 'You've not checked your phone this morning? I sent a message from the boss. And voicemail to go with it when you didn't answer.'

Jenkins fished the device out of her pocket and tossed it onto her desk unchecked. She stood up and removed her coat, letting it drop alongside her phone. 'Oh, well. Too late now, I suppose.'

Morgan rested a buttock on the edge of Jenkins's desk, finishing the crust of toast only after dunking it deep into the depths of her coffee. 'He was annoyed he couldn't get hold of you,' she said, licking melted butter from one of her fingers. 'Not his usual apeshit, in fairness to him. But pissed off, nonetheless.'

Jenkins didn't look away from her laptop screen. 'It'll give him something new to moan about.'

'This isn't new, though, is it? Lately you've been all over the place. And not only that—'

Jenkins raised a hand and lowered her head. She took a breath. 'Don't go there, okay? Just don't.'

Morgan gripped her mug in both hands and rested it beneath her chin. 'But you *are* all right? You'd tell me if something was wrong?'

'I'm as *all right* as I'm ever going to be.' Jenkins took a white envelope off her desk and turned it over. 'What's this?' she asked, tapping it against the scratched wood veneer.

'No idea. I've been downstairs getting my breakfast.' Morgan slipped off the desk, but didn't move too far away. 'Shall I go back down and get you a coffee, or something else?'

Now that Jenkins recognised the foreign postmark, she knew exactly what it was. She put the envelope away in her drawer, unopened. Even if it was good news, the time was no longer right for a year's secondment abroad.

Chapter 9

'THERE'S NO DOUBTING THIS being a deliberate act.' Reece poked at a stray hair circling the surface of his coffee. It didn't look like one of his own. He caught it between a finger and thumb and flicked it to one side of the room with little care for what might be in its path. 'There was some type of binding fixed to the victim's ankles. Bag-ties by the looks of it. We'll know a bit more later.'

Chief Superintendent Cable was repositioning herself after ducking out of the way of the flying strand of hair. Steadying her teacup and saucer, she checked herself over before answering. 'It all sounds awful. What's your next move?'

'Uniform will speak to people in the area obviously, but you know what it's like with these things? No one will admit to seeing or hearing anything. And then there'll be the usual nutters and other time wasters.'

'An unusual place for something like this to happen,' Cable said. 'So close to the new housing developments. It's a very nice area over there.'

'I'd hardly call it *housing*,' Reece scoffed. 'Not in the way we'd think of it. Some of those unfurnished apartments are going for upwards of four-and-a-half grand in rent each month. Who around here can afford that?' He stared at the floor, his mind wandering. It was doing that a lot in recent days. More than usual. He blamed it on the pressure of the coming weekend. 'Mind you, I'm sure Douglas Hames's PR team will manage to squeeze something positive out of it all.' He shook his head. 'That man could sell sage and onion to a turkey.'

Hames was an MBE and local property developer. A man with links to people in high places, including several members of the nearby Senedd. Reece imagined him being someone used to getting his own way.

'Not so much lately.' Cable moved her cup and saucer to one side of the desk and filled the empty space with her elbows. 'He's having serious financial difficulties getting this one completed. That's what I've heard in private circles.'

'My heart bleeds for him,' Reece said, unable to contain a grin that almost split his face in two.

'Why the sour grapes? The likes of Douglas Hames have transformed the area in recent years, and very much for the better, I'll quickly add.'

'Superficially, maybe.'

'Nonsense. The regeneration itself cost well over two billion pounds.'

'And who's benefiting from it?' Reece asked. 'People who can afford to squander four grand a month on a flat barely larger than your average cell downstairs. That's who.'

'You're being silly now.'

'Maybe,' he conceded. 'But you get my drift?'

'I'm really not sure I do.'

He puffed his cheeks and tried again: 'It's only the likes of Douglas Hames and his cronies who've truly benefited from the regeneration. You've got wealthy people dishing out the contracts. Wealthy people doing all the building and selling. And it's only their sort who can afford to buy those properties when they're finished.'

'I don't think that's true at all.'

'No? What's that housing minister's name?' Reece clicked his fingers and tried to remember. 'Always on the telly and done up like a dog's dinner most of the time.'

'You mean Bridget Payne?'

'That's her. More interested in getting herself in front of a camera than she is in doing good for the people round here.'

Cable pointed a finger in warning. 'You stay away from Senedd Member Payne. I don't want you going over there rattling your sabre about local causes when you should be concentrating on the case in hand.'

Reece threw his empty paper cup at, rather than into, the bin. 'I'll go wherever the evidence takes me, thank you very much.'

'Not without discussing it with me first.' Cable pressed him when he didn't reply.

'I won't be pussy-footing around anybody if I think they're involved in this. No matter who they are.'

'That's not what I'm saying.'

'But you do want to pick and choose who I talk to?'

Cable massaged her temple and opened her desk drawer with her other hand. 'I don't want you making a nuisance of yourself over there, is what I'm saying.'

'I'll tear the place apart if I think there's a good enough reason to.'

She slammed the drawer shut and popped the lid of an aspirin bottle. Shaking out two, she swallowed them without water. 'Can we please move on?'

'You brought up the Senedd thing, not me.'

'Post-mortems. When are they due?'

'Cara Frost wasn't exactly forthcoming on that front,' Reece said. 'If you ask me, all's not well between her and Jenkins.' He made no mention of his detective sergeant's repeated late starts.

'Ah yes. Nice Segway. I wanted to talk to you about her. She's eligible for promotion soon.'

'I know that.'

'So what are you doing in preparation?'

'I've been busy.' Reece said. 'Besides, if she was to leave, then it would mess with the dynamic of the team.'

'You can't use that as a reason to slow the career progression of a capable detective. HR and the Federation would have a field day.'

'I'm not, but we've got the makings of something special developing downstairs and I wouldn't want to spoil that.'

'And Ginge's trial period with you is soon up for review. How's he getting on?'

'He's nothing like his uncle, that's for sure.' Reece pulled a face. 'That's not a bad thing, I'll hasten to add.'

'A serving officer? I don't think I know him.'

'Retired. The old guard type who jumped before they were pushed.' He left it at that.

'The reason I ask about Ginge's position is because we might not have adequate funding to keep him next year.'

'Bloody hell!' Reece thrashed about in his seat. 'Has Harris been up to his old tricks again?'

'That's *ACC* Harris.'

'Can't help himself, that one. Even after having his arse slapped, he's still trying to break us up.'

Cable shot to her feet, knocking the bottle of aspirin onto the floor. 'Remember where you are and who you're talking to. This has nothing to do with the Assistant Chief Constable.'

'You'll be finding those things for months to come,' Reece said, nodding at the spilled tablets. 'Treading them into the carpet every time you get up.'

'Shut up.'

He drummed his fingers on the desk. 'Does that mean I can go now?'

Cable was down on her hands and knees, collecting as many as she could find. 'You stay put until I tell you we're finished.'

Chapter 10

THE DECISION TO ACT and clear her name hadn't been an easy one for Mali Ingram to make. Her world had spiralled out of control at a breakneck speed following the incident on the quarry in North Wales.

That's what most people had called it at the time: an *incident*. Others: an *accident*.

Only she and the scheming couple knew the full truth. The awful truth. That they'd been willing to ruin her life because it served their purpose. Whatever that was.

She hated them.

Despised them with all her being.

Her job at the climbing centre was first to go, unsurprisingly. Management quick to show their hand and distance themselves from any association with her.

Jobless, she quickly burned through what little savings she had in her building society account.

Without money, she was unable to pay the rent and soon lost her flat.

With nowhere to live, friends became conspicuous by their absence. All except Lisa, that is. A good school friend, who despite her own hardships, had allowed Mali to couch-surf at hers whenever there was room.

It was while at Lisa's she felt suddenly compelled to pick herself up and fight back. There was a news broadcast on daytime television. Senedd Member Bridget Payne was being interviewed over the impending relocation of a Cardiff drop-in centre for rough sleepers. A move that was deeply opposed by relevant charities and all those using the facility.

It struck an obvious chord with Mali.

Payne spoke in a condescending tone. Perfect makeup and a model's smile doing nothing to hide her disdain for all those she considered beneath her. She was at it again. Stepping all over the little guy. Mali had to put a stop to it.

She had no solid proof of guilt; only heavy suspicion; the letter she'd sent being somewhat premature. But it was done now. She couldn't change that, even if she wanted to. There would be danger ahead. A powerful politician wouldn't stand back and watch a successful career fall apart. Not one who'd been willing to kill her own husband.

And so Mali arrived in Cardiff in the cab of a Polish trucker's lorry, frightened, yet determined to succeed. Piotr, the lanky driver, had kindly promised not to molest or murder her during the four and a half hour journey south, and in fairness to him, had kept his word.

The silence shared between them had suited her. She wasn't in the mood for deep and meaningful conversation. Rather, wanted to work over certain details in her mind. What would she do when she got to the Senedd? How would she approach Bridget Payne? And what would she say when she confronted the politician with the truth?

Piotr had smoked the whole way there, frequently taking calls on a hands-free phone that stuck out of his dashboard like a witch's claw. He'd glanced at Mali on several occasions, leaving her in little doubt that she was often the topic of conversation.

That was nothing new to her. The villagers back home had done a similar thing. But they'd also point and make snide remarks. Talk about kicking a person when they were down. Most of them had laid into her with everything they had.

Dreaming she'd been drugged and trafficked to continental Europe to be sold into the sex trade, she'd awoken with a violent start, only to catch sight of the towering uprights of the Severn Bridge. Piotr had even draped an old coat over her while she slept.

Cardiff was less than thirty miles away.

The Albanian border nowhere in sight.

When they got to the busy city centre, she thanked Piotr and wished him a safe journey onward, sliding from her seat to the pavement below. Her left foot was numb from where she'd had it tucked under her. It took a shake and a fair amount of persuasion before it was willing to take its share of the weight. Piotr lit another cigarette and pulled off into the traffic with a wave and the minimum of fuss.

Mali was in Cardiff and properly alone, with nothing but the clothes she wore and an old sleeping bag containing all her worldly possessions. She slung it over her shoulder and shivered without the coat and the warm air of the lorry's heater-blower.

There was a dirty blue tent pitched on the wet grass in front of the castle; a couple of empty sleeping bags and a few sheets of folded cardboard positioned only a short distance further on. Two middle-aged men were sitting with their backs against the damp stonework, sharing stories of woe and a bottle of something inexpensive.

Following its humble beginnings as a Roman fortress in AD 55, William the Conqueror had rebuilt the castle over a thousand years later, only for it to be stormed by Owain Glyndŵr in 1404, in a final revolt for independence from the English.

Someone bumped against her, walking on without apology, sipping a takeout *crappuchino* only because just about everyone else in the country did.

Mali didn't. Those prices were way beyond her means. Besides, who *really* needed to drink on the go?

Someone else gave her a wide berth when approaching from the opposite direction; a woman who pulled her child close to her side and didn't let go again until they'd safely made it past.

"*I won't eat him*," Mali wanted to say, but didn't.

There were looks of loathing. Some of pity. Many of complete disinterest. She was no stranger to any of them. Turning away from the castle, she entered Queen Street, stopping briefly to read from the inscription on a plinth supporting the statue of a man wearing a smart suit.

Aneurin Bevan
1897 - 1960
Founder of the National Health Service

Mali remembered something from her school days about Bevan resigning from office once a labour government began charging for dental work and prescription medicines. From what she'd read and heard in the recent press, the NHS was now too broken to fix. Ambulances were taking almost as long responding to a stroke or heart attack victim as Piotr's journey back to Poland. Not quite, but it painted an accurate enough picture.

Everything in the world, it seemed, was going to shit.

Chapter 11

REECE HADN'T STAYED UPSTAIRS with Chief Superintendent Cable for any longer than he needed to. As soon as she'd given him the green light to leave her office, he'd scarpered before she was able to change her mind and start on some other topic of conversation.

On entering the incident room, he tapped his watch and put it to his ear, making a point. 'What time do you call this?' he asked, going through the routine for a second time. 'You need to get yourself one of these for Christmas.'

Jenkins waved her phone at him. 'Already got the newest model, and it doesn't need winding like that antique on your wrist.'

'Doesn't bloody work though, does it?'

She rubbed her eyes and failed to hide a yawn behind her free hand. 'I slept in this morning. It won't happen again, I promise.'

Reece went over to his office, half in and half out of his suit jacket. 'I'd like a word,' he said before going inside. He hung the jacket over the back of his swivel chair and asked her to close the door and sit down once she'd joined him. He went over to the window and opened it, looking down on the car park and street below.

She had her back to him and hadn't yet let go of the handle. 'I know I haven't been pulling my weight lately, but—'

'This isn't a bollocking,' he said, and stopped her when she attempted to finish the sentence. 'I want you to hear me out first.'

She accepted the chair opposite and lowered herself onto it with the mannerisms of someone anticipating bad news. 'If it's not a telling off, then what is it?'

'I've been upstairs with the chief super. Having a chat. Talking about you, actually.'

'There's nothing wrong with me.' She shifted position and sat on her hands to keep them still. 'I can do my job perfectly well. It's just that I—'

He leaned towards her. 'Relax. We all know that.'

She crossed, then uncrossed her legs, swinging them with a pendulum motion under her chair. 'What did the chief super want? Was it anything to do with me being late for work? Because if it was, then you can tell her I'm getting it sorted. Honestly, I *will* be getting things sorted.'

'You're eligible for your promotion exam,' Reece said in a gentle voice. 'What are your thoughts about that?'

She blew air through pursed lips. 'The Belle Gillighan fiasco ruined any chance I ever had of progressing in this Force. A colleague died because of my actions and you got shot.'

'We've been through this a million times or more.' Reece massaged his injured shoulder. 'I got myself shot. My actions, not yours, put me in front of that gun.' He clasped his hands together and wheeled his thumbs. 'I'd be sad to see you go when the time comes. You're a good copper. Better than that—an excellent detective. But I'd never stand in the way of your career. You're going places, Elan.'

She looked away. To what might have been her safe place on the far wall. 'Right.'

Reece frowned. He'd expected more than that. 'Is that all you have to say?'

'Can we do this another time? My mind's a bit ...' she whirled a finger at the side of her head. 'You know? All over the place at the moment.'

Reece had no idea what was going on. It wasn't at all like her, and that concerned him. 'I saw Cara today,' he said, using a different approach.

Jenkins tensed, her gaze quickly shifting to focus on him. 'What did she tell you? What did she say?'

'Very little, in fact. Said I should speak to you if I had a problem.'

'Nothing else?'

Reece shook his head. 'Should she have?'

Jenkins relaxed and looked away again. 'No.' It didn't sound at all convincing.

'Do you need time off to get something sorted between the two of you? I'll have a look at arranging cover if it's needed.'

'That's not what this is about. It's not Cara. Not all of it, anyway.'

'If I can help, then I will. But there's nothing I can do if you don't ask.'

'I'm fine. Or will be soon. There's no need for you to worry about me.'

'You're sounding a little like I did. And I can tell you now, I was anything but fine.'

She got up without warning and turned towards the door. 'I'm not sleeping very well. That's all it is.'

'It's always open,' he said from his chair. He didn't get up, and made no attempt to stop her. 'And I meant what I said about you having time off.'

Jenkins stopped in the doorway, and for a moment, looked like she might say something in response. It clicked closed again behind her, leaving Reece alone with his thoughts.

Chapter 12

Mali needed to get out of the cold, and quickly. A relentless combination of freezing air and wet pavements had numbed her toes. If she didn't find somewhere to warm up soon, she'd be in real trouble. A heavy glass door led the way inside a large retail store. She entered and stopped beneath the down-draft of warm air coming from a ceiling vent. It felt so good she was at risk of never again stepping out of it.

Someone asked her to move.

Another *told* her to move, before pushing past, clucking their tongue and shaking their head.

She was getting in everyone's way. Weren't they feeling the cold as much as she was? Of course they were. But unlike her, they had some place to go home to afterwards. Lucky them.

Store security had spotted the logjam at the door and was already heading in her direction. He was short and round and in no fit state to chase anything but his own shadow if the need ever arose.

'Here we go again.' She had enough time chalked up on the streets to know what was coming. 'Same old. Same old,' she said, getting louder as the distance between them decreased. 'What?' she asked, glaring at him. 'I've not done anything.'

His reply was simple: 'You can't come in here.' He didn't give a reason.

'Why not?' Mali pointed at several shoppers in quick succession. 'What makes me any different from that lot?'

'They'll pay for whatever goes in their basket.'

'And you're saying I won't?'

Security pointed at the door. 'Out. Now.'

Mali stood her ground. 'I could have loads of money, for all you know. Why do you assume I've got nothing?'

He looked her up and down and rolled his eyes. 'I said, *out.*'

'And I said, you can't make me. So go bother someone else.'

The man spoke into a radio and when finished, came closer. 'Back-up is on its way.'

She gave him the middle finger and went running towards the escalator. Several shoppers got out of her way. Several more stopped to gawp. Rounding off on the First Floor Level, she was met by two more security staff. 'What *is* this?' she asked, checking in all directions. 'I didn't come here to cause trouble. I needed to warm up before I froze to death out there.'

'Show us inside the sleeping bag,' one of them said. 'What do you have in there?'

Mali used both arms to hold it against her body. 'What's it got to do with you?'

'Empty it, or one of us will.'

She twisted her body away from them when a struggle started up. It soon degenerated into a violent tug of war. 'Get off.' She slapped the man's hand and screamed at him: 'I said leave it alone. Sod off, will you!'

He let go and stepped out of reach, apologising to the growing crowd of onlookers. 'We can involve the police if you'd prefer? It's your choice entirely.'

Mali glanced over her shoulder. 'I think Officer Lorenzo might have already done that.' She helped them out when they didn't get it: 'The dumb airport cop from the second Die Hard film.' She leaned on the balcony rail and waved. 'Look at him—no clue how to get up here. You step on the moving bit,' she shouted in his direction. 'Both feet, not just the one.'

'You're doing yourself no favours, shouting like that,' the nearest security guard said. 'Open the sleeping bag and then leave.'

Mali threw it at his feet. 'I want it all back,' she said, watching him empty her belongings onto the shop floor. 'Satisfied?' she asked after one of them used his foot to thin things out. 'Could have saved you the bother, if only you'd listened.' She turned to the crowd. 'How can you people shop in here?' Not one of them came to her defence.

Security went and waited on either side of the down escalator. 'We'll show you out.'

'Get your hands off me,' Mali protested, stuffing the last of her things into the bottom of the sleeping bag. 'I wouldn't shop here, even if I had the money. There's bugger all suitable for anyone this side of the grave.'

'The door's just there.'

'I know which way to go,' she told him. 'I'm potless, not lobotomised like your pal Lorenzo.'

The doors to the outside opened, letting in a cold breeze. There was a man crouched in the doorway; a towel draped around his shoulders and gripped in a fist jammed beneath his chin.

'I could have spared you the bother,' he said, grimacing as he moved out of her way.

'Who the fuck are you?'

He let go of the towel and held out a hand. 'Cory. What's your name?'

Mali crouched over him and ignored the greeting. 'You don't need to know that.'

Chapter 13

Pinned to the evidence board behind Reece were several photographs taken at that morning's crime scene. A few of them captured the location while others were of the charred body and the scorched ground beneath it. He put the last of them up and faced the assembled group. 'It doesn't make for pleasant viewing.'

'Looks like one of my father-in-law's barbecues,' said a uniform, slouching with his legs stretched out in front of him. The accompanying laughter was very short-lived.

Reece singled out the culprit. 'A person lost their life in this fire. We don't yet know who, or how old they were. You want to tell the rest of us what you find funny in that?'

The man turned several shades of red and squirmed in his seat. 'Sorry, boss. I meant nothing by it.'

Reece watched every man and woman in turn. 'Anyone else thinking of playing the comedian today?' He came back to the joker. 'Looks like you're the only one.'

The officer folded his arms and lowered his head. 'Boss.'

'Let's go through what we know so far,' Reece said, finally looking away.

Ffion Morgan leaned forward in her chair, craning her neck while trying to focus more clearly on something. 'The second photo down. To your right. What's in the white bag?'

'A roasted duck,' Reece said. 'Or half of one, to be exact. And a few shots of cooking sherry.'

'A rough-sleeper, do you think? Or a drunk who fell asleep on the way home?'

'Homeless is a reasonable shout,' Reece said. There was some cardboard alongside him that hadn't contacted the fire.

'Shall I start looking at CCTV for the area?' Ginge asked.

Reece nodded. 'Ask at the bars and restaurants. I want to know who saw him. If he was with anybody at the time. Was anyone else in the area acting suspiciously or causing trouble? You know the usual drill.'

Ginge made a couple of entries in his pocketbook. 'Boss.'

'Ffion, I want you on the post-mortem. I've had word saying it'll be done first thing tomorrow morning.'

Morgan flopped like a rag doll and groaned. 'I swear to God, I've been to more of those things than half the pathologists working there. I'm telling you – it won't be long before the hospital asks me to have a go whenever it gets busy.'

'That's why we keep sending you,' Reece said. 'You ask all the right questions.'

'Want to borrow my cycle helmet?' Ginge teased. 'It'll save you another egg on the head.'

Morgan gave him a playful slap. 'That happened just the once. Maybe twice,' she admitted, when he challenged her on it.

Even Reece laughed at that. Everyone in the room did. Everyone, that is, except the joker. 'We need to find out who this person was.' Reece tapped the photographs with the end of a pen. 'Who they were. Known associates and feuds. Anything that might give us a name or motive to follow up on.' He nodded when Ginge raised a hand.

'This might be a daft question, but why are you so sure this is murder? Couldn't he have had an accident with lighter fuel or the bottle of spirits he had with him?'

It was a fair enough question. Reece had once read a newspaper story about an elderly gentleman who had accidentally dropped the contents of his pipe into his lap. When he'd panicked and tried to put out the smouldering pile of tobacco with what was left in his brandy glass, he'd gone up in flames and died as a direct result of his horrific injuries.

Reece told them about the victim's ankles. How the plastic had melted into the underlying flesh. He pinned a close-up shot to the evidence board. 'As you can see from this, someone made sure our victim couldn't get away.' He waited for everyone to quieten down and fully comprehend what they'd heard. 'Thoughts?'

'Is there anything to be gained by us giving Shaun Kendle a tug?' Jenkins asked. 'I'm not saying he's our perp, but he might have overheard something in the circles he keeps.'

'Who's Shaun Kendle?' Morgan asked. 'I don't think I've ever come across the name.'

'He's a lowlife and serial arsonist,' Jenkins explained. 'With a festering grudge against any employer stupid enough to piss him off.'

'Council buildings are his usual thing,' Reece said. 'Those and small business premises.'

'Sounds like a right one.' Morgan again. 'But this wasn't a property fire?'

'And the last I heard, he was doing time for previous,' Reece said.

Jenkins shook her head. 'He's been out on licence for more than six months. I've already checked.'

Reece put the pen down and wiped ink off his fingers. 'Let's pay him a visit. If only to rule him out early.'

'When were you thinking?' Jenkins asked, dealing with an incoming message that lit up the screen of her phone.

'You and I can do it once we're finished here.'

'Can Ffion go instead?' Jenkins asked, typing a reply without looking up. 'There's something I need to do.'

'Related to the case?'

Her silence and general demeanour suggested it wasn't. 'It won't take me long.'

Morgan pushed her chair under the desk. 'I've never met this Kendle guy. It might be useful for me to put a face to a name.'

'All right,' Reece said, heading over to his office. 'You come instead.'

She caught up with Jenkins on the way back to their desks and leaned in close. 'What are you up to?'

Jenkins shifted a pile of paperwork from one spot to another. 'I'm not up to anything. I've got things to sort out, that's all.'

'You didn't want to spend time with the boss. That much was obvious.'

'Ffion, will you please leave it.'

'He asking too many awkward questions—is that it?'

Jenkins slammed a file down hard, knocking over a framed photograph of her parents. She picked it up and stared at it before putting it back in its place. 'Like you, you mean?'

Morgan went over to her own workstation and grabbed her jacket off the back of the chair. She forced an arm through the sleeve and snatched up her phone and bag. 'I thought we were friends? No problem. I'll keep my mouth shut, shall I?'

Chapter 14

MALI STARED THROUGH THE wide window of a busy burger bar, salivating at the sight and smells of greasy fast food. Each time the door swung open, she had to fight the overwhelming urge to run in there and grab lunch out of some young kid's hands. The last thing she'd eaten was a bruised apple Piotr, the lorry driver, had given her the day before. That and a piece of furry blue cheese she'd only had the stomach to nibble round the edges of.

'Smells very good, doesn't it?' The woman wore a red tabard and carried a shoulder bag full of *TheBig Issue* magazines. 'You like this kind of food?'

Mali had cramps and the beginnings of a dull headache. She'd eat just about anything right now. 'I don't have the money to buy a magazine. I'm sorry.'

'No problem,' the woman said with a heavy Eastern European accent. 'You live here?'

'Just visiting.' Telling a complete stranger she was in Cardiff only to expose a murdering politician was unnecessary. 'I'm looking for the Senedd.'

'You're a tourist, then?'

'Hardly. I'm also looking for the main homeless drop-in centre for the area. Isn't there one in the bay? The one they're trying to close or move elsewhere? It's been on the television recently.'

The woman banged the shoulder bag against her hip. 'I don't have many of these left to sell. If you can wait, then I'll take you there?'

Mali said that she could and thanked her. 'And I can walk in off the street?'

The woman didn't understand.

'I don't need a social worker referral? I can go there myself.'

'Ah, I see. Yes, you can—how you say again—walk in off road?'

Mali thought it rude to correct her. 'And I can get something to eat there? Without having money?'

'And shower if you sign book to take key for washroom.'

Mali's knees almost gave way beneath her. The last shower she'd had was nearly a week ago. At a local leisure centre back home. The receptionist had temporarily left her post to help a couple of kids with a chocolate bar stuck in a vending machine. Mali had taken the opportunity to skip past and race upstairs to one of the empty changing rooms, where she found an abandoned towel and a few squirts of cheap body wash and shampoo on top of a locker. She'd stood under the hot jets of water until the skin on her fingers and toes turned white and wrinkled.

With her consignment of magazines sold, they made their way to the drop-in centre.

'I'm Mali. Thank you for helping me. It's very kind of you.'

'Agnieszka. But most people call me Aggy.'

'I can see why they might. But you speak very good English.'

'I try,' Aggy said, rolling the *R*.

Mali cleared a dirty puddle only just ahead of a blue Edwins bus speeding past like it was on the wrong end of a police chase. Several other pedestrians were not so lucky and got soaked in punishment for a moment's hesitation. '*Idiot!*' she screamed as it rounded a bend in the road without slowing. 'Did it get you? Are you wet?'

'Not really.' Again, the rolled *R*. A green Telecoms box next to a lamppost had shielded Aggy from the worst of the spray kicked up by the bus's wheels. She shook her bag. 'It's not too bad.'

Mali gave the bruised sky a once over. 'It's going to rain again. I thought it was supposed to be drier down south?'

'It's not much further now,' Aggy promised.

Mali could smell the sea, and the gull activity overhead was certainly more frantic. There were several advertisements for the local restaurants, pleasure boat trips, and high-end apartments for sale or rent. 'This place must be lovely during the summer months.'

Aggy stared across the wide expanse of the man-made lake; out towards the barrage; the white Norwegian Church; then round to the Pierhead building. She pointed toward a predominantly glass structure that had a metal roof overhanging its frontage. 'That there is the Senedd.'

Now that Mali knew where it was, she let her gaze wander over a skyline dominated by a pair of tower cranes that reached across it like they were claiming it as their own. 'And that building site belongs to the developer who's trying to get the centre moved?'

'Mr Hames. Yes.'

Mali read the name from a white board opposite. **'Douglas Hames - *MBE*.'** She shook her head. 'No surprise there, I suppose.'

Aggy frowned. 'I don't understand.'

'The MBE bit. Their sort always make the most noise.'

The *Big Issue* seller looked none the wiser. 'There have been several council meetings already. But I don't think they're listening to anything we have to say.'

'And a final decision to be made soon, according to news channels?'

'At the end of this month.'

'What are you all doing about it?' Mali asked. 'Not just talking, I hope? As you say, no one listens to any of that.'

'There were protest marches,' Aggy said.

'I saw those on the news.' Mali smacked her lips. 'You could have done with a bigger turnout.'

'Would it matter? Isn't the saying: *money talks the loudest?*'

Mali had to concede the fact it probably did.

'And that's how they silence us. They drag everything through the courts, using expensive lawyers. We don't have a chance to win. It's hopeless.'

Mali didn't subscribe to the model of rolling over and giving in whenever things got tough. 'We'll see about that.'

Aggy stared out to sea a little while longer, then turned her back to it. 'Maybe we go to centre now?'

Chapter 15

THEY FOUND SHAUN KENDLE lying under a car with only the bits from his knees down visible. He was singing away to something on the radio, oblivious to their presence. Reece turned the volume off and gave the man's foot a kick. When that failed to provoke the desired reaction, he caught hold of his ankle and gave it a firm tug. 'Get out here where I can see you,' he said, not bothering with pleasantries.

The grease monkey's body came into full view. A faded red boiler suit to go with black boots that were missing patches of leather over their metal toe caps. He raised his welding visor with a pair of gloved thumbs while remaining flat on his back on a wheeled trolley. 'What the fuck do *you* want?'

Reece introduced Morgan, who showed her warrant card as proof of identity. He swooped to grab Kendle's leg again when he tried scuttling back under the car, up-ending him onto the oil-stained floor. 'On your feet and stop messing me about,' he said, looming over the man.

Kendle got up with a groan, mumbling obscenities. He gripped a gas welding torch in a tight fist, its limp flame flickering yellow. 'I'm warning you,' he said, aiming it like a handgun. 'I've nothing to say to you lot.'

'Whoa,' Reece said, moving clear of it. There were two men eating sandwiches on the other side of the office window. Both were preoccupied with their own conversation. Neither of them yet aware of what was happening only ten to fifteen feet from where they were sitting. 'That pair must be on drugs, letting you loose with a naked flame.'

'Keep your voice down.' Kendle checked neither man was watching. 'You're going to get me sacked.'

'I get it,' Reece said with a brief chuckle. 'You neglected to disclose your pyrotechnic tendencies on the application form?' There were numerous containers of flammable liquids dotted about the garage. He went and examined a few at random. Picked some up and put them down again. 'Hilarious if it wasn't so bloody serious.'

'Who do you think you are?' Kendle challenged. 'Coming here to cause trouble when there isn't any to be had. Say what you've got to say and then piss off.'

Reece took a couple of paper tissues from Morgan and wiped a smear of grease from one of his hands. He went and put them in a bin on the other side of the room. 'A man died in a fire last night.'

Kendle extinguished the torch and put it down. 'What does that have to do with me?' He thrust his hands into the pockets of his overalls and shook his head. 'Oh, no you don't.'

'Looks like someone emptied petrol over him and set it alight.' Reece made no mention of the bag-tied ankles. Only the murderer and those attending the crime scene in an official capacity were so far aware of that fact.

Kendle backed away, still shaking his head. 'Well, it wasn't me.'

'Convince me,' Reece said. 'Because so far, you haven't come close.'

Kendle came to a stop only when the cluttered workbench dug into the small of his back. 'I never hurt anybody with what I did. Those buildings were always empty when I torched them. Every one of them.'

'Now you've moved up a notch and started chasing a new adrenaline rush.'

Kendle ripped off the headgear and slammed it down on the workbench behind him. The noise it made was like a shotgun blast reverberating around the compact garage. The office door opened with a rattle of the slatted blinds.

'You okay, Shaun?'

A second man stood behind the speaker, trying to get a better view of the visitors. 'Is everything all right?'

'I dropped something,' Kendle said. 'Go finish your break. We're done here.' The men went, but only when they'd been told for a second time.

'Where were you last night?' Reece asked.

Kendle walked the short distance to the open shutters at the garage entrance. 'Get out here. Both of you.' He waited for them to join him on a slab of cracked concrete. 'I was at home.'

'Can anyone vouch for that?'

'The cat.'

Reece's face was impassive. 'You'd rather do this down the station?'

'I was on my own.' Kendle bowed his back until their eyes were on the same level. 'I'm always on my own.'

'Convenient.'

'We can't all be shacked up at home with the missus. Some of us aren't so lucky.'

Reece fought the urge to slam his forehead against the other man's broad nose. Morgan got in front of him before he could.

'Answer the question,' she said, stepping to the left when Reece tried to get round her. Then to the right, when he had another go.

Chapter 16

JENKINS MADE HER WAY home from work a few hours earlier than she would normally have done. Orders from Reece to get her head sorted before she forced him to intervene for the good of the team. It was damage limitation, for want of a better term. She'd offered little in the way of explanation or apology for her behaviour towards Ffion Morgan. Instead, she'd collected her belongings and left before anyone caught sight of the flood of tears.

She'd sat in her car and bawled. Slid down behind the steering wheel each time anyone went by, and when she could cry no more, she'd tidied herself up and driven off.

The short drive home did nothing to improve things. Finishing before time meant sharing the roads with the rush hour traffic and drivers who changed lanes as frequently as most people changed their minds. She resorted to acting like Reece did on such occasions: banging the horn and shouting insults at them.

It was during one such angry lapse of concentration that she failed to notice the illuminated brake lights of the vehicle in front, rear-ending it with a heavy and expensive sounding thud. The bump jolted her, but thankfully, there was no painful airbag deployment. No shunting into the path of anything travelling alongside. The Fiat came second place in the exchange; a fist-sized dent in the off-side wing and a strip of plastic bumper trim left dangling onto the tarmac road.

The van had a cracked rear-light casing and little more than a few scuffs in its paintwork. Jenkins accepted all liability immediately and offered to settle without involving insurance companies. But it really wasn't her day. She'd hit a company vehicle and there was a formal process to be followed.

With full contact and insurance details exchanged, she completed the rest of the journey home with the broken car parts crammed into an undersized boot.

'What alternative is there?' Jenkins paced the length and breadth of the kitchen, her tone sharp, her mannerisms bordering on aggressive. 'Mam's getting worse by the day and becoming a real danger to herself. We'll have to move her in with us.'

Cara Frost used a blue-and-white striped glove to transfer a tray of smoking oven chips to a cleared space on the work surface. 'They're overdone,' she said, pushing them to one side. She tossed the glove into the empty sink and grabbed for a wine glass, taking a hefty gulp of its contents. 'Don't you think that time might already have come and gone?'

Jenkins stopped pacing. 'Meaning what?'

'There are plenty of excellent nursing homes in the area. We could both go and—'

Jenkins spat air through her front teeth. 'You want to lock Mam away and forget she exists? Is that it?'

'Not at all.'

'It's what happens though, isn't it?' Jenkins stood on one foot and leaned her hip against the kitchen cabinets. 'Everyone's keen to visit in the beginning. Two or three times a week. It's not long before that's down to weekends only. Give it a few months and we'll be dropping off cheap toiletries on our way to the pub.'

Frost lowered the glass. 'I see no reason for that to happen.'

'It's not happening, full stop!' Jenkins screwed her eyes closed and took a moment to reboot. 'I couldn't afford to pay for it, even if it was an option.' She opened her eyes again and quickly added: 'Which it isn't.'

'You'd use the money raised from the sale of Margaret's house,' Frost said. 'Not dip into your own savings.'

'I was born in that house. Grew up and lived there until I could afford somewhere of my own.' Jenkins came away from the cabinets and wandered as she spoke. 'My parents worked hard so they could leave it to me when they were both gone. It should be mine. It *will* be mine.' She knew how that must have come across. Her whole body was shaking, and not only with rage. 'What I meant is: why do hard-working people have to use every penny they've ever put away, when others—parasites who've never got off their arses—take everything there is for free?'

'I can't answer that?' Frost said, staring into the bottom of her glass. 'But I know Wales has made a recent change in that regard. They've capped the amount you're liable for, to around fifty thousand pounds, and not the full cost.'

'Pocket change.' Jenkins scoffed at the remark. 'Start checking down the back of the settee for stray pound coins.'

Frost drained the dregs of her glass and poured herself a refill. 'Not exactly pocket change, but it's nowhere near what many have had to pay for nursing care.'

'I'll be looking after her here.' Jenkins pointed at the floor she stood on. '*Here*. You got that?'

'You're in full-time employment, working unsociable hours, a police detective with a promising career pathway ahead of you. How on earth would that work?'

'I'll ask the boss for time off. Maybe unpaid leave for a few months. He's as good as agreed to it already.'

'It's not just the time factor,' Frost said. 'There's the space and equipment required to care for Margaret in a new environment.'

'Okay then. We'll move over to her place. It'll be far less disorientating for her and a better idea all round.'

Frost spilled wine on the countertop and put the bottle down. She took a paper towel to the spillage and chased the small puddle across the polished surface. 'Elan—'

'There's a spare room for us upstairs at Mam's place. Cooking would be easy enough, and—'

'Margaret's going to require care that you're not trained to provide.' Frost spoke quickly, leaving Jenkins with little time to interrupt. 'I don't just mean feeding and basic hygiene needs. There will be more specialist intervention needed as time goes by.'

'You're a doctor,' Jenkins said. 'How difficult can it be?'

'Margaret's condition is only going to get worse.'

'People manage.' Jenkins lay her hand on Frost's and squeezed gently. '*We'll* manage. We always do.'

'This is life changing. Life limiting. It's not possible.'

Jenkins withdrew her hand. 'I see.' She moved to the other side of the kitchen. 'Reading you loud and clear.'

Frost dropped the saturated lump of kitchen roll into a pedal bin and tore off another couple of sheets. 'My work commitments have me in and out of the house at all times of the day and night. I don't think I'd be of any use to either of you.'

Jenkins grabbed for the handle of the kitchen door, missing on the first attempt. 'You never are.'

'Please don't say that.' Frost followed a short distance only.

Jenkins marched through the living room, grabbing for her car keys on the way. 'You only ever care about yourself. It's always you, you, you.'

'That's not true. Where are you going?'

'Over to Mam's.'

'You haven't eaten yet.'

'And who's to blame for that?' Jenkins slammed the front door and caught sight of the damage to her car. She held a hand to her forehead. 'What a fucking day this is turning out to be!'

Chapter 17

THE DROP-IN CENTRE WAS built mostly from red brick and glass and could easily have doubled up as a public library or community arts centre in any British town or city. It was tired-looking from years of use, and in need of a good jet wash and a fair bit of TLC.

Mali had fully expected it to have metal bars or wire caging bolted over the windows like some she'd used in the past. It didn't. There was a line of concrete bollards on the pavement directly outside, though she could think of no reason why anyone might want to ram-raid the place. 'We just beat that rain,' she said, rushing into the doorway with her sleeping bag protected from the worst of the sudden onslaught. 'Another couple of minutes and we'd have been properly soaked to the skin.'

Aggy wasn't listening to anything she had to say and was more interested in finding out what the police were doing there. She wandered towards a noisy gathering near the far wall, Mali following in the spotlight of multiple pairs of prying eyes. She was a new face. A potential ally or enemy. The jury would be out at this stage.

'There was a fire last night,' Aggy said, twisting her upper body. She was standing on tip-toe, peering over the shoulders of those at the back of the group. 'Someone died.' She put a hand to her mouth. 'How terrible.'

Although Mali wasn't acquainted with the victim, learning of their death in such horrific circumstances was understandably upsetting. 'Did you know them?'

Aggy's heels rose and fell repeatedly on the marked vinyl flooring; her head moving side-to-side as she struggled to see and hear it all. 'She turned again, a look of worry on her face. 'They don't know who it is. A rough-sleeper, they think.'

That made it more personal. A loss that was far closer than if the victim had been a tourist or your average Jane or Joe making their way out of the city after a hard day's graft.

'They're saying it might have been deliberate.' Aggy crossed herself. 'I can't believe anyone would do such a thing?'

Before Mali could respond, Aggy had already turned away again. A police officer was asking if anyone had witnessed suspicious persons or criminal activity in the area. Had they themselves been threatened or assaulted recently? Numerous people appeared to have an opinion.

The officers left only a short while after that, running across the road to their parked van, seeking shelter from the deluge. Several of the group stayed put. Huddled in nervous conversation.

'Why don't you get some soup?' Aggy suggested. 'And bread, before it's all gone.'

'What about you?' Mali asked.

'I can't eat after hearing this.' The *Big Issue* seller was crying. 'Who would do such a thing? Tell me, who?'

Mali couldn't. It seemed disrespectful to sit down and enjoy a meal like nothing had happened, but she was beyond hungry and didn't know when or if another opportunity would present itself. 'Can't I get you anything at all?'

'Just tea. Milk no sugar.'

Mali joined the queue, her legs almost buckling now she was within touching distance of hot food. 'One soup and two teas, please. The second tea is for that lady over there.'

'I've not seen you here before.' The woman behind the serving counter was middle-aged and wore a yellow tabard over a knitted jumper. She had a face that had clearly known hard times.

'It's my first visit to Cardiff,' Mali said, stirring sugar into one of the teas.

'You chose a hell of a time to come here.' The woman ladled soup into a chipped bowl and added two rounds of white sliced bread to a plate. 'That's one-fifty if you have it.'

Mali apologised for not being able to cover the cost. 'I can wash a few dishes, or tidy up once everyone's done?'

'The charity will see to it,' the woman told her. 'If it wasn't for public donations, I don't know what we'd do.'

Mali struggled to carry the soup, bread, and teas in one go. 'There are some good people out there still.'

'Thankfully,' the woman said. 'If everyone was like Douglas Hames and that *witch*, Payne, then the country would be in a far worse mess than it already is.'

Mali almost dropped her soup. Even the mention of the politician's name had her coming out in hives. 'Do you see her out and about much?'

'Only when there are television cameras in the area. A right prima donna, that one.'

'So I've heard.'

'But she's due a fall. And I only hope I'm there to witness it.'

Mali came away from the serving counter thinking what an interesting turn of phrase that was. 'Watch this space,' she said, looking for somewhere to sit.

Chapter 18

REECE NEEDED TO CLEAR his head before making his way home to Brecon. The coming weekend was weighing heavily on his mind, making him short-tempered and argumentative with most people he came into contact with. Chief Superintendent Cable had even offered him leave, which he'd firmly declined.

The simple fact was, he'd have been far worse if left alone to dwell on things at home. Work gave him a sense of purpose and kept his mind occupied. It also kept most of his demons away until night-time fell.

It was only a short walk from the police station over to Mermaid Quay in the bay. His thin coat was doing little to keep out a wind that whipped across the water. He'd forgotten his scarf and couldn't be arsed to turn back and fetch it. Raising his collar was as good as it was going to get. He shoved his hands deeper into his coat pockets and stooped.

A skateboarder rattled past, catching him unawares, the rider's body moving in a serpentine fashion as he went. Reece turned to watch for as long as the teenager remained in sight, scaring off a flock of gulls busily tucking into a chip supper on the paved walkway. The feathered diners flew off, only to return once the detective had moved on and posed them no further threat.

He wasn't alone on the quay. People seldom were. Even with summer well gone, Cardiff Bay remained a popular place to get out and spend time with family and friends. He stopped to buy himself a flat white and stood staring at his own reflection in the café window. He turned side-on to it and examined himself in profile. There was no need for him to pull in his belly or puff out his chest and shoulders. Men twenty years his junior worked hard in CrossFit gyms across the country for a physique similar to the one good genes and a daily run had given him.

He stirred a trio of sugar sachets into his coffee. Two wouldn't have cut it. Not with Anwen and Idris on his mind.

As he exited the café, he almost fell over a young woman sitting in the doorway.

'Watch where you're stepping,' she said, shifting a tatty sleeping bag out of his way. 'It might look like nothing to you, but it's all I've got.'

She was young enough to be his daughter. He hated the inequalities in life. Despised how society sat back and let so many people get chewed up and spat out like lumps of unpalatable gristle. 'That must be tough?' he said with a genuine sincerity.

'It's not by choice.'

He couldn't imagine it would be. He went to take a sip of his coffee, but thought better of it. 'Can I get you one of these?' he asked. 'Or something else to help warm you up?'

The young woman shied away from him. 'You've got the wrong end of the stick, mate. I don't turn tricks in exchange for gifts.'

'Just as well then,' he said, with the makings of a grin, 'because I've never been a man who accepts them. Do you want that coffee or not?'

'No strings attached?'

'Tell you what,' he said, struggling to take a twenty-pound note from his wallet, one handed. In the end, he used his teeth. 'If it makes you feel any safer, go in there without me and get yourself something to eat with it. If they give you any hassle, tell them Brân Reece sent you.'

The woman took his money. 'Are you sure about this? That's twenty quid you've given me.'

'I must be going soppy in my old age,' he told her. 'Seriously though, you need to get in out of this wind. It's biting.'

'I will. Thanks for the money. You're the second decent bloke I've met this week.'

'Ssh,' he joked, stepping around her with a finger planted firmly to his lips. 'I prefer people to think I'm a grumpy old bastard. They tend to leave me alone that way. Stay safe.' He was on his way again, the new focus of his attention being the small white church on the edge of the water. Its arched windows glowed with a soft orange light that gave it a homely and welcoming look.

'What about the change?' the young woman called after him.

'Get yourself some breakfast in the morning,' he replied without looking back.

The church was over one hundred and fifty years old. Built on land kindly donated by the 3rd Marquess of Bute. There to serve the religious needs of past Norwegian sailors and expatriates alike. Although the darkness obscured his view of the flag flying above it, he could hear its thick material flapping in the breeze, as though in conversation with the water lapping against the wall on the other side of the safety railing.

The church had been one of Anwen's favourite places to spend time, and Reece gained great comfort in being there. Wiping droplets of rain from the surface of a solitary wooden bench, he lowered himself onto the wet smudge of paintwork, alone with his coffee. His teary eyes made the bright lights of the nearby city blur into one colourful blob. He wiped the back of his hand across them and sniffed more than a couple of times. The lights didn't sharpen up any.

To his left was the absolute darkness of the sea and the Somerset coastline on the other side of it. The waves spoke to him. Begged him to join them. Promised to free him from his pain and loneliness. He'd almost given in and answered their call several times previously. A pact made with his dead wife's father, the only thing preventing him from seeing it through.

He got up off the bench and blew a kiss at the church and all it represented for him. When he walked into the wind, it was with hunched shoulders and a heavy heart.

It was time to go home.

Chapter 19

ABEEKU QUAYE WAS IN trouble. Deep trouble. And well overdue a visit from those further up the food chain. He skulked along the empty pavements with a short-bladed knife hidden from view in his jacket pocket. Size alone was no guarantee of safety. Not in the murky depths of the drug dealer's world.

His route home involved stopping to wait in doorways and on the blind side of parked cars. It didn't hurt to be cautious. Complacency was a foe that got people killed.

Home for the past few months was an empty end-of-terrace house in a street strewn with overturned bins and boarded-up windows. A pair of scruffy running shoes hung from a cable spanning the width of the road, attached to a pair of street lamps that offered no light.

Nobody came to complain about any of it. No one cared. It wasn't that sort of neighbourhood.

He stopped at his end of the street to check the ply boards were secure on the downstairs windows and front door. Satisfied, he turned into the adjacent alleyway, keeping close to the broken brickwork as he went. Someone approached from the deeper shadows. They bumped fists. 'Any heat?' Quaye asked.

The teenager handed over a wedge of folded banknotes. 'Nah, man. It was cool.'

'Sweet.' Quaye counted off payment and pocketed the rest.

'Same time tomorrow?' the youngster asked.

'I'm lying low for a while,' Quaye told him, and handed over a burner phone. 'I'll let you know when I'm in town again.'

'You in trouble?'

Quaye grabbed hold of the teenager. 'That ain't any of your business. Know what I'm saying?'

The teenager straightened his hoodie and threw a leg over the seat of his bike. Then pedalled a slow and meandering route out of the alleyway and along the centre lines of the road until completely out of sight.

There was a rusted sheet of corrugated roofing resting against the garden wall, concealing a gap only just wide enough to squeeze through. Quaye was careful not to cut himself, but not in avoiding the sharp edges of stonework that broke the skin on his back and hip.

He repositioned the metal sheet, doubling it up with a thick board of marine ply. Then a wet and heavy fence post, two car batteries, and an old bathtub. Only then did he make his way down a garden path that was overgrown with filth and weeds.

Squatting at the back door, he slotted his fingers the other side of a board that was missing a few screws along its lower right edge. He pulled it back, and with a struggle, crawled inside.

A woman waited in the darkness of the mould-infested kitchen, stick-thin in a tracksuit several sizes too big for her. She tucked a carving knife—one she'd only moments earlier been brandishing at the back door—down the hip of her waistband. 'It's you,' she said, breathing heavily and wiping sweat from her forehead. 'Thank fuck for that.'

He caught her chin in a pincer-like grip and jerked her head to the midline. 'Who did you think was coming?' he asked, relieving her of the weapon.

She closed her hand around his thick forearm but couldn't budge it. 'There's been some weird shit goin' on since you went out.'

He pushed her against the wall and put the tip of the knife to the underside of her left eyeball. 'What you been up to, bitch?'

The blade punctured the skin and drew blood. The woman sucked in a lungful of damp air. 'Nuffin. I swear.'

He forced his head against hers. 'I'll kill you if you're lying.'

She stroked his arm. 'Iss you and me, babe.'

Loosening his grip, he backed away.

'There was someone out there,' she told him. 'They was tryin' to get in.'

'How many?'

'One, I fink.'

'Where?'

'Where you was just now. I could hear him breevin' and everything.'

'Was it one of them? The Liverpool crowd?'

'Couldn't see. It was too dark.'

He dropped to his knees and stuck his head outside. 'You sure you weren't tripping?'

The woman shook her head hard enough to rattle her brain. 'The board was movin' and stuff. He was deffo tryin' to get in.'

'Well he ain't here now,' Quaye said, wrestling a battered washing machine across the room. He set it against the kitchen door. 'One more night. Then we're off.'

'Where to?'

'London. I know some people there.' He checked the doorway one last time. 'Nobody's getting in or out of this place tonight,' he said, pulling her towards the stairs.

Chapter 20

THE HEADLAMPS OF REECE'S Land Cruiser cut through what would otherwise have been an impenetrable darkness on the Brecon Beacons. His old Peugeot had travelled the same route, and on countless occasions, but unlike the battered 205, the Toyota's heating worked perfectly well. Its windows didn't lower themselves under the command of every bump in the road, letting in rain, sleet, or snow. And the very best thing of all was the fact the radio worked without him having to stab it with the pointy end of a short screwdriver.

This radio had knobs and all sorts of twiddly bits to fiddle with. Yanto had installed an aftermarket upgrade that paired with a phone. Jenkins had set up a Spotify account and put together a half-tidy playlist for him to listen to. Reece had admitted to the whole thing being *"Bloody brilliant,"* causing everyone involved to fall about laughing.

The youngsters at work found his lack of tech-savviness both hilarious and worrying at the same time. But George, the desk sergeant, knew where he was coming from. The pair of them were cut from the same cloth.

"Bluetooth?" George had asked when Reece first mentioned it. *"Isn't that what happens when you've been on the ole Vino Rioja?"*

It wasn't far off midnight. He'd briefly contemplated sleeping in his office back in Cardiff, but thought better of it. It was a slippery slope, that one. He had a home to go to and decided he should damn well use it.

It being too late to pick up Redlar from Yanto's farm, he'd phoned and apologised. The farmer had complained as he usually did, claiming Reece was taking liberties and should pull himself together. Then he'd agreed, as was always the case.

Queen's *Don't Stop Me Now,* was just beginning in the background. Reece turned it up and pressed his right foot almost to the floor. The Land Cruiser grunted and duly obliged, speeding him along and into the night.

Mali had bought a steak sandwich and a flat white, courtesy of the guy calling himself Brân Reece. She'd eaten only half of it. The rest was knocking about in the bottom of her sleeping bag and would make a welcome breakfast the following morning. Always one to pay her way when able, she'd donate the change to the drop-in centre when next there.

The bright lights of the high-rise apartments lit up the waterfront. 'You're no better than we are!' She leaped up and down, the sleeping bag and its contents slapping against her hip. 'Do you hear me, people? No better at all.'

A dog barked somewhere. Maybe in agreement.

Another answered. One for the opposition, perhaps.

Hames's company moniker was just about everywhere she looked. Fancy artwork depicting expensive interiors and communal gardens. Not much further along from where she was were scorch marks burned into the ground and up the side of the concrete bus shelter. Broken lengths of police tape hung limply from the wonky fencing. A yellow card was nailed to it, stating: **POLICE. SERIOUS INCI-DENT.** There was a date and time, as well as a request for potential witnesses to come forward with information.

The entire building site was surrounded by a wall of boards standing eight feet or more in height. Mali jumped and wrapped her fingers over the top of it, pulling herself upward until her chin was level with her thumbs. Her arms lacked their former climbing strength, but the action remained simple enough for someone of her expert ability.

There was nothing extraordinary to be seen on the other side. Only heavy plant hire, gantry lighting, and more mud than a WW1 battlefield. Everything was shut down until morning. Everything but the lights.

There was a Portakabin next to a makeshift road, representing a checkpoint of sorts. Two men were visible inside. Both wearing the unmistakable uniforms of security staff. They'd surely see her crossing the open waste ground and give chase. But the rewards of making her first foray into Douglas Hames's world by far outweighed the risk. If the developer was in some way involved in a business deal with Bridget Payne, then he, too, was fair game.

Mali lowered herself and tossed her sleeping bag over the boarding. And without a moment's hesitation, hoicked herself up again and followed after it.

Chapter 21

IT WAS A CURIOUS whirring sound that first got Abeeku Quaye's attention. Coming from somewhere downstairs. Possibly near the kitchen. It repeated itself a few times before he was sure it belonged to a drill or an electric screwdriver of some sort. Someone was messing with the ply boards on the back door. Had the Liverpool crew arrived to punish him for creaming off a little of the profit? Who else was it going to be?

He rolled over and shoved the snoring woman next to him. 'Wake up. We've got ourselves some trouble.'

She stirred, but did little more than that. Even when he repeated himself, all she did was complain and change her sleeping position. The movement released an empty vodka bottle from somewhere beneath her body. It rolled out of the sleeping bag and onto the wooden floorboards with a dull thud and a full rotation before it came to a complete stop in the middle of the room.

He took her by the shoulders and shook her violently. 'They've come for us.' He gripped his knife between clenched teeth and did up his jeans and belt.

'*Whaat?*' she asked with a throaty groan, and twisted her fists against her bloodshot eyes. 'Where you off to, babe?'

He was busy collecting rolls of banknotes from beneath a loose floorboard. Stuffing as many as he could into his pockets and underpants. When they'd take no more, he tossed a few at the woman, who was still struggling to get upright without falling onto her hands and knees.

'What's that smell?' she asked, now staggering in circles.

Quaye went over to the far wall and crouched again to force an arm behind a rotten length of skirting board. 'Fire.'

The woman caught the empty vodka bottle with her bare foot, setting it rolling towards him. It got only halfway there before coming back on itself. 'How's that?'

He was no longer interested in any unclaimed bounty. Survival was his priority. He bounded over to the bedroom door, thick dreadlocks trailing behind him. The pungent stink of petrol was a clear indicator of what was going on downstairs. He caught hold of the door handle and cried out when it burned the skin of his palm.

'We've gotta get out of here,' the woman said, trying to force her way past. She banged her fists against his chest when he wouldn't let her. 'We gotta get out,' she kept repeating between bouts of hysteria.

He grabbed her hands and held them against him. 'They've screwed down the back door,' he said, dragging her away from the exit. 'I heard them.'

The woman pulled free and gripped her head in her hands. 'Fuck. Fuck. *Fuck!*' She stopped and pointed. 'It's comin' through the gaps in the floor.' That set her off again.

Quaye pulled their sleeping bags over the rising smoke. It was a temporary measure and one that was hopelessly ineffective. He went to the window and used his knife to stab at the plyboard covering the otherwise empty frame. The screws had rusted in the damp air, making it impossible for him to loosen them with the point of his knife. He kicked at them instead, using his height and physical bulk to do them some serious damage. 'Get over here.'

The woman refused to budge until he told her what he had in mind.

'Are you nuts?' she screamed. 'I can't jump.'

One edge of the ply board split along most of its length and broke free of its fastenings with a loud snapping noise. 'You can,' he said, giving it one last kick.

'I can't. I can't.' The woman reversed all the way over to the bedroom door. 'I'm goin' this way.'

'Don't open it.' Quaye manoeuvred himself along the narrow windowsill, dangling his legs outside. There was a sound not unlike that of storm winds whipping their way through the rooms below.

'We can use the stairs,' the woman said through more bouts of phlegmy coughing. 'If we're quick, we can.'

The drop to the pavement below looked far greater when viewed from above. If he could land on the overturned bin, then maybe the soft plastic would break his fall and minimise injury. 'The rest of the money,' he said, holding an arm out towards her. 'Give it to me!'

'If I wrap my hoodie round my hand ...' The woman grabbed hold of the doorknob.

'The money,' Quaye shouted above the din of the staircase collapsing. 'Don't open it. *Don't!*'

Too late.

The woman turned the glowing handle with a fist wrapped in her clothing. 'See,' she said, pulling on it. When the door blew in, her hair ignited almost immediately. Not that Abeeku Quaye got to witness much of what happened next. The pressure wave that surged through the bedroom catapulted him way beyond his intended landing zone. By the time he came to a messy stop on the hard road below, the woman had already stopped screaming.

Chapter 22

MALI LANDED ON THE other side of the boarding, slipped and toppled backwards with her arm outstretched. She got to her feet and massaged it. There was nothing broken or dislocated, as far as she could tell. The sleeping bag was soaked and filthy from where it had been pressed into the mud. Next to useless for its intended purpose of keeping her warm and dry overnight.

She'd freeze without adequate shelter from the elements. But the main high-rise development was too far away from where she was, especially with the amount of lighting in the area. A row of yellow excavators, each with **JCB** stencilled along their sides, was a much safer option. She chose one that was partially hidden from the view of anyone watching from the security hut. The machine's glass cabin would provide a welcome break from the wind and rain.

She checked for the presence of security guards, and even from her current distance, saw one man holding a mug of something to his mouth. 'Lucky sod.' She took her chance and went.

Close up, the digger smelled of oil. Its metal scoop rested on the ground like a fist at the end of an arm crawling with hydraulic pipelines. She put a foot on the bottom step and reached for the handle of the cab.

Was it alarmed?

Would it give her away when she opened it?

She held her breath, closed her eyes, and pulled.

———◆———

Jenkins awoke with a violent start. Drawers opened and closed in the room next to hers. It was dark outside. She checked the time on her phone, waiting for the blurred numbers to morph into something more legible. It wasn't yet two-thirty in the morning.

She threw back the quilt and swung her legs out of bed, rubbing her eyes and swaying towards the door like one of the living dead. She found Margaret standing in the far corner of her bedroom, a blank look on her face, a clean nightie and underwear gripped in her hands.

'I was just …' Margaret glanced at the bed. Then away again. 'I was …'

Jenkins could see the yellowing wet patch from where she was. 'Your nightie's soaking,' she said, crossing the room. 'Let me see to it.'

'I tipped my cup of tea.' Margaret tried to shoo her away. 'I didn't burn myself this time.' She went over to the bed and pulled the duvet into place. 'No harm done. You can go back to sleep now.'

'It needs changing,' Jenkins said. 'Do you still keep the spares in the airing cupboard on the landing?'

Margaret was on her way to the door. 'I can do it. There's no need to fuss.'

'You're shivering.' Jenkins rubbed her mother's back. 'I'll run a nice warm bath and get this sorted while you're in there.'

Downstairs a short while later, Jenkins shoved the soiled clothing into the drum of the washing machine and set the program to start. She put the wet bedding in a separate pile to go in next. Then sat at the kitchen table, supporting her weary head on a fist. It was a difficult thing to accept, but Cara might be right after all. This wasn't in any way sustainable. Not for the long term.

There was movement upstairs. And the gurgling sound of a bath plug pulled. She shot out of the chair and shouted at the underside of the ceiling: 'Don't get out yourself!' She raced up the stairs and burst through the bathroom door. 'I told you not to stand up. You'll fall and break something.'

'I've never fallen before.' Margaret looked startled. 'Why would I start now?'

'Wrap this towel around you.'

'I know what to do.'

'I know that, but—'

'Stop babying me. I'm the mother, not you.'

Jenkins backed slowly out of the bathroom, allowing Margaret more space to step out of the tub. 'Hold on to the basin. It'll steady you.'

'I don't need to hold on to anything.'

'You'll slip.'

'I won't. I've done this a thousand times or more.'

Jenkins curled an arm around Margaret's waist and steered her into the bedroom, dripping frothy bath suds and water onto the carpet. 'I've turned the mattress over,' she said, patting it. 'Nothing came through this side. And that's a clean sheet and duvet cover.'

Margaret hugged herself. 'It's cold in here. You've left the window open.'

'I'll shut it again once you're back in bed.'

'I'll be needing a pair of your father's thermals, if you keep this fresh air thing up.'

That brought a smile to Jenkins's face. 'What are we going to do with you?' she asked, embracing her mother as they settled onto the bed.

'They'd shoot me if I was a horse.'

She rested her chin on top of Margaret's head and gave it a gentle kiss. 'I love you, Mam.'

'I love you too.' When Margaret looked up, she was crying. 'Growing old is no fun, Elan. I'm frightened.'

Chapter 23

MACHINERY STARTED UP ALL around Mali. This was no dream. It was morning. There were voices belonging to dozens of men wearing heavy boots and hard hats. One of them was walking towards her excavator with his head lowered while he negotiated a safe path through the mud and ice.

Mali clicked open the cab door and stuck out a leg. The man didn't look up. Even if he had, he'd have seen little of her through the condensation on the windscreen. But that in itself might have alerted him to things not being as they should.

She slid to the ground, her clothing riding up her back while the mud sucked at her feet. She kept the sleeping machine between herself and the oncoming worker. With the filthy sleeping bag thrown over a shoulder, she made her getaway like a thief with a bag of swag.

'Oi, *you!*' Someone was trying to get the driver's attention by waving his arms above his head. 'What are you doing in here?'

Legging it in such treacherous conditions was easier said than done. It was more of a slip and slurp as the ground threatened to pull her under.

'Somebody stop her.' Several tried.

'I've got her,' one of them shouted. 'She's coming your way now,' he corrected, when Mali altered her course.

'Stay put.' A third worker widened his arms and bent his legs like he was about to face a penalty kick. 'The game's up, love.'

'I wouldn't bet on it.' Mali swung the sleeping bag with all the force she could generate. It bounced off the man's shoulder and caught the side of his head, knocking him flat in the mud. He lay there like an overturned beetle. His legs pedalling the air.

She was heavily outnumbered. Even Bill and Ben had dragged themselves away from the security hut. But they were no threat to her. No threat at all. There was only one way she was getting off the building site without being apprehended, and that was the same way she'd come in.

'Those boards are close to eight feet tall,' someone said. Nobody there could have accounted for Mali being such an accomplished climber. Most of the workers slowed until realising their mistake, and by then it was already too late.

She swung a leg and quickly followed it with the other. Dropped roadside, hitting the floor harder than she would have liked, stumbling forward and into the cycle lane.

'Get out of the way!' The passing cyclist swerved in a failed attempt to avoid a collision, the derailleur of his gears catching the sleeping bag, dragging it until the bicycle came to a full stop. 'Idiot!' the cyclist shouted, hurling the bag over the side of the quay and into the water. 'You could have killed me.'

Mali stared in disbelief as the bag bobbed on the surface until sufficiently soaked to sink out of sight. 'I wish I had!' she screamed at him. He was already pedalling away and gesturing obscenely with his free hand. 'That was everything I had. Everything,' she said, settling onto her haunches and pulling at handfuls of hair.

Jenkins flew out of bed. She was late. Again. She'd either not set an alarm in the first place or had somehow deactivated it when she'd got up to see to her mother during the night.

And where was Margaret now? Not in her bedroom. Bathroom neither.

'Oh, God. Not again.' Jenkins descended the stairs. There wouldn't be time for a shower, and she still needed to call at her own house for a change of clothes. That would mean bumping into Cara.

She couldn't face another row and would have to go to work in the clothes she was wearing—as grim as that was.

But first. Where was Margaret?

Jenkins burst into the living. 'There you are.'

Margaret was sitting comfortably in her favourite armchair, wearing a nightie together with a fleece dressing gown. Balanced on the arm of the chair was a cup of tea and a plate of toast with butter and orange marmalade. 'Where else did you think I'd be?'

Jenkins went over and gave her mother a peck on the cheek. 'You got yourself breakfast.'

'Would you like some? There's plenty of bread there.'

'No time. Tomorrow. I promise.'

'That'll be nice.'

'Have you seen my car keys?' She wandered the room, hunting for them. 'I'm sure I put them next to the telly last night.'

'I hung them up on the key rack in the kitchen,' Margaret said. 'Didn't want you losing them again.'

Jenkins checked. That's exactly where they were. It might be a good day after all. It was certainly easier to leave Margaret alone for a few hours when she was more switched on. 'I'll ring you later, just to be sure you're all right and don't need anything.'

'I'll be fine. Don't worry about me,' Margaret said, finishing the second round of toast. 'I'm not planning on doing anything as silly as I did the other night.' She hid her face in her hands. 'What was I thinking, wandering off like that? And with the front door left open.'

'Just a funny five minutes,' Jenkins said, more for her own peace of mind. 'I'll try to get back at lunchtime and then again tonight.'

'Phone me beforehand,' Margaret said. 'Why don't we play it by ear?'

Jenkins breathed an enormous sigh of relief. This was the best her mother had been in weeks. 'Right,' she said, stopping briefly for another kiss. 'I'm off.' She got as far as the front door before Margaret called her name.

'Best be quick to the bus stop, sweetheart. You're going to be late for school.'

Chapter 24

FFION MORGAN HATED HAVING to attend post-mortem examinations. Everyone had something they didn't get on with in life, and PMs were, without a doubt, hers.

She hadn't slept well the previous night. An hour or so here and there. Images of the dead and the horribly injured had played on her mind for most of it. So much so, she'd given up and climbed out of bed to stand next to the window, staring at the empty street below. It was quiet and restful, but not nearly enough to help her get back to sleep.

She'd watched Josh, her fiancé, dream like the proverbial baby. His eyelids quivering, his breathing slow and shallow. No nightmares there.

She went downstairs for a while and watched television without the sound on. Then tidied up in the kitchen. Ironed Josh a clean shirt for the morning. And eventually, went back to bed.

Being sent to the morgue was a stark and unpleasant reminder of her own mortality. A dragging up of the breast cancer scares that had so far proven to be nothing more serious. But the dreaded BRCA 1 gene was never going away.

Life was a numbers game. A thing of statistics and percentages. She remained thankful that the big bingo caller in the sky had yet to select hers.

The hospital corridors were endlessly long and narrow. Draughty and poorly lit in places. The windows were dirty and the pigeon deterrent systems did no such thing.

She knew the exact route to where she was headed, but wished with all her being she didn't. And to make matters worse, today's corpse was burned beyond all recognition. Yay! A first for her. She swallowed and sucked on her lips.

Ginge, her junior colleague back at the station, had bragged about holding a chilled brain when he'd last been at the mortuary. He'd revelled in getting up close and personal with the cutting table, watching in awe of the pathologist as she dug fragments of bone and bullet out of some poor sod's chest and shoulder. He'd even relived the ghastly experience in front of the entire murder squad while tucking into a tuna sandwich and a packet of crisps. The man was immune to anything that might put a normal person off their dinner.

Morgan, on the other hand, wouldn't be able to look at a scrap of food for the best part of twenty-four hours. During which time, she'd launder all her clothing and shower on multiple occasions. *"To get the smell of death off me,"* she'd explain to anyone witness to the ritual.

And there she was. ***Authorised Personnel Only*** it read on the overhead sign. Was she authorised? Should she be there? She was still pondering those questions, and others, when the sound of heels on tiles announced the arrival of Doctor Cara Frost.

'Morning,' Morgan said in a nervy tone. She attempted a smile to go with it, but managed only a lip-tremble. 'I'm here on time for once, as you can see.'

'You're not changed yet.' Frost pushed on the door and waited. 'After you.'

'Oh, I'm not changing.' Morgan ducked under the outstretched arm. 'I'll be watching from the viewing gallery.' Again, the smile failed her. 'In my usual spot down the front. It's not nearly so smelly behind the glass.'

Frost raised her eyes to the ceiling. 'Suit yourself.'

Morgan watched as the pathologist slipped out of a raincoat and collected a pair of black scrubs from a tower of shelving in the room's corner.

'How is Elan today? She seemed a bit ... under the weather yesterday.'

Frost supported herself against a grey, metal locker and sunk a good two inches in height once free of her shiny shoes. 'Why don't you ask her mother?'

'Margaret?'

Frost pulled the scrub-trousers over her legs and tied the strings at her narrow waist. 'There *is* only one mother, unless you're privy to something I'm not.'

'I don't think so.'

'Margaret, it is then.'

Morgan stopped in the doorway leading to the viewing gallery. 'There's no need to be rude to me. I was only being polite and friendly.'

Frost sat down on a wooden bench, half dressed, with her hands pressed between her knees. 'I'm sorry. Things are a bit tense at home. Neither of us are at our best right now. But I shouldn't have snapped at you.'

'No problem. Is Margaret unwell?'

Frost was on her feet again, slipping into a pair of white clogs. She pulled the scrub top over her head and put her hair right. 'She's taking up a lot of Elan's time at the moment. I don't think she'd want me saying any more than that.'

'No. I can imagine.' Morgan pushed on the door. 'I hope everything is back to normal again soon. You two are good together.'

Frost secured her locker door using a key on a lanyard sporting a rainbow of coloured stripes. When she caught Morgan's eye again, it was only fleetingly.

Chapter 25

THERE WERE THE USUAL rubberneckers congregating on the civvy side of the crime scene tape. The type drawn to other people's tragedy. Several of them were busy filming anything that moved—or didn't move—one or two of them gesturing aggressively at anyone they believed to be in a position of authority.

'About time.'

'Stop for breakfast on the way, did you?'

The taunts a seasoned police officer got used to. As it was, the traffic from Brecon had been busier than most days; something to do with a temporary road closure in the Merthyr Tydfil area.

Reece said nothing in response and ducked beneath the tape in search of a CSI. It took him only a couple of minutes to sign in and get dressed in head-to-toe PPE.

'You wouldn't be dragging your arse like this if it was one of their lot over there,' someone shouted at him. That got a few more in the crowd riled up in agreement.

Reece knew only too well that such bad feeling could easily spark a riot and extensive damage to public property once night fell. The criminal element always felt emboldened by the cover of darkness. And the disillusioned needed no encouragement to take matters into their own hands whenever they believed they were not being treated equitably.

The assembled crowd had a point, though. There had been no urgent phone call from police headquarters that morning, demanding he get over there and see what was what. No summons to the chief super's office. Just a nod from an inspector in uniform suggesting that he *"Might want to take a look at this one, given what happened the other night."*

There was a tent billowing in the middle of the road, opposite an end-of-terrace house with little more than black holes for windows and doors. Above the openings in the brickwork were areas of V-shaped dirty sooting. The roof was completely absent. As was a good half of the property's next door.

Reece showed his ID to a firefighter wearing a white helmet and raised his voice to be heard over the clackety noise of a diesel engine. 'A high suspicion of arson, I'm told?'

'Definitely,' the other man answered, alternating his attention between the detective and everything else that was going on in the immediate vicinity. 'Plenty of evidence of accelerant used at both main exits.'

'No way out of there?'

The firefighter cast an eye over the external walls. 'Not with everything boarded up like it was. The occupants didn't stand a chance.'

'Two fatalities,' Reece said. 'Is that still the total number?'

'We're having a proper look around with the structural engineer now the fire's out. It's little more than a shell in there.'

'One victim inside, the other out in the street?' Reece asked, wagging this thumb in alternate directions.

'Looks like the male tried to jump for it. I can't give you the sex of the other victim with any certainty, but they're a fair bit smaller. Female is my best guess.'

'Please tell me it wasn't a child?' Reece couldn't bear the thought of that.

The firefighter removed his helmet to finger-comb hair that was soaking wet and stuck low on his forehead. 'I really can't say at this stage.'

Reece estimated the distance between the house and the position of the CSI tent to be twenty feet at the very least. 'How did he get all the way over there?' He supposed the man could have hit the ground and then staggered a few steps before succumbing to his injuries.

'There must have been some blast activity in the bedroom. To the right, as we view it. Sudden changes in air pressure and the dispersal of hot gases will have been enough to propel him in that direction.'

Reece gave the firefighter his contact details and instructions to keep him up to date with any new developments. He made his way over to the tent while gulls circled overhead, waiting for the humans to clear off. 'Ouch,' he said upon entering. 'That looks painful.'

'It wasn't the prettiest of landings, I'll give you that,' was the duty pathologist's opinion. The victim's head was folded underneath his chest, dreadlocks trailing like the tendrils of a giant squid. His buttocks were forced into the air, giving him the appearance of a toddler that had fallen asleep on its face. But the man wasn't asleep. He was dead and leaking clear fluids from his nostrils and ears.

Reece didn't go too close. Head injured people always had a distinctively unpleasant odour to them. 'The fire team say he was blasted out of one of the upstairs windows.'

The pathologist—Reece hadn't previously met him, looked up from whatever he was doing—and said: 'Either that or his Spidey-web let him down.' He laughed through his nose. An act that made him sound both nerdy and irritating.

'Dead before or after he landed?'

'Alive when he hit the ground, I'd say. But not for long.' Snort. Snort.

Reece squatted. 'What's he got in his pockets?'

'Several thousand pounds in rolled-up bank notes.' The patholo-gist prised open the deceased man's fingers to show the contents of the clenched fist. 'A rival wanted this dealer out of business.'

Reece refused to jump to such early conclusions. 'And leave that amount of money behind? I don't think so.'

'Fair point, Chief Inspector.'

'Have you seen the other victim yet?'

'They're next on my list.'

Chapter 26

REECE FOLLOWED THE PATHOLOGIST out of the tent, leaving the dead man alone with a photographer struggling to capture his best angle.

'I'll come across with you, if that's all right?' he said.

The pathologist told him it was and then went on to make bizarre small talk about his fascination with cemeteries. 'A *taphophile* is the official term for it,' he said. 'Most of us have an additional interest in funerals and the ceremonies that go with them. Do you know how many types of funeral ceremony there are in this country alone?'

'Can't say I do.' Reece tried to imagine himself lying down in the middle of the road—any road—during school-run traffic. 'Here we are,' he said, cutting the pathologist off in full flow.

A young firefighter supplied them with hard hats and plenty of instructions to keep them out of harm's way when negotiating the downstairs area of the burned out terraced house. The same man would act as a chaperone, providing an extra layer of safety.

The smell as they entered the building was overpowering. 'It's like being in the belly of a whale,' Reece said, studying the bare walls and the few charred rafters that hadn't burned through and fallen to the floor.

'Your best guess or are you speaking from personal experience, Chief Inspector?' Snort. Snort.

Reece didn't answer. You needed to be somewhere beyond odd to want to spend an entire career in the company of the dead, and the pathologist oozed that particular quality in bucketfuls.

Reece was long enough in the job to know that the smell of pork crackling was the doing of the balled up victim in the far corner of the room. 'You found no one else in your search of the property?' he asked the chaperone, and was told they hadn't.

'We think this person fell through when the upstairs floor gave way,' the man said. 'See how the remains of those rafters are piled beneath the body and not on top?'

It was like a funeral pyre. Reece stared into the smoking void above them. Visible were the same gulls he'd seen circling from the street view outside. There was dirty water dripping from what little remained of the upper floor and attic space. Steam rose all around them and most things in there creaked and hissed.

The corpse was more extensively burned than the one with the roasted duck supper. This victim was also missing its nose, lips, and eyes. The pugilistic pose was a given for anyone so badly affected by heat. A large lump of something crispy and yellow bulged out of a hole in the left side of the upper abdomen. The charred skin was split and pink in places over both shoulders. Few people ever deserved to die like that. There were a few Reece had caught over the years that were. But not many.

He shook his head and whispered. 'What an awful way to go.'

Mali could tell something was wrong as soon as she arrived at the drop-in centre. Deciding it best to stay clear of any brewing trouble, she joined the breakfast queue and waited for her turn to be served.

'I still don't know your name?'

The voice startled her and belonged to the man standing directly behind. She shuffled forward as far as the gap would allow.

'Just being friendly,' he said, quickly filling the space between them. 'I'm Cory. We almost met yesterday.' When he smiled, the creases around his eyes sank deeper into the skin. It was difficult to pin an age on him.

Mali guessed he was somewhere around thirty.

'Are you going to tell me your name this time or are you still playing hard to get?'

She shuffled another inch or two before there was nowhere left to go. 'Leave me alone.'

'Come on.'

'Get your hand off my shoulder.'

'Listen—'

She spun and almost snapped his arm. 'Why couldn't you fuck off, like I told you to?' She left the queue and banged her way between the tables and chairs. When he looked like he might follow, she wagged a finger in warning. 'Don't even think it.'

She wasn't far from the centre when a feeling of lightheadedness came over her. For a moment, she thought she might pass out and caught hold of the metal railing to steady herself. It was cold to the touch and enough of a stimulant to jerk her back to the present. 'That's all I need,' she said as the aura slowly subsided. She straightened, took a few deep breaths, and then caught sight of a man watching her from his window seat in a nearby cafe. A glare of sunlight on the glass made it difficult to get a proper look at him.

At first Mali thought he was some middle-aged perv who fancied his chances. He was paying her far more attention than he should have been. 'What?' she mouthed in his general direction. 'Get lost, creep.' When he pushed his coffee cup to one side and stood, she got a better view of him and froze.

Chapter 27

Tommy Hemlock hadn't followed Mali. Not as far as she could tell, anyway. But what was he doing there in Cardiff? The last time she'd seen him was when he'd given evidence against her at the coroner's inquest in North Wales, spouting a mouthful of lies and pointing the finger of blame. He and the scheming politician with him.

There was a large gathering in the street ahead and no obvious way to get past now that the police had just about everything cordoned off with blue and white tape. She pushed through a small gap in the crowd, as interested as everyone else to know what was going on.

There were three fire appliances and at least two ambulances she could see from where she was. A tent was pitched in the middle of the road. People in hooded paper coveralls came and went with monotonous regularity.

Several members of the press were already present, their television cameras pointed at just about anyone claiming to have something to say.

'What happened?' Mali asked the woman standing next to her.

'There's been a house fire.'

Ask a daft question. 'Is everyone okay? Did they all get out alive?'

'They reckon there's at least four dead,' the woman said without taking her eyes off the busy scene. 'Couple of kids as well. Tragic innit?'

'Kids. No way?' Mali's stomach turned over.

'That's what they're saying.'

Two men in white coveralls exited the burned-out house, one of them carrying a metal case, the other holding a phone to his ear. The second man lowered his hood and removed his face mask. Even from that distance, Mali recognised him as the provider of the steak sandwich and coffee. Police. Who'd have believed it?

The detective must have had a sixth sense. He glanced in her direction and, at first, slowed his pace before speeding up again. He was coming towards her now and offered a wave of acknowledgement.

Mali turned away and forced a path through a crowd that was growing by the minute. The police officer was calling her. Not by name. But she knew who he meant.

Someone tugged at her arm and pulled her to one side. The grip was firm. Not friendly by any means.

'Let go of me,' she squealed and tried to pull free. When he didn't respond, she sought the help of the policeman, but the crowd had totally obscured him from view. 'What are *you* doing here?' she demanded to know.

'I could ask you the same question.' Hemlock forced her against the wall and pressed his forehead tight to hers. 'But Bridget's already told me about your letter.'

Reece saw them from where he was standing in the middle of the street. The interaction between the bearded man and the young woman wasn't friendly by any means. She was trying to get away, while Beard was doing all he could to stop her.

But why? Was he her pimp, or a prospective punter pushing his luck? The answer mattered little to Reece. Those people were all the same to him. Exploiters of vulnerable women. He went after them with his phone still held to his ear, catching only sporadic glimpses between heads and shoulders in the crowd. When he next got a proper view, Beard was bent over, clutching his groin. The woman was nowhere to be seen.

'Ffion, what's up?' Reece asked. 'I'm busy right now. Can it wait?'

'The post-mortem's all done, boss. And there might be something for us to work on, ID-wise.'

Reece had only momentarily taken his eye off the injured man. But that's all it took. He was gone, along with the young woman before him.

He pushed through the crowd, continuing the conversation, and got to the spot where the brief altercation had taken place. 'I'm listening. What did you find out?'

'The victim had a tattoo,' Morgan said. 'On his lower back. Some of it survived the fire thanks to the damp ground he was lying on when he died.'

Reece wasn't fully concentrating on their conversation. He was well beyond the crowd and checking in all directions. The pair of them had definitely disappeared. He turned and retraced his footsteps. 'When you say, "*Some of it* – how much, exactly?"'

'Numbers. A two and a nine. Pretty much everything else was lost to horrific tissue damage.'

Even though the information was limited, it gave them something to explore. 'Okay. Excellent work. See you back at the station when you're done.'

'I'm already finished at the hospital,' she said, sounding relieved. 'And survived to tell the tale.'

'I'm glad to hear it,' he replied. 'Because we've got ourselves another couple of bodies over here. I'll pencil you in for an introduction.'

Chapter 28

REECE CROSSED THE LANDING with a spring in his step, whistling something he'd heard on the car radio on the short drive back to the station. The artist and title of the song were already forgotten, but the tune, he couldn't get out of his head. The incident room was empty, save for Ginge and one or two others busily tapping away at computer keyboards.

'Is Ffion not back yet?' Reece asked, slipping out of his suit jacket. He'd taken the stairs and the building's centrally controlled heating made the room uncomfortably warm. 'She was done at the hospital when I last spoke to her.'

Ginge checked his watch. 'She phoned twenty minutes ago, saying she was about to leave. Should be back anytime soon.'

DEVIL'S BREAD

'Did she tell you about the victim's tattoo?' Reece asked. 'Or what was left of it?'

Ginge told him she had. 'A nine and a two. A date, maybe? Or a password for something?'

'Could be a child's birthday,' Reece said. 'Could be anything, in fact.'

Ginge agreed. 'I've already started running searches on the numbers, using *tattoo* and *homeless people* as additional filters. I haven't found any useful matches as yet.'

'Keep trying.' Reece scanned the room. It was unusually quiet in there. 'Jenkins not in?'

'I thought she might have been with you,' Ginge said, still concentrating on his search through the HOLMES 2 database.

Reece went over to his office. 'What's that on my desk?' he asked, reappearing in the open doorway only seconds later. He hadn't noticed it the first time he went in with his jacket. 'There's a box in brown wrapping paper. Looks like it might be a bottle of something.'

Ginge went over to take a look for himself. 'No idea. I didn't see anyone put it there.'

'And you were first in this morning?'

'Pretty much.'

'So how did it get there? It wasn't there when I left last night.'

Ginge shrugged. 'Dunno.'

'You're a big help.' Reece normally preferred to pick up his own mail from the downstairs post room. That way, he could call in and

127

chat about the rugby with George, the desk sergeant. Everyone knew that. At least, he thought they did.

Ffion Morgan breezed in through the door just then. She removed her long coat and did a slow pirouette at the centre of the room. 'Come on then, boys. Ask me who it was that got all the way through a post-mortem on a burns victim without puking or sparking out. Not even once.'

'Do you know anything about this?' Reece took her by the shoulders—while she was still babbling on about earning herself a Blue Peter badge—and walked her sideways towards his office. 'The box. That tall one in the brown wrapping paper.'

She poked her head through the open door. 'What's in it?' she asked. 'Something nice?'

Reece only just managed not to swear at her. 'I'm asking you.'

'Why would I know? I've only just got back from the hospital. Maybe Elan does. Have you asked her?' She looked towards her colleague's empty desk and chair. 'Where is she, anyway?'

Reece gave up. 'Your guess is as good as mine.'

Morgan grabbed him by his arm. 'Hey, hang on a minute. Are you thinking what I'm thinking?'

Reece pulled away. 'It's very unlikely.'

'That could be a homemade bomb sat there on your desk,' she said, her eyes widening. 'Shaun Kendle was none too pleased with you yesterday. He looked like he could be a nasty piece of work if someone provoked him enough.'

'A bomb.' Reece scratched his head. 'You can't be serious?'

'I am,' she told him. 'The anti-corruption review that's going on at the minute – that's all down to what you uncovered in the Brogan case.'

Ginge agreed. 'You'll have made no shortage of enemies there.'

His junior colleagues were right. There'd be rogue officers who'd slipped through the net, either by retiring or transferring to other forces. Any one of them might have decided to take him out in the most effective and permanent of ways possible.

'But a bomb. In my office?'

Ginge and Morgan had already started backing away from the open doorway.

'What are we going to do next?' Morgan asked.

'We should escalate it,' Ginge said.

Reece stared at the package, and against his better judgement, reluctantly agreed.

Chapter 29

MALI RUSHED ALONG THE waterside path, checking over her shoulder every few seconds. She had no idea where it led, but there were plenty of people about and that meant safety in numbers.

But even a growing crowd hadn't put Tommy Hemlock off dragging her to one side to make threats through clenched teeth. He might have done a damn sight more had the two of them been some place else on their own. The short episode had frightened and angered her. More anger than fright now she'd had an opportunity to reflect on it. How dare he watch her every move and follow her. Who the hell did he think he was?

He was rattled. *They* were rattled. He'd admitted to hearing from Bridget Payne. The letter to the scheming politician had fulfilled its intended purpose, but had also telegraphed Mali's intentions, making it far easier for them to launch a counterattack.

And now she couldn't get Lisa—her friend in North Wales—off her mind. Had Hemlock been there too? He was quick following to Cardiff, and only Lisa had known when she was leaving. There was a sick feeling in the pit of Mali's stomach. She had to know her friend was safe and well.

Her escalating fear was in part driven by a nagging doubt over Rhydian's untimely death. Him committing suicide only a day after the fatal fall had never sat right with her. It wasn't his way. Not something he was ever likely to do.

Two police officers, calling at his home to take a formal statement, found him hanging from a tree in his garden. Pinned to the trunk, next to his limp body, was a typed suicide note. Mali had always considered that odd. Typed, not handwritten. Why such a formal method of explaining away what had been a very personal act?

No one other than she had questioned it. It was an open and shut case, much like her own.

Rhydian had explained, in clear detail, the reasoning behind his final actions. And at the same time, implicated Mali in the climber's death. He blamed himself for what had happened that day. *Guilty by association* was the term he'd used to describe his part in it. The husband's preventable death had overwhelmed him to the point whereby he could do nothing but take his own life in an act of penance.

His outpouring—read at Coroners' Court—had gone some way in reinforcing the account given by the two surviving climbers. They'd even claimed that Mali been acting oddly during the entire climb. That she'd taken three attempts to fix the nut in the crack in the rock face; dropping the first two she'd attempted. Worried she was climbing under the influence of alcohol or drugs, the couple had been on the verge of descending to safety only moments before the fatal fall occurred.

But subsequent blood analysis had found no evidence of intoxicants of any kind.

Mali, having not previously been diagnosed with a potentially incapacitating illness, meant she hadn't breached any employment or health and safety law. And when physiological testing conducted by a hospital neurologist confirmed a diagnosis of absence seizures, it was ruled that she could not be held accountable for her actions, or lack of them, at the time of the climb.

That simple fact alone meant she'd narrowly avoided the case being handed over to the CPS for consideration of a criminal prosecution.

Bridget Payne—the dead man's wife—was apparently okay with there being no further investigation. And why wouldn't she be? She'd even sent flowers and a card saying that given full disclosure of the circumstances, she no longer blamed Mali for what had happened to her *darling Jonathan.*

Mali had stamped all over the expensive bouquet. Every petal torn and crushed beneath the soles of her boots. The card was similarly dealt with and discarded like confetti at a wedding.

The more she thought about it, the more convinced was she of the couple's involvement in Rhydian's death. They were cleaning up. Taking no chances. Mali had to warn Lisa to lie low.

Chapter 30

THE SNIFFER DOG AND bomb team were long gone. Laughter and a few snide remarks, still making their rounds of the Cardiff Bay police station. There couldn't have been anyone working there who hadn't heard or seen what went on that morning.

'I should never have let you talk me into calling them,' Reece said, staring at the unopened bottle of Penderyn Sherrywood whisky on his desk. 'The pair of you made me look a right idiot.'

'I still think it's better to be safe than sorry,' Morgan said. 'That's always been my motto in life.'

Ginge agreed. 'You read about these things all the time.'

'Where?' Reece wanted to know. 'I haven't seen it.'

'On the internet. Awful things happen to anyone who stands up to the Mafia or the Colombian drug cartels.'

'You do know this is Cardiff?' Reece reminded him. 'Not bloody Sicily or Bogotá.'

'We were right to get it checked,' Morgan insisted. 'There's no harm done that way.'

Reece massaged the back of his neck. His head was pounding. 'Not to you, maybe.'

The inner silver wrapping paper and gift card lay on his desk. The brown paper in the bin. He turned the card over and read from it: 'Does 'M' mean anything to either of you?'

'Didn't miss your birthday, did we?' Morgan asked, leafing through her pocket diary. 'I thought that was in—'

'Not for a few months yet,' Reece said, dropping into his chair behind the desk. He rocked back and forth, rolling the unopened bottle between his hands like a man with too much on his mind. 'Who the hell is 'M'?'

'Stop pretending you don't already know,' Morgan said, slotting the diary into her back pocket. 'It's from Miranda Beven.'

Reece put the whisky down. 'Miranda? Why would you think that?'

Morgan folded her arms and guffawed. 'As if . . . ?'

'As if what?' Reece had no clue what she was getting at.

'She fancies you.' Morgan nodded. 'And that bottle of whisky there is a present. It's her way of asking you out on a date.'

Reece squirmed in his chair. 'Don't be so bloody daft.'

Morgan stuck her head through the open doorway. '*Oi* Ginge, doesn't Miranda Beven fancy the pants off the boss?'

Several of the other staff raised their heads, both in interest and amusement. Reece almost dropped the bottle in his haste to keep her quiet.

Ginge was already on his way across the incident room, grinning like a simpleton. 'I've seen the way she looks at him. I bet she can't wait to—' He fell instantly quiet again when Reece rounded his desk, gripping the bottle by its neck, like an improvised club.

'I might not get away with belting her,' he said, barging past Morgan. 'But *you*, matey, are expendable.'

There were a handful of boats on the lake. One of them making its way out towards the open sea. Mali could find no trace of her sleeping bag. It hadn't washed up on the shoreline, as she'd hoped. Her medication and belongings were still hidden somewhere beneath the water, and she had no clue how deep that was.

The bag would be at the mercy of the tides, and at some point get dragged towards the barrage. But how long might that take? Days, weeks, years even?

She wasn't far from the barrage now and broke into a trot. There were other people jogging. Most of them wearing expensive running shoes and branded exercise gear, not heavy boots and dungarees purchased from a charity shop.

The sound of water gushing through the sluice gates was audible even before she got anywhere near them. A noise not unlike that of a crashing waterfall after several days of heavy rain. She gripped the railings and stared into the churning torrent below. There was no bright blue sleeping bag to be seen anywhere.

Moving further along the road, where it formed a flat bridge, she got her first proper look at the sea. The light on the horizon caught her eye and cast a hold over her.

She could hear nothing else as she stared into it.

Could see nothing else.

There *was* nothing else.

Someone tapped her on the shoulder.

'Are you okay?'

Mali blinked repeatedly. 'What?'

'We're raising the bridge.' It was a man's voice, and he was talking to her.

'What did you say?'

'Can't you hear the alarm?'

'Alarm?'

He took her by the elbow and led her away to a point behind the safety barriers. She offered no resistance.

'There's a boat going out.' His voice was now louder than it had previously been.

Another man wearing the same hi-viz gear came towards them. 'Is everything okay here?' He looked at Mali for an answer.

She told him it was. She needed that anti-seizure medicine, and soon.

Chapter 31

REECE CHECKED HIS PHONE for missed calls or texts from Jenkins. Seeing there were none, he put it on charge under his desk. The lead was stupidly short, meaning he had to scramble under there to plug it in. He hit his head on the way up and swore. 'And their plugs are too slippery to pull out of the socket without having to stick your foot against the wall,' he said, unable to remove it again. 'How difficult can it be to design something that works as it should?' He clapped his hands as he made his way across the expanse of the incident room. 'Looks like we'll have to do this without her. I want everybody ready in five minutes.' He'd barely finished speaking when Jenkins wandered in. She didn't stop at her desk to put her things down, and walked on past.

'Can we use your office, please?' was all she said. It was short, matter of fact, and not at all like her.

Reece called everyone's attention again. 'Make that fifteen minutes.' He let Jenkins walk in front of him. 'Coffee? Or do I need something stronger for this?' he asked, putting the bottle of whisky away on a shelf.

'I owe you an apology.' She closed the door behind her and pressed her back against it. 'I owe everyone here an apology.'

'Elan, what's wrong?'

'I've been a total shit.' Her speech was punctuated with episodes of gulping. Her body trembled as she spoke. 'I've been taking advantage of my rank and not pulling my weight.'

'That isn't true. You haven't been yourself lately, but—'

'Will you hold me?' she sobbed. 'I need a cwtch right now.'

He went over and hugged her while she cried. 'Let it out,' he whispered. 'It helps more than most things.' He said no more than that. Kept quiet until she was ready to talk.

'I should have told you sooner, instead of taking liberties by coming in late and sneaking off early.' She blew her nose in a paper hanky, twice folded it over and blew again. 'My mam's a proud woman and she'd be mortified if she knew I'd been talking about her like this. She's losing her mind and resents anything I do to help her. I don't know how I'm going to manage.'

'I lost my father to dementia,' Reece said, surprising himself for being so open. 'Watched him go from being a school headmaster to a nappy-wearing shell of the person he once was. The man had no idea who I was in the end and started calling *me* Dad in the weeks before he died. It was a blessing when he went.'

'That's awful.' The hanky took another bashing. 'You've never mentioned him before now.'

'Mental decline in a parent still carries a stigma for most people,' Reece said. 'It shouldn't, but unfortunately, it does.'

Jenkins nodded. 'And yet if it's heart disease or bad hips they've got, everyone wants a good old moan.'

'True.'

'What's it all about?' Jenkins stuttered. 'Life's a fucking car crash for most of us. Ffion's cancer scares. You losing Anwen. We've all been screwed over good and proper. This place is hell, not Earth. It has to be.'

'I suppose there are a few good bits thrown in along the way,' Reece said, unable to remember many he'd experienced in recent times.

'Listen to us. We sound like a couple of old winos wondering where it all went so horribly wrong.' She attempted a chuckle, but it didn't sound right with her nasal passages packed full of snot. 'The only time we're truly happy is when we're still young kids. When our parents are the centre of our world. No troubles or worries. Just playing in the park, riding bikes, and climbing trees. Even school was a doddle at that age – painting pictures and sculpting dinosaurs made from dried lumps of coloured plasticine.'

'You made dinosaurs, not cute little kittens?'

Jenkins clucked her tongue. 'I was a tomboy even then.' She took a deep breath and sighed. 'And then it all starts going to shit when you get that bit older. There's the pressure of changing schools and working for exams. Hormone surges that turn us into self-loathing maniacs. Boys can't go anywhere near each other without fighting like dogs in the street. Next come the university applications, job interviews, and leaving home. Parents divorce. Then they get sick and die.'

'Wait till you get to my age,' Reece said, shaking his head. 'That's when you start losing friends to all sorts of illnesses. You know you're on the last lap of life when that happens.'

'And what's there to gain from any of it?' Jenkins lifted her arms and let them slap down against her thighs. 'Sod all, as far as I can tell.'

Reece went back to his chair. 'You know your mum will only get worse over time? And when she really starts to deteriorate, it'll happen fast?'

'I need to get her seen and assessed properly,' Jenkins said. 'Not only by the GP. Maybe there's something they can do to slow it down? You read all sorts in the papers these days.'

'Don't be buying anything spur-of-the-moment from the internet,' Reece warned. 'Nothing but snake-oil merchants lurking there. People who enjoy profiting from the misery of others.'

'I know. I'll go through the right channels before I do anything.'

'Cara being a doctor, must help?'

Jenkins turned away. 'You'd have thought so. But sadly not.'

Chapter 32

'WHAT CAN I GET for you, young lady?'

The man's question was delivered in a polite and cheery manner. But it still irritated Mali. After many months of couch surfing, and then living rough on the streets, she knew she looked anything but young and ladylike. She scanned the length of the serving counter and saw very little to choose from.

'You're way too late for breakfast,' he said. 'And a bit early for supper.' He waved the blunt end of a butter knife at her and offered some toast and jam while she waited. 'Orange juice too,' he added, disappearing for a moment. 'Nope, it's apple,' he corrected, squinting to read from the side of the carton. 'I'm Itchy.' He swapped the knife over and held out a hand in greeting. 'Pleased to meet you.'

Mali wasn't at all sure about accepting his hand in hers. 'Itchy? That's nice.'

'It's only a nickname,' he said, waving the knife again. 'Charles Rash is my proper name. Rash and Itchy – get it?'

There was some logic to it, she supposed. 'Sort of.'

'You can call me Charlie if you'd prefer. Lots round here do. I'll answer to most things,' he told her. 'Been called all sorts over the years.'

'I'll take you up on the toast, if that's okay? Butter with no jam, thank you.'

Charlie took two slices of bread and waited next to the grill until they were done. 'I've not seen you here before,' he said, opening a new pack of butter. 'How did you find us? We're a bit out of the way, down here.'

'I met someone called Aggy yesterday, in the main shopping centre. An Eastern European lady with short, dark hair. You might know her? She brought me here.' Mali couldn't see the *Big Issue* seller and decided she was likely to be on her rounds of the city at that time of day.

'Aggy's always saving lost souls, bless her,' Charlie announced loudly.

'That's not what I am,' Mali said, sipping her tea. 'There's a reason for me being here in Cardiff. I'm not lost.'

'That's good to hear.' He handed over two rounds of buttered toast on a clean plate. 'Everyone loses their way in life, at some time or another. And most of us need help getting back on the right tracks.'

Mali feared the conversation was about to degenerate into some sort of religious sermon. It sounded like the usual opener for such things. 'I need medication,' she said, not taking the bait.

'Methadone?' Charlie asked.

'No. Nothing like that.' She wasn't overly offended by the assumption. Other people there would have been asking Charlie a similar question on a daily basis. The brief absence episode on the barrage had been a warning, and one serious enough to have her returning to the centre, seeking help. 'I have a form of epilepsy,' she said. 'Not your full-blown type. But it still causes me problems if the blood levels of my medicines drop too low.'

'You don't have a GP here in Cardiff?'

She shook her head. 'I'm passing through. Once I'm done, I'll be going home again.'

'That's a fine accent you have there. North Wales, isn't it? I've been to Snowdonia many times over the years and love it there.'

Mali felt a sudden pang of homesickness. Followed by a wave of overwhelming nausea. Not knowing if Lisa was safe was still weighing heavily on her.

Charlie wiped his hands dry on a tea towel and came closer to the counter. 'There's a substance abuse nurse here most Mondays. I know it's not the same thing, but you could ask him about your medicine. Or wait for Janice to come in.'

'Who's she?' Mali asked.

'Janice runs this place,' Charlie explained. 'I only do a couple of hours here and there to help out when she needs me.'

Monday. Mali did the maths. Having to wait another five days for anti-seizure medicines posed a real risk of something more serious happening next time.

Chapter 33

Reece settled into his seat at the head of the briefing table. His phone was fully charged and face-down in front of him. He'd given Jenkins the option of busying herself elsewhere, but she'd insisted on being present, even with eyes that looked like she'd been pepper-sprayed. 'I'll do a quick recap for all those of you just joining in,' he said. He'd recently taken to wearing glasses for reading, much to his annoyance. He opened a pewter case and gave them a quick clean with a cloth before putting them on.

Morgan wolf-whistled from only a few seats away. 'Looking good, boss. Very sexy. They suit you.'

Reece chuckled. 'Thank you, Ffion.' She winked and he blushed more than he already was. 'There were two victims this time,' he said, swiftly moving things on. 'Squatters, by the early signs of things. One fell to his death from a bedroom window. The other died as a direct effect of the fire and fumes inside the building itself.'

Jenkins raised a hand, but didn't wait before speaking. 'You say that, but it's possible the victim on the road murdered the other one and died while making his escape. Didn't uniform find a lot of cash and drugs on him – or did I get that wrong?'

Reece hadn't considered that particular scenario. It was a plausible enough angle. The bigger man might well have seen an opportunity to make a move on what was obviously a lucrative business. And him being out in the street suggested he hadn't stuck around to help the other person. 'That's a fair point.'

But then there was the role of the blast activity to consider. The firefighters had said the man would have been expelled from the building at force and without his consent. Maybe he'd been climbing over the windowsill, waiting for the other victim to join him, when the fatal blast separated them for good. It was impossible to know for sure. Most of it remained guesswork.

'So we're saying motive was robbery?' Ffion asked.

'*Might* have been,' Jenkins corrected. 'I'm only putting that out there as an alternative.'

'And a reasonable one.' Reece got up and penned a new entry on the evidence board. 'Anything else?'

'There could be a racial angle?' Morgan suggested without any real conviction. 'Given the ethnicity of the man found in the street.'

Reece added it to the list. Even though that particular area of the city was diverse in both culture and religion, it only took one numpty to harbour a grudge. He stepped away and read out what they had so far: 'Robbery, drugs dispute, or race crime.'

'It could have been a random act,' Jenkins said, swinging on the back legs of her chair. She brought the front legs down to rest on the carpet tiles. 'Or something made to look random, but part of a bigger purpose.'

'Hang on now,' Morgan said, scribbling something in her pocketbook. 'You're losing me. What do you mean by a *"Bigger purpose"*?'

Jenkins joined Reece in front of the evidence board and took the marker pen from his hand. He sat down and gave her space. 'Who misses a prostitute or someone who's been living on the streets for months or years?' she asked.

'No one,' Morgan said under her breath.

'Exactly. Their deaths often go unnoticed by crime agencies. And if the killer moves from city to city, targeting the same demographic of victim, then historically, they've tended to get away with it – sometimes for years.'

'I get that bit.' Morgan again. 'It was the *"Bigger purpose"* comment I was unclear about.'

'The driving motive behind the action,' Jenkins said, taking the top off the marker pen. She wrote **PROSTITUTE** on the board. 'If *they* are the only victims in a spate of killings, then it would be reasonable for an investigator to think the killer hates women who sell sex. For religious or moral reasons, maybe. But that can be a red herring. The *bigger purpose*,' she said, singling out Morgan, 'is to rid the world of women who show no love or affection towards men. Think of our dealings with Richard Wellman – the anaesthetist who murdered women because his own mother put him in care when he was a kid. The chosen victims are surrogates for the true problem.

There was a brief silence in the room.

'I think I get you now,' Morgan said, slowly nodding. Then a blank look descended over her again. 'So what's the bigger purpose of someone killing rough sleepers in Cardiff Bay?'

Jenkins returned to her seat. 'That, my friend, is the million-dollar question.'

Reece's mind was racing. 'Questions, anyone?'

Chapter 34

THERE WERE QUITE A few questions. Some more worthy of discussion than others. Reece listened to them all, answered whenever he could, and made a couple of new entries on the evidence board. He brought order back to the room once he'd heard enough. 'I want everyone to keep an open mind still,' he said, tapping the board with the end of the marker pen. 'Everything we have on this list has to be properly considered before ruling it in or out. No jumping to any early conclusions, do you understand me?'

Morgan had her phone screen lit up and turned it towards Reece. 'I knew I'd read it somewhere. It was on the Wales Online site. They've been trying to get the drop-in centre moved.'

'What did you think the recent protest marches were about?' Jenkins asked.

Morgan shrugged. 'I didn't pay them much attention, to be honest with you. I thought it might be those idiots gluing themselves to everything again.'

'Who's trying to get it moved?' Ginge asked. 'Wales Online?'

'Don't be so bloody stupid,' Jenkins told him. 'They reported on it.' She pointed a finger at the young detective and stared at Reece in disbelief. 'Did you know he was this thick before taking him on?'

'He hid it well,' Reece replied with a shake of his head.

Morgan thumbed through the article, stopping in places to read out loud. 'Local businesses were in favour of the centre being relocated to an alternative location in the city.'

'Where?' Ginge asked, with a nervous glance at Jenkins.

'It doesn't say. What it does say is: Bridget Payne, Senedd Member and Chair of the Local Government and Housing Committee, will be making an announcement in the coming weeks.'

'Right pain in the arse, that one,' Jenkins said. 'No pun intended. I had dealings with her when I was trying to get Charlie somewhere more permanent to live. It's only when I threatened to get the newspapers involved, and expose her for going against the party line, that she backed down. She didn't like it. Didn't like me. A nasty piece of work hiding behind a fake smile, if you want my honest opinion.'

'A smiling assassin,' Morgan said. 'That's what they call them where I grew up. You don't ever want to turn your back on one of those.'

'And the party line is what?' Reece asked.

'That Welsh government operates a *no-one-left-out* approach to homelessness. All those who need help and shelter, get it – just as long as Bridget Payne doesn't stick her nose where it's not wanted.'

Morgan closed her phone and lay it on the table top. 'That there could be your bigger purpose. Local businesses with a secret agenda.'

'Or a rogue politician,' Jenkins said, adding an air of drama.

Reece puffed his cheeks. 'I think we're at risk of wandering way off piste now.'

'Why do you say that?' Jenkins asked. 'What puts Payne or anyone else at the Senedd above suspicion?'

'I don't trust any of their sort,' Morgan said. 'And that shower in Westminster . . . don't get me started on those.'

'No one's above suspicion,' Reece replied. 'Far from it. All I'm saying is, we seem to have taken a huge leap from where we were.'

Jenkins closed her pocketbook and lay her Biro on top of it. 'I was only reacting to the news story Ffion showed us.'

'You can understand why local businesses wouldn't be happy,' Morgan said. 'It can't be easy trying to sell a nice dining experience with people dossing on your doorstep, begging for change.'

'They're not *dossing*,' Jenkins snapped. 'They're trying to survive in a world that's screwed them over. Most of those poor bastards are running away from something awful in their lives. Things that would drive anyone to drink and drugs.'

The comment got Reece thinking about the young woman he'd met on Mermaid Quay. The same one he'd since seen tussling with a man who looked anything but homeless. Maybe this *was* an angle that deserved more consideration. It was certainly up there with the current number one theory of it all being part of a local drugs war. 'Any business in particular, making the most noise?' he asked.

'It wasn't the restaurants that kicked this thing off,' Morgan said from memory. 'It was Douglas Hames. The property developer on the waterfront.'

'Interesting,' Reece said. 'It's rumoured he's struggling to finance completion of that project.'

Morgan pulled one of her *doesn't-that-sound-suspicious* faces. 'So, he's struggling financially and blaming slow sales on the homeless population.'

Jenkins threw her arms wide open. 'And that there could be all the motive we're looking for. Hames knows he can't win in his bid to get the centre moved, so he blindsides us by taking the official route of lobbying the Senedd while he deals with the problem himself.'

'I like it.' Morgan clapped her hands. 'Shall we bring him in, boss, and see what he's got to say for himself?'

Reece shook his head. 'We need more than a few ideas knocking around a table before we speak to him. If he is involved, and we let on before we have anything more concrete, then we risk scaring him off. Ginge, when we're done here, get onto your contacts in uniform and ask if they're aware of any serious assaults recently that wouldn't have been be flagged up to us.'

Ginge scribbled an entry in his pocketbook. 'Does it have to involve fire, or is it any type of assault on rough-sleepers you're interested in?'

'Any, to be getting on with,' Reece said. 'But if there's a fire element, then I want those reports on my desk, pronto.'

Chapter 35

MALI DRANK HER TEA with one eye fixed on the front door. Not only was she watching for the woman named Janice, but Tommy Hemlock was also out there somewhere, and he had the advantage over her. 'Hurry up,' she mumbled, struggling to remain calm.

'You talking to me?' The woman wore leggings and a tight cropped-top. She was standing behind Mali's chair, dry-smoking a cigarette that was only a quarter of its former length. Much of her abdomen was on show, pink baby-creases giving it something of a marbled appearance.

It was all Mali could do not to snatch the cigarette from the woman's scabbed lips. She'd almost smoked herself to death in the weeks and months after the fall. Then, all of a sudden, she couldn't stand the sight of them. That was just as well, because they were long since out of her price range. But now she had the craving again. Things were turning full circle. 'Nothing,' she said. 'I was talking to myself.'

'All right if I sits down by yer?' The 's' added to *sit*, was a prominent feature of the local dialect. "I *goes* to the pub," and "I *loves* my girlfriend," were others Mali had heard since arriving in Cardiff. The woman didn't wait for an answer and dragged a chair from under the table.

'Come sit by me,' said an old man in an ill-fitting suit and flat cap. He tapped his thigh. 'There's plenty of room on this.'

'*Jack!*' warned one of the volunteers from behind the serving counter. She waved a soup ladle at him. 'You'll be getting your marching orders if you don't leave the girls alone.'

He turned to Mali. 'She keeps promising to put me over her knee.' He rubbed his hands together. 'Today could be the day.'

'I'll smack you round the head with this,' the woman said, swiping the air in front of her like Zorro on amphetamines.

Jack leaned towards them. 'I likes a woman with a pair of balls.'

Mali couldn't go there. 'I'm leaving soon,' she told the dry-smoker. 'Waiting for Janice and then I'm off.'

'What do you want with her?'

Mali had no intention of sharing details of her medical condition with a complete stranger. 'Advice, that's all.'

LIAM HANSON

The woman couldn't keep still. She was picking and poking at herself, and gurning like she was in a national competition. 'You got any skunk on you?'

'I don't do drugs.'

'Your fella been smacking you about, has he?'

Mali checked the door for the umpteenth time. How much longer was Janice going to be? 'I'm single.'

'Don't blame you. Men are only good for one thing, and most of them are shite at that.'

'Do you want something?' Mali asked. 'Because I don't have it. Apart from the clothes I'm wearing, I've got nothing to show for my name.'

'Chill, girl.' The woman got up slowly, fighting to keep her balance. 'Only being friendly.' Off she went with the cigarette hanging from the corner of her mouth, and her leggings riding low on her skinny buttocks.

———⋯⋯———

Reece knew something was up as soon as he saw Chief Superintendent Cable loitering at the foot of the stairwell. She had the door open and looked like she was on the hunt for someone.

Someone like him.

'Out the front way,' he told Jenkins, redirecting her with a poke in the back. 'Sharpish.'

'Chief Inspector.' Cable's call was loud and shrill. 'Chief Inspector!'

He was already through the sliding doors and almost dragging Jenkins out of the building with him.

'What's the hurry?' she asked, scrabbling to free herself of his grasp.

'Can't you hear her? She's after me again.'

Cable was at the top of the steps leading to the pavement and street. '*Reece!* Get back here,' she called, breaking into a trot.

He turned into the car park at the side of the building, shouting: 'I'm in a rush. There's been a development in the case.'

When the Land Cruiser rounded the corner, Cable was waiting for him—hands on hips and blocking the exit. 'What if I claimed I never saw her?' he said, not slowing down. 'She can't be more than five feet and a fart tall.'

'Brake,' Jenkins told him, drawing her legs up and forcing herself into her seat. 'For Christ's sake, *brake!*'

The Land Cruiser slid to a halt. Reece stuck his head out of his window. 'You could cause a nasty accident, messing about like that.'

'Out.' Cable squatted to retrieve her service hat. She slapped it a few times to get the grit off and didn't put it back on.

'Can't it wait?' Reece asked, opening the door, but remaining inside.

Cable grabbed the handle and yanked it the rest of the way open. 'DS Jenkins, give us a moment, will you?' She waited for Jenkins to do as she was told. 'What do you think you're playing at?'

'You'll have to explain.' Reece shook his head. 'You've lost me?'

'If only it were that simple' Cable got so close she was almost touching him. It made Reece feel uncomfortable, but that was her intention. 'You're going to the Senedd.'

'Am I?

'Don't fuck with me.'

'Who told you?'

'Never mind that. Did I not make it perfectly clear that you were to give that place a wide berth?'

Reece's eyes widened. 'And I told you, I'd be going wherever the evidence took me.'

'And you have evidence?'

'It's more of a theory in progress,' he admitted. 'But it's starting to look like it might be a decent one.'

'A theory?'

'That's right. Anyway, I was off to the drop-in centre, not the Senedd, if you must know. Cable didn't stop him when he climbed into the driver's seat and closed the door. He leaned across the passenger side and whistled to Jenkins. When he got her attention, he turned to Cable again. 'You might want to move out of the way this time.'

Chapter 36

'Calm down.' Reece pulled away from the junction with only a cursory look left and right. He honked his horn at a trio of cyclists riding side-by-side and accelerated past them. 'I thought she'd move out the way when she saw us coming.'

'She didn't though, did she?' Jenkins fiddled with the clip of her seat belt. Her hands were still shaking and she couldn't get the mechanism to engage. 'And if I hadn't pulled on the handbrake, she'd have been toast, and you'd have been nicked for dangerous driving.'

'Don't be so dramatic.' Reece checked the rear-view mirror, watching the cyclists hold up the traffic as they usually did. Few things irritated him more than the Lycra brigade and the way they insisted on sprawling all over the road like they were competing in some international peloton. He didn't get in people's way when he went for his morning run. What made their lot feel so bloody entitled? 'There was plenty of room for me to swerve round her.'

'Me? Dramatic? That's rich coming from you.' The seat belt engaged with a reassuring click. 'It's like you're on a self-destruct mission most of the time and sod anybody who gets in your way. Like her or not, Chief Superintendent Cable is our commanding officer, and there's no sign that I can see of that changing anytime soon.'

'I do like her. Most of the time,' he added as an afterthought. 'But having to tell her everything I'm doing, gets on my tits.'

'Do what you want when you're in your own company,' Jenkins said. 'But when I'm with you, just try to be normal.'

'Normal?'

'You know what I mean.'

Reece wasn't sure he did and decided it wasn't a conversation he was willing to have. 'Feeling any better for our chat earlier?' He flicked the stalk of the windscreen wiper, clearing the first spots of rain.

'I'm not sure.' There was a brief pause. 'I suppose so.' Jenkins's reply was accompanied by a deep sigh. She stared out of the side window at someone cleaning up after their dog. 'I'm still surprised by what you said about your father.'

Reece kept his eyes on the road ahead. The cyclists had since taken an alternative route and were no longer playing on his mind. 'Surprised I told you, or that he had dementia?'

Jenkins steadied herself with a hand pressed against the dashboard when the Land Cruiser slowed. They went round the front of a car that had overshot the *Give Way* lines on the junction. Reece silently eyeballed the driver as they passed, but reacted no more than that.

'Dunno. Just surprised, that's all. You don't normally give much away about yourself. And yet, that's a pretty big thing you shared with me.'

There was nothing for Reece to say in response. He watched the traffic go by and got lost in a succession of daydreams. Some of them involved happier times with his father. Fishing trips and Sunday morning rugby. 'Did you say something?'

'I was going to ask about your sister again, but stopped myself.'

Reece worked his hands back and forth on the steering wheel and pulled up in front of the drop-in centre. 'There's nothing more to say.'

Chapter 37

'Long time, no see,' Reece said, blowing on his hands as they entered the drop-in centre. 'How often do you work here?'

Charlie closed the fridge door with a thunk and turned to face them. 'Hey, how are my favourite detectives?'

'He's talking to me,' Jenkins said, barging her way to the front.

Charlie disappeared through a door and joined them on their side of the counter only moments later. He hugged Jenkins, raising her a few inches off the floor. Reece got a heavy pat on his good shoulder. 'What brings the two of you here?'

'We came for a tea and a chat?' Reece said.

'I'll have to charge you for them.' Charlie disappeared again. 'That's one pound fifty each,' he called from somewhere behind the counter.

'How much?' Reece leaned into Jenkins. 'No wonder this lot are homeless.'

'Tea and coffee normally come free,' Charlie explained. 'But I've got to charge food prices on account of you not being clients. Sorry about that. Just the way it is.'

'Give me ten quid,' Reece said, going through his wallet.

'Do you want change of something?' Jenkins asked, handing over a couple of five-pound notes.

He gave them both to Charlie and added a ten of his own. 'Consider that your good deed for the day.'

Jenkins looked as though she might snatch them back, but didn't. 'My car's running on fumes.'

'Jog home,' Reece told her. 'You can't keep crashing into things that way.'

'Ha, bloody, ha.'

Charlie collected the money and put it away. 'That's very kind of you, Mister Reece.'

'And me,' Jenkins protested. 'Half of that was mine.'

'And given so willingly.' Reece led them to a table and pulled three chairs before sitting down.

'So what can I do for you?' Charlie handed out the teas. 'I'm thinking this might have something to do with that fire round the corner.'

'And the one a few nights ago,' Jenkins said.

Reece sipped his tea. It wasn't as sweet as he normally took it, but he didn't make a fuss. 'Tell us how this place works. Before we get going on the other stuff.'

'Janice would be the best person for that,' Charlie said. 'She's the centre manager. Has her fingers in all sorts of pies, does Janice. Needs to slow down though, if you want my opinion.'

'Where is she?'

'Should be here anytime soon.'

'Tell us as much as you know,' Reece said. 'Janice can fill in the blanks when she gets here.'

'It's run by a charity organisation,' Charlie began. 'Hubbard. Have you heard of them?'

Reece hadn't. Jenkins had briefly come across them when helping Charlie as a rough-sleeper himself.

'Here she is now,' Charlie said loud enough to catch Janice's attention before the front door closed behind her. She slowed, then changed direction to head towards them, and was only halfway there when a younger woman got up and made a beeline for her.

'Are you Janice?' Reece heard her ask.

He got to his feet. 'Excuse me.'

She glanced in his direction. Twice more before moving sideways towards the door. 'Leave me alone.'

He slowed, not wanting to alarm her any more than he already had. 'If you're in trouble, let me help you.'

'There's nothing to say.' She forced herself through the front door; between people who were trying to get in. 'I'm not ready yet,' she shouted, before disappearing from sight.

Reece returned to his seat and sat down. 'What do you think she meant by that?'

'Beats me,' Charlie said.

'Do you know her?'

Charlie skimmed over the events of earlier that morning. 'I didn't get her name,' he said. 'But she seemed pleasant enough.'

'The two of you spoke?'

'Only briefly. She's from up north, but didn't say where.'

'Like Cumbria, you mean?'

Charlie put him right. 'This is Janice,' he said, introducing Reece and Jenkins. 'I told them you knew the ins and outs of this place far better than me.' He got up to fetch Janice a coffee.

There was a few minutes' delay while she went to deal with something that couldn't wait until later. When she rejoined them, it was with the enthusiasm of someone who revelled in being in the thick of it. 'What can I do for you?' she asked.

Reece gave her the short version.

When he'd finished, she sat there shaking her head. 'Do you really think these fires are somehow connected to what's going on with the centre?'

He hadn't said that. Had been careful not to. 'It's only one line of enquiry we're following.'

'But you've come here asking questions. Which means you consider it a possibility?'

'We're being careful to remain open-minded at this point.'

'The first victim had a tattoo on his lower back. Numbers, including a nine and a two,' Jenkins said. 'Have you seen anything like that here?'

'Most people have tats of some sort,' Charlie said, exposing his upper arms and calves.

'But numbers on the lower back. I can't imagine that being a regular thing?'

Janice and Charlie shook their heads. Neither of them could remember seeing anything similar at the centre.

'Do you know of anybody here assaulted or threatened recently?'

Charlie chuckled. 'That comes with the territory. There's not a day goes by without someone having a dig at folk here.'

'I mean a serious incident,' Reece said. 'Threats to life and suchlike?'

Janice stirred another sugar into her coffee. 'There's Dale, I suppose.'

Jenkins made a written entry in her pocketbook. 'Do you have a surname for him?'

'Dale Lynch. I haven't seen him for a few days, come to think of it.' Janice turned to fully face Charlie. 'Have you?'

He shook his head. 'Me neither.'

'What happened to him?' Reece asked.

The front door opened to reveal a youngish man with a drab beige towel draped across his shoulders. Charlie got to his feet and called Cory Cullinane's name. 'Here's the man who can tell you.'

Chapter 38

'LEAVE HIM BE,' REECE said when Charlie started after the fleeing man. 'Have a word with him next time he's in? Tell him I want to chat. Off the record for now, if that makes it any easier.'

'Who was he?' Jenkins asked, readying her pen.

Charlie returned to his seat. 'That there was Cory Cullinane. He and Dale Lynch were pretty close. You'd always see them about together.'

'An item?'

Charlie shrugged. As did Janice when he checked with her. 'I don't think so. Just good friends, as far as I know.'

'So what happened to them?' Reece asked, concerned they might never again set eyes on Cullinane.

'The pair of them got into a spot of bother the other night, is what they said.' Charlie wrung his hands. 'Dale more than Cory, from what I could tell.'

'Bother with whom?'

'Hames's men were throwing their weight about. Security is the official term they go by, but thugs is all they are. Roughed the boys up good and proper, they did, and warned them they wouldn't get off so lightly next time.'

Reece glanced at Jenkins, who had her head down while she made entries in her pocketbook. 'You're sure they were employees of Douglas Hames?'

'As sure as I can be,' Charlie said. 'And them dogs don't bark unless they're thrown a bone.'

Reece thought for a moment. 'Let's say this first victim turns out to be Dale Lynch.' He raised his hands. 'And I've no way of knowing at this stage that it is. Then why do you think he would have gone back after being warned off?'

'Because he's a bloody-minded so and so,' Janice said. 'It's exactly the sort of thing he'd do. Not Cory though. He's the quieter of the two.'

'Couldn't knock his way out of a wet paper bag, that one,' Charlie agreed in a lowered voice.

Janice shifted in her chair. 'I'll have to be getting on soon,' she said. 'Fighting against this move is taking up far too much of our time.'

'We won't keep you any longer than we need to,' Reece promised. 'The male in the house fire was around six-four. Afro-Caribbean, with long dreadlocks. The other victim was much smaller. We're guessing female unless the post-mortem examination says otherwise.' He didn't show them the crime scene photographs.

Janice spoke to Charlie. 'Sounds like that couple you had a to-do with a few days ago.'

'Not him so much,' Charlie replied. 'But that girlfriend of his was a right piece of work.'

'Wouldn't happen to have names for either of them, would you?' Jenkins asked.

'None that'll stand up to proper scrutiny, I bet.' Janice excused herself to fetch a large black diary from her office. She sat leafing through its pages and turned it for the detectives to read for themselves. 'We make people sign for the key to the shower room. And again when they bring it back.'

'But they could write anything,' Jenkins said. 'If you're not checking it against any official documentation, then . . .?'

'That's not the real purpose,' Janice told her. 'It's more to keep track of where the key is and who had it last. In case there's a mess in there. You wouldn't believe the problems we had before we started doing this.'

Reece was keen to know what names the couple had used. Even if they were aliases, it could be assumed they'd previously used them elsewhere. He put his glasses on and ran a finger down the page. Janice told him to stop when he got to the relevant entries. 'I can't read it.' He took the glasses off and squinted. There was no improvement. 'What does it say? Can you tell?'

Jenkins brought her face to within a couple of inches of the scrawl. 'Abeeku Quaye.'

'That'll be right,' Charlie said. 'I remember her calling him Abu, the night she was having a go at me. I won't tell you word-for-word what she said, but it's safe to say she had a foul mouth on her.'

'I've heard most things,' Jenkins told him. 'And been called a lot of them.'

'What was her problem?' Reece asked.

'I was sure she'd taken a knife from the kitchen,' Charlie said, using both hands to estimate its length. 'A proper big carving one. She denied it, of course. When I asked her to open her jacket and show me, that's when the big guy got involved.'

'Was he violent towards you?'

'I told them to leave and stood my ground.'

'And did they?'

'After promising to catch up with me sometime.'

'I guess you're safe now they're both dead?'

Charlie swallowed. 'I didn't kill them.'

Jenkins put her hand on his shoulder. 'We're not saying you did.'

'But we will need to ask your whereabouts for last night,' Reece said. 'It's standard procedure. You said yourself you had an altercation with them.'

Jenkins made a note of Charlie's alibi. They'd have to check, but for the time being, it was accepted without question. She swapped her pocketbook for the diary and rotated it at arm's length before giving in. 'I can't read it.'

'She was from the Bristol area,' Charlie said. 'I can tell you that much from her accent.'

Reece got to his feet and thanked them both. 'Come on you,' he said to Jenkins. 'We've got plenty to be getting on with.'

Chapter 39

'I've seen that young woman three times already this week,' Reece said on their way back to his car. 'And twice she's run away from me.'

'Told her one of your jokes, did you?' Jenkins asked.

'One of yours, actually.'

'Touché. So why did she do a runner?'

'You tell me.'

'And the time she didn't run away?'

Reece recounted the brief conversation they'd had over on Mermaid Quay.

Jenkins tapped his arm with the back of her hand. 'You big softy. You'll have no money left, you keep giving it away.'

He stared at the skyline. 'It's the inequality in life that makes me angry. Working-class people will never get a look in. Not when the country is run by the privileged few.'

'That's very deep and philosophical.'

'It's not meant to be. Common sense stuff, isn't it?'

'I suppose so.'

'There's no supposing about it.' Reece watched the tall cranes at work and wondered what it took to climb one of those things and do a full day's work up there. His fear of heights meant he'd never know the answer to that question. 'You tell me how a politician born into a wealthy family; sent to prep school from the age of five; then graduates from an Oxbridge university, can have any clue what it's like to grow up on a council estate in the South Wales valleys, or anywhere else in the country, for that matter?'

'They're not all from privileged backgrounds,' Jenkins argued. 'Some come from areas like ours, and will have gone to ordinary schools.'

Reece stopped and blocked her way past. 'The token gestures to make peasants like us think times are changing for the better. Take what's happening with sports pundits as an example. They frogmarch a couple of women into the studio and call it progress. It's not. It's bollocks. Everyone sees right through it. The number of women involved. The ethnic mix. Or sexual orientation. There are quotas for everything now—clipboards and tick boxes—and that's not how it should be.' He shook his head and got walking again.

Jenkins shoved her hands deep into her jacket pockets. 'And your point? Because I can't remember how this conversation started.'

'My point is: it's the same with politics. All token gestures and quotas. The posh lot will never be on the same page as the likes of you and me.'

Jenkins nodded. 'I'm glad you got that off your chest. Feeling any better now?'

'You asked.'

'I bloody well didn't. Not in that much detail, anyway.'

Reece opened the Land Cruiser's passenger door, bent over, and made a stirrup shape with both hands. 'In you get.'

'Cheeky sod.' She playfully bumped him out of the way.

He went round the other side of the vehicle, chuckling to himself. 'The Force has a quota for short arses, and you've ticked somebody's box.'

'I could have you cancelled for that,' she said, climbing in.

'Don't get me started on that lot,' Reece said, buckling up. 'They'll have us living in caves again within a couple of generations.'

'Now that's something I'd never be able to unsee. You in a loincloth.' They both laughed. Reece started the Land Cruiser and steered it in a wide arc turn. 'Seriously though, what do you think that woman's problem is?'

Reece described the altercation he'd witnessed at that morning's crime scene. 'The only time she stayed put long enough to talk was when she didn't know I was a copper.'

'Do you think the pair of them had anything to do with the fire? Perpetrators returning to the scene of the crime, and all that.'

'Not from the way she reacted to him.'

'Shall I get uniform to keep an eye out and bring her in?'

'Not for the moment.'

The waterside development went by on their right. Neither of them made any further mention of it.

'You didn't finish telling me about your sister,' Jenkins said.

'Because there was nothing else to say.'

'What's she like?'

'Horrible.'

'Be serious.'

'I *am* being serious.' She was staring at him. He turned the radio off and gripped the steering wheel with both hands. 'The two of us had been drifting apart ever since we were kids. Dad getting ill was what finished us off in the end. There was no good reason to try to patch it up after that.'

'Was your mother gone by this stage?'

'Gone is the right word for it,' Reece said. 'Buggered off when we were in school one day.'

'You're kidding me?'

'Couldn't write this stuff, could you?'

'I'm so sorry. I feel like I'm prying now. I should have kept my mouth shut.'

Reece waited for the lights to change. 'I was only twelve when it happened. A year into comp. She was there when I left one morning and gone by the time I got home.'

'A MISPER?'

'She wasn't missing as such. We all knew she was with Dai The Milk.'

'An affair?'

Reece nodded. 'He was a dairy farmer in Builth. We'd see him on market days, mostly. Only my mother was seeing him at other times of the week as well.'

Jenkins put a hand to her mouth. 'Your mother literally ran off with the milkman?'

'Wasn't so much of a run as an awkward hop.' Reece glanced to his left. 'What with her having only one leg and a clubbed foot.'

'Aw, sod off.' Jenkins looked away and crossed her arms tight across her chest. 'Bloody wind-up merchant.'

'Stop being so nosy then.'

'Says you.'

'The long and short of it is: Dad went into hospital after assaulting the GP. He thought the man had broken into his house to steal his things. After that, the care agencies refused to send their staff. In the end, the decision was taken out of my hands, no matter what fuss Becci made.'

'And how long did it take him to settle?' Jenkins asked.

There was a silence broken only by the noise of the traffic on the road outside.

Chapter 40

MALI HADN'T GONE FAR after leaving the drop-in centre. She'd holed up in what she considered being a safe spot, ready to watch the detective when he came out. Three sightings in a little over twenty-four hours were unlikely to be a coincidence. He'd even come to the drop-in centre and tried to speak to her.

What was his agenda?

Was he working with Bridget Payne and Tommy Hemlock?

Mali was understandably confused and only wished she knew.

Her gut feeling said he wasn't. That he was all right. If he'd wanted to harm her, then he could have done so the night they first met over on Mermaid Quay. But he hadn't. Neither had he come on to her, like most older men she'd met on the streets. Instead, he'd given her money and seemed genuinely concerned for her welfare on what had been a hideously cold night.

She was still trying to make sense of things when the doors to the centre flew open. It wasn't the detective. It was the man who'd twice introduced himself as Cory. He was running with his towel clutched in one hand and the other gripping his side.

Mali watched and waited for the detective to follow, but again, he didn't. She went after Cory and called his name. At first, he didn't slow and turned up a side-street, obviously spooked. She called again. 'The police aren't following. I just want to talk.'

He stopped to catch his breath and looked to be in a fair amount of pain. He squinted at her and edged his way closer. 'You're the woman from the shopping centre?'

She nodded. 'If you'd only warned me about the shitty reception I'd be getting in there.'

Cory's breathing was slowing, his grip on his side, looser. One end of the towel was draped across the wet pavement. He didn't appear to care. 'You weren't willing to listen to anything I had to say. Not even when we were queuing for breakfast this morning. What's changed so quickly?'

Mali introduced herself by her full name. 'I was on my own at the time. Scared and with no idea who I could trust round here.'

Cory rescued the towel and slung it over his shoulder. 'My question was: what's changed?'

'The detective. He's interested in the both of us. I'm trying to work out why that is?'

Cory shrugged. 'Don't ask me. I've never seen him before.'

'But you ran away, just the same?'

'I didn't need to know who he was, to realise *what* he was.'

'Are you in trouble with the police?'

'Not anymore. And I intend to keep it that way.'

They walked side-by-side. 'I meant no offence this morning,' Mali said. 'I'm just a bit overwhelmed by everything at the minute.'

'Want to tell me about it?'

Having an ally and an extra pair of eyes on the street might come in useful. She nodded. 'But can we go find somewhere to sit down first?'

They were on their way back to the station when Reece got a call saying there was room on that day's schedule for the post-mortems on the house fire victims. He considered it unfair to send Morgan again so soon. Ginge was preoccupied with other things. And Jenkins wasn't at all keen once she knew the pathologist for at least one of the cases was going to be her partner, Cara Frost.

It was during times like these he was reminded of how much he'd enjoyed working with Twm Pryce. He'd met up with Twm on only a handful of occasions since the pathologist's sudden retirement the previous year. Reece promised himself he'd attend to that sometime soon and arrange a day's fishing. Yanto could join them if he had the time.

Pryce had been a remarkable pathologist in his day. A proper trailblazer. But the man—unlike so many others—had instinctively known when the time was right to stop and hand the scalpel over to a new generation. So many people fell into the trap of hanging around for far too long, attracting the label of *has been*. Twm Pryce wasn't one of them.

Reece waited in the air-conditioned gallery for Cara Frost to begin. She was working on the man assumed to be Abeeku Quaye. Her snort-snort colleague was carrying out the post-mortem on what was believed to be the Bristolian woman.

The cutting tables were in close enough proximity for Reece to keep track of what was happening on both. He was more interested in the burns victim ever since Jenkins floated the possibility of Quaye having murdered her. Or was it Morgan's idea? It didn't matter which. They'd hopefully have an answer soon enough.

Having a better understanding of how a victim died often led to knowing the reason why. And then, who was most likely to have committed the act? Detective work wasn't that dissimilar to medicine. Presented with available evidence, the expert methodically examines what's available to them, compiling a list of plausible differentials to be tested until the most likely decision is arrived at. None of it was rocket science.

Ruling out Quaye as the perpetrator early on meant the team could concentrate on the developing angle of investigation. There was still no absolute connection between the house fire and the death of the man found at the roadside – not beyond their social circumstances. That didn't mean Reece was having a rethink about Douglas Hames's possible involvement. If the property developer *was* encouraging his employees to assault rough-sleepers and squatters in the area, then Reece would be doing some roughing up of his own.

Chapter 41

MALI'S LOWER JAW FELL open. 'You're kidding me, right? You're going to buy me a burger?' Her salivary glands went into instant overdrive, causing a painful ache in her neck and jaw. She put a hand out and steadied herself against the wall. 'I can't remember the last time I had one of those.'

'Burgers, it is then,' Cory said, leading the way.

'How are we going to pay for them?' Mali asked, catching up.

Cory rattled the change in his trouser pocket. 'I did all right yesterday.'

'You beg for money?'

He slowed. 'I don't beg. I ask. If people don't want to give, then I leave them alone.'

She knew where he was coming from. The word *beg* carried all sorts of unwanted connotations. She wished she hadn't used it. 'Sorry. I've been there too.'

They arrived at the same McDonalds she'd stood in front of—salivated in front of—when Aggy had stopped to speak with her. But this time, instead of watching through the window, she was going inside to eat a meal with other people. Her legs were weak. Her head light. None of it the fault of a warning aura.

She almost passed out when they entered the burger bar, and at that moment, would have gladly swapped her right to oxygen for the smell that greeted them.

'What would you like?' Cory asked, looking up at the menu board.

Mali cast her eye over the cheaper options. 'One of those, please.'

'I didn't bring you in here for that,' he said with a firm shake of the head. 'Get a grip and choose a proper meal.'

The wait for their order to be processed seemed endless. In reality, it took less than a minute between payment and the arrival of two paper bags. Mali found somewhere to sit and ripped at the wrapper like a child on Christmas morning. 'Oh my God,' she said, with a handful of French fries hanging from her mouth. People were watching. She didn't give a damn. 'This is better than sex.'

'You're not going to do the Meg Ryan thing, are you?'

She started on the burger and shut her eyes. 'It's going to be a close call.' They both laughed. It had been far too long since she'd last done that.

'So,' Cory said, dipping a wonky fry into a tiny pot of barbecue sauce. He held his other hand underneath it to catch the drips when he brought it to his mouth. 'What's up? Why so scared?'

She saw no reason to hold back and told him everything about that summer's day three years ago. Her suspicions over Rhydian's apparent suicide. Her fears for Lisa's current well-being. Right through to exposing Bridget Payne for what she really was.

When she'd finished, Cory sat back and puffed air. 'That's one hell of a story you've got there.'

'It's no story,' she said, sucking Coca Cola through a straw until it made loud gurgling noises. 'It's what happened. You don't have to believe me.'

'And do you think that's why the detective keeps following you? Because he suspects what you're up to?'

'I don't know what he wants. All I know is his name and that he was kind to me when we first met.' She recounted the events of the night on Mermaid Quay.

'Sounds like he might be a decent bloke,' Cory said. 'Either that, or he's setting you a trap.'

'I don't think he is, you know. I think it's something else altogether.'

'Like what?'

She shrugged. 'I don't know. What's he want with you?'

'No idea. Honestly, I really don't.'

'So why run away from him?'

Cory looked away, and then slowly redirected his gaze towards her. 'Because I don't need any more trouble from Hames's people. If someone sees me talking to the police and word gets back to them, then . . .'

Mali scrunched up their food wrappers and paper bags ready for the bin. 'So what exactly did they do to you?'

—◆◇◆—

'Let's be clear about this,' Reece said, pressing against the glass of the viewing gallery. 'You can find nothing to suggest this woman was murdered? Nothing at all?'

The pathologist removed his gloves and used his foot to raise the lid of the bin. 'I'm satisfied with my conclusion that she died as a direct consequence of smoke inhalation and heat damage.' He went over to a scrub trough and soaped his hands. 'She'd have been dead within a matter of seconds. Which would obviously have been something of a blessing, don't you think?' Snort. Snort.

Even that was far too long for Reece to contemplate. He couldn't imagine what pain and suffering she'd experienced, if only for the shortest time. 'And mid-twenties? You're still going with that?'

'Age can usually be estimated following examination of the pubic symphyses; the sternal rib ends; the auricular surface of the ilium, and—'

'Yes or no,' is fine,' Reece said.

'The body was extensively fire damaged, but mid-twenties is where I'd put her.'

'Anything else you think I should know?'

The pathologist had dried his hands and was filling out a form attached to a clipboard. 'We already spoke about the tox screens earlier. They're going to take a day or so to turn around.'

'This man has no track lines on any of the usual needling sites,' Cara Frost said, circling her cutting table. 'Though the tissue overlying his nasal septum suggests a history of moderate cocaine use.'

'We did find a few wraps on him,' Reece said. 'And the money he had won't have come from a window cleaning round.'

Frost looked up but didn't say anything in response.

Her colleague handed his clipboard to a shorter man wearing similar clothing. 'Is there anything else, Chief Inspector? I have a meeting to attend at the Deanery?'

'Only to ask when I can expect your full report?'

'I'll get it typed up and pinged across to you later this afternoon.'

Frost's shake of the head didn't go unnoticed by Reece. 'And yours, Cara?'

She visibly stiffened at his lack of formality in addressing her. 'When it's ready. I have this morning's case to report on first.'

'Later today would be good,' Reece said in as grovelling a voice as he could manage.

'Tomorrow then,' Frost replied. 'Somewhere around lunchtime.'

Chapter 42

MALI LISTENED WHILE CORY described the beating he'd sustained at the hands of Douglas Hames's security staff. It made her angry. She gripped the edges of the table. 'Why the hell didn't you go to the police?'

'Dale didn't want anyone else involved. He said he wasn't going to be scared off by the likes of them.'

'And where is he now?'

Cory shrugged. 'I haven't seen him these past few days.'

'Sounds like he wasn't as brave as he made out?'

'That's not true.'

Mali had never met the man and only had Cory's word for it. 'What about the next person they do this to? And those after that?'

'Bruises soon heal,' he told her. 'It's not worth the hassle.'

'They could kill someone. One punch is all it takes.'

'It's just a warning to stay away,' he said. 'And that's what I'm intending to do.'

She watched him get to his feet, stifling a groan. 'Where are you going?'

'Back to the drop-in centre. I want to find out from Charlie why the police were looking for me. You never know, Dale might be there. Want to come and meet him?'

Mali didn't want to take the risk of the detective still being there. She thanked Cory for the meal and let him go by himself.

⸺◆⸺

The Senedd was only a short distance from where Mali stood on Mermaid Quay. Between the famous red brick Pierhead Building and the whitewashed Norwegian Church. Although Aggy had previously pointed it out to her, it was easily recognisable from the numerous newsreel images she'd seen on television.

Understated when compared with buildings of similar function and importance elsewhere in the United Kingdom, the Senedd remains impressive by design. Officially opened on St David's Day 2006, it is self-cooling; self-warming; and its use of rainwater for toilet flushing and maintenance activities gives it a mains water bill comparable to that of a large domestic property.

Mali stood on the water's edge and got her bearings. The cold wind whipped in off the choppy water, all-but stripping her naked. She moved to a more sheltered area and sat on a damp bench, shivering while staring at the building's main entrance. There were people inside, going about their daily business in shirtsleeves. They were talking together. Laughing and smiling in many cases. Munching on an apple or drinking tea and coffee during their break. How she envied them those simple things. They'd be going home later in the day. *Home.* To friends or family. Doing things they wouldn't have to give much thought to – like vegetating on comfy sofas, watching sit-coms with takeaway dinners on their laps.

It all sounded perfect to Mali.

Just perfect.

She sat there daydreaming. Listening to the call of the gulls until they fell silent. Until the wind lost its voice. She pulled at the neck of her hoodie in an attempt to cool down. Someone went by, saying something she couldn't hear. Someone else walked towards her, moving their mouth, but speaking no words.

Man or woman?

Hemlock or the detective?

She really couldn't tell, and blinked in a failed attempt to improve her vision. And once she'd started blinking, she found she had no control over it.

There was something warm and soaking wet running down her legs and into the fabric of her socks and boots. 'Oh God no. Not now,' she said, before lurching forward onto the hard slate floor.

Chapter 43

REECE WAITED IN THE hospital car park, snatching a few minutes for himself. The Land Cruiser's radio played low in the background while he thumbed through his contacts list. It had been more than two months since he'd last spoken with Miranda Beven. One final meeting in an official capacity before she'd submitted her report to the pen pushers at Police Headquarters in Bridgend.

He'd played the game and said the right things. His prize was to be left to work mostly unchallenged. Chief Superintendent Cable was annoying him in the run up to the anniversary of Anwen's death. Playing mother by offering leave he neither wanted nor needed. She'd be operating under orders from ACC Harris, of course.

Watching and waiting for a spike in volatility. Why couldn't they all sod off and let him get on with things the only way he knew how?

The last time he'd met Miranda Beven in an unofficial capacity was at a dinner party thrown by Jenkins and Cara Frost. When both women were on far better terms. He hadn't wanted to go. Was freaked out by the very thought of socialising with a group of people who were younger, happier, and far more outgoing than he was. Last to arrive and first to leave, he'd mostly enjoyed the experience, even with Jenkins and Morgan plotting to pair him up with his counsellor.

With his thumb hovering over the *Call* prompt, he ran the potential scenario over in his mind, trying to decide on what to say beforehand. He'd thank Miranda for the kind gift of whisky. She'd tell him not to mention it. He'd say she shouldn't have gone to the trouble and expense. There would be an awkward silence between them when he couldn't think of anything else to say. And that's when he'd hang up. Abruptly, in all likelihood. Then he'd slump in his seat, breathing heavily and wishing he hadn't bothered in the first place. He chose not to make the call. It wasn't the right week to do such a thing. Would it ever be the right week? Scrolling further down the list, he tapped Ginge's number and waited.

'Yes, boss?'

'Have you been across to the restaurants yet?'

Ginge said he wasn't long back. 'And got lucky with the first one I tried.'

Reece could almost see the smug grin on the young detective's face. 'Let's hear it then.'

Ginge gave the pronunciation of the chef's name his best shot. 'He wouldn't admit to giving our man the duck and cooking sherry—not at first—but once I got him outside and on our own, he confirmed he did.'

'Did he get a name for him?'

'No, but there was a pretty good description. And of another man who chef thought might have been watching them from the railings at the far end of the alley.'

'Watching?'

'That's what it looked like to him. He was worried he'd get into trouble for giving food away, so he sent our man packing after that and went back inside.'

'Did he notice if this person said anything to the victim? Or followed him?'

'He thought they might have spoken. That's when he left them to it and went back to his work in the kitchen.'

'What did he look like? You said there was a description.'

'It was dark—street lighting only—and there was a fair distance between them. But slim and tall, with black hair that might have been curly. Definitely a beard, though.'

It fit the appearance of the man at the crime scene that morning. 'What was he wearing?'

'Jeans, shirt, and what might have been a leather bomber-style jacket.'

'Bingo,' Reece whispered. 'You checked with the other businesses?'

'Like you told me to, boss. There was a man matching the description in one of the cafés this morning. Had a window seat and looked like he was waiting for someone to pass in the street. One of the staff remembered him because he just about went running out of there.'

'Was there a girl with him?'

'Not when he was inside. And after that, the staff were more concerned with him not having paid for his breakfast.'

'Fair enough. Did you ask them for any CCTV footage they might have?'

Ginge told him he had. 'And from the area directly outside.'

Chapter 44

MALI WOKE UP IN a daze and with a crowd of anxious-looking people surrounding her.

'Where am I? What happened?' She tried to move, but it wasn't an easy thing to do.

There was a woman on her knees next to her, holding her hand. 'Take it easy. You fell off the bench and hit your head.'

Why would she have fallen off a bench? That made no sense. And why was she soaking wet from the waist down? Had she landed in a puddle? It was too warm for that. She tried to sit up. There was a jacket that wasn't hers draped over her shoulders. Was Piotr the lorry driver back?

Nothing was adding up.

'You've cut your head,' the woman said. 'Just above your right eye.'

Mali put her hand to it. The woman wasn't wrong. It hurt when she touched it.

'It's stopped bleeding, but might need a couple of stitches to hold it closed.'

'I'm all right,' Mali mumbled. 'No stitches.' Someone tried to pass her a clear plastic cup filled with water. She shook her head. 'I'm okay now. I need to leave.'

'Let's get you inside first,' the woman told her. 'I've sent someone to look for a change of clothes.'

Mali was sitting on the slate floor, her back pressed against the bench she'd tumbled off. She'd had a fit. A full-blown fit. Her first ever. That explained why she'd wet herself. 'This can't be happening. Is there somewhere I can shower?' she asked.

'Change into something dry while we wait for the ambulance,' the woman told her. 'It's so cold out here.'

'I don't need an ambulance. I'll be okay after a shower.'

'That's a nasty bump you have there. Why don't you let them take a quick look at it?'

Mali's protests were drowned out by the approaching siren.

'Here it is,' the woman said, getting to her feet. 'You stay put until they're ready.'

'What about the dry clothes?'

'You can take them with you. They'll be from the lost and found cupboard. You never know, there might be something in there that'll fit.'

There were two people walking towards her. Both were dressed in dark green uniforms and yellow hi-viz jackets. One of them was carrying a white cylinder with clear plastic tubing and an oxygen mask.

'I don't need that,' Mali said to the approaching paramedic. 'I banged my head. There's no problem with my breathing.'

'She's peed herself,' the woman told the other member of the ambulance crew. 'I wasn't here at the time, but it sounds like she had an epileptic fit and fell off that bench.'

The paramedic shone a pen torch in both Mali's eyes. 'Have you taken anything recently?' he asked, repeating the examination. 'Any drugs or over-the-counter medicines?'

'Of course not.'

'Alcohol?'

Mali shook her head.

'Have you ever previously fitted?'

'No.'

'Absence moments? Visual issues like tunnel vision or floaters in front of your eyes.'

'Yes.'

'What medication do you take for that?'

'It starts with a *zed*, I think. And another one with a *vee*.'

'Did you take today's tablets?'

'I lost them.' She raised a shaky hand and pointed at the dark expanse of water opposite. 'They're in there somewhere.'

'You threw them away?'

'It was nothing like that.'

'Speak up if you can. I can't hear you properly.'

'I don't need this.' Mali lifted the oxygen mask out of the way. 'I said I dropped them in the water. It was an accident.'

'How often do you get your blood levels checked?'

'It used to be a regular thing, but not anymore.'

'When was the last time?'

'Six months. Probably longer.'

'Are you able to stand if we help you up?' the paramedic gave her room. 'Let my colleague get the other side before you try.'

There was a trail of urine snaking to the gutter and her dungarees were wetter than she'd first thought. 'Can I have a blanket instead of this?' she asked, looking for the owner of the jacket. She was cold and shivering, but the blanket would do a better job of hiding her embarrassment.

'Can you walk?' the paramedic asked, wrapping one around her. 'We can't get the van any closer because of the security barriers. There's a wheelchair, if you'd prefer?'

'I'm all right.' Mali shuffled her way closer to the waiting vehicle. She turned with the intention of thanking all those who'd been kind enough to stop and help, but never got past the deadpan faces of Bridget Payne and Tommy Hemlock.

Chapter 45

REECE MADE A QUICK stop at the front desk to talk to George. 'You're losing weight?' he said, and was nowhere near quick enough to get out of the burly desk sergeant's way.

George grabbed him by the shoulders and landed a wet kiss on his forehead. 'You're the first to notice,' he said with a beaming smile. 'Cheers Brân.'

'What the hell are you doing?' Reece wiped his head with the cuff of his jacket. 'I'd have kept my mouth shut had I known the response I'd get from you.'

George leaned an elbow on the counter. 'It's all because our Julie's going to have a baby.'

'Who with?'

'Her husband.' The desk sergeant straightened and stared at him. 'Who did you think it would be?'

Reece scratched his head. 'Do I know him?'

'Didn't make the wedding reception, did you?'

Reece couldn't remember when that was and managed little more than a shrug in response.

'You won't have met him then,' George said. 'Mable doesn't fancy the idea of me corking it when I take the little one over the park with a ball.'

Reece frowned. 'Can't imagine you fancy it much yourself?'

George looked like he might cry. 'She's got me on one of them low-carb diets. All salad leaves, veggie soups, and skinless chicken.' He shook his head and sat on a stool. 'Being dead probably isn't such a bad thing. At least I wouldn't be farting every couple of minutes. I almost followed through yesterday? Can you imagine how I'd have coped with that?'

Reece backed away. 'Too much information. Catch you later.' He took the stairs and marched along the landing and into the incident room.

Ffion Morgan approached as soon as she caught sight of him. '*I* didn't let her in, boss. She was here before me.'

Reece peered through the open door of his office. 'Put the whisky back where you found it,' he said, tossing his jacket onto his desk. 'Who let you up here?'

Maggie Kavanagh held an unlit cigarette between her crooked fingers. Her red hair was pinned up in its usual beehive style. 'Can't say I've ever seen him before,' she answered with a dismissive wave of the hand. 'He must have been a newbie.'

'Don't give me that. You know every person working in this building. And most of them by name.'

'God's honest truth.' She crossed herself and then pinched Reece's cheek. 'Would I lie to such a hottie?'

'Maggie, I haven't got time for this.'

'What have you been up to?' she asked, not yet free of the bottle.

'Give me that.' He snatched it from her grasp. 'It was a present,' he said, putting it out of reach under his desk.

'I can see that.' Kavanagh squinted while she read from the gift card. 'But from her, of all people.' She winked. 'You really are a naughty boy.'

'There's nothing going on between us,' Reece blurted and went over to the window and opened it. The day's light was fading quickly. Some of the streetlights below were already on. 'It's purely platonic, I can assure you.'

Kavanagh helped herself to a seat and took a few dry puffs on her cigarette. 'Even so, I can't see the chief super being happy with you accepting gifts from members of the criminal underworld.'

Reece spun around. It suddenly dawned on him who 'M' was. How could he have been so stupid in thinking it was Miranda Beven?

'Marma Creed, sending your favourite whisky.' Kavanagh took a hand-held recording device from the pocket of her Colombo-style coat and placed it on the desk. 'I'm thinking there's one hell of a story behind this?'

'And I'd like to hear it myself, Detective Chief Inspector?'

Reece recognised the voice even before Harris and Cable appeared in the doorway. 'Aw, shit.'

Chapter 46

MALI SLID OFF THE uncomfortable hospital trolley wearing little more than a thin gown with a tie at the back. She'd seen plenty of people wandering the Emergency Unit wearing a similar thing, every one of them flashing body parts at anyone who cared to look their way.

The linoleum flooring was cold beneath her bare feet. A nursing assistant had hunted for spare slippers but could only find a pair of men's that were at least two sizes too big. Mali had thanked her and declined the offer.

There were two radiographers, dressed in black, waiting beside a machine that looked like a large Polo mint stood up on its end. The Polo hummed while it patiently waited for her.

'Do you have a cannula?' one radiographer asked.

Mali's chaperone answered on her behalf. The cannulation process had been an exercise in how not to do it. The junior doctor had given up after five, maybe six, unsuccessful attempts, returning sometime later with a nurse practitioner in tow. A cannula was then inserted into a vein at the elbow – all others lower down the arms being "*Totally messed up.*"

'Does it flush?' the same radiographer asked.

Mali looked to her chaperone for help and nodded with her. If a shake of the head had meant she'd need another one, she'd be walking out of there, regardless of what anyone else had to say.

She climbed onto a horizontal surface in front of the Polo and put her arms down by her sides. A worryingly large syringe of clear fluid was then connected to the cannula at her elbow. 'Anaesthetic?' she asked.

'You'll be awake for this,' the radiographer said with a brief chuckle. 'The fluid goes into your blood vessels and shows up any leaks on the inside.'

'In my head?' Mali hadn't considered that before now. The skin above her right eye hadn't needed suturing, but she could be bleeding into her brain and not know it. 'What if there *are* any leaks?'

The nearest radiographer wrapped a wide Velcro strap around her and didn't answer the question. 'We'll be next door and just behind the glass. It'll take less than a couple of minutes to get this done.'

Mali heard the door close and the humming get louder. There were clicking sounds and then the surface she was lying on moved into the open mouth of the Polo, taking her with it. She shut her eyes and held her breath.

'Breathe away normally.' The radiographer spoke through a PA system that changed her voice to something more official sounding. 'Relax. Nearly done now.'

The door to the other room opened, releasing both radiographers and the chaperone in green. The whole process reversed itself until Mali was back on the original trolley.

'Was it okay?' she asked. 'Were there any leaks that you could see?'

The radiographer's face remained impassive the whole time she spoke. 'Your scan will be reported on and then one of the doctors in the Emergency Unit will discuss the findings with you.'

'For Christ's sake,' Reece said, pacing the carpet of Chief Superintendent Cable's office. Assistant Chief Constable Harris was looking none too pleased. 'I didn't know it was from Marma Creed. How the hell could I have done when there was only an 'M' as a clue?'

'Who *did* you think sent it?' Harris demanded to know. 'How many 'M's are there?'

'Miranda.' Reece looked away. 'I thought it was from Miranda Beven.'

Harris turned to Cable. 'Isn't she one of our contracted counsellors?' He pointed a finger in Reece's direction. 'Your counsellor?'

Reece wandered the room with his hands planted firmly on his hips. 'You know I don't have counselling these days.'

'And wasn't Beven the one who wrote the final evaluation report?' Harris asked. Cable nodded and glanced at Reece. 'We'll need a second opinion, in that case. There *has* to be a second opinion.'

Reece glared at him. 'In your dreams. I'm done with that shite.'

'You'll do as you're told, Chief Inspector.'

Reece balled his fists. 'Nothing happened between us. We're friends. Nothing more.'

'Yet she sends you random gifts at work. Sounds to me like there's more going on than you'd care to admit.'

'I saved her life once. It's an act of gratitude on her part.'

'I want her reported to her governing body,' Harris told Cable. 'This is highly unprofessional behaviour.'

'Can't help throwing your weight around, can you?' Reece said, glaring at him. 'You're never going to change.'

Harris went a deep shade of purple. 'Get out!' He pointed at the door. '*Out!*'

'Try stopping me.' Reece banged it against the wall as he left.

'You've not heard the last of this,' Harris shouted after him.

'You know where to find me,' Reece called over his shoulder. 'Even *you* can't fuck that up.'

Chapter 47

BY THE TIME REECE got back to his office, Maggie Kavanagh was nowhere to be found. His phone log showed three missed calls from the reporter, plus a text he was far too angry to open and read.

'You couldn't have known,' Morgan said, putting a mug of steaming coffee on his desk. 'None of us twigged who that whisky was from.'

'But we should have known Harris would soon get wind of a sniffer dog team going through this place. That's why he was over here. To see for himself what was going on.' Reece slid into his chair. He rocked back and forth, making the swivel mechanism squeak. Something wasn't right about the whole affair. The more he thought, the more unlikely it was Marma Creed had anything to do with it. He stared at the wall and a daddy long-legs slowly making its way towards the ceiling. It was doing no one any harm, and he left it alone. Someone was setting him up. Payback for the harm he'd done them. There were a thousand or so officers currently under investigation in the Metropolitan Police Force alone. It was unlikely Wales would have got rid of all its bad eggs in one hit. Grudges and loyalties were something that went hand in hand.

He'd be bagging the card, bottle, and all its packaging, once he was alone; sending it over to the lab to have it checked for prints. He wasn't going to sit back and let someone sully his reputation.

Ginge appeared in the open doorway. 'What's up?' he asked. 'Did I miss anything?'

'The ACC had a right go at the boss,' Morgan said. 'We should have kept our mouths shut.'

Ginge looked none the wiser. He cleared his throat. 'Someone came to the front desk when you were upstairs. Says he wants to talk to you about an assault the other night.'

'Cory Cullinane, by any chance?'

'That's him. George put him in an empty interview room.'

Reece got to his feet. 'You two carry on here.'

Ginge moved out of his way. 'Problem?'

Reece walked slowly past him. 'Only time will tell.'

Jenkins exited the village chip shop to the sound of a bell chime from her phone. She dug it out of her back pocket and checked the text message from Ffion Morgan. *The boss is onto you. Knows you've left early. Been bollocked by Harris and in a foul mood. Something's up. Something big. He's paranoid all of a sudden. I'll explain when I see you next. Shit – I hope it's not about to kick off here!*

Jenkins texted back: *Tell him I was following up on something that can't wait.* She deleted the text. There was no reason to ask a colleague to lie on her behalf. *Thanks for the heads up. Back within the hour.* She pressed send and got in her car.

Margaret was buttering bread when she got there.

'It's just you and me for tea,' Jenkins said, putting the lid on the butter dish. 'You've done enough to feed the entire street.'

'Dad likes his bread and butter,' Margaret said. 'And so does Mam.'

Jenkins's movements slowed as she unwrapped dinner. Surely her mother wasn't now mistaking her for a sibling? She took two plates from the cupboard, thinking about Reece's father calling him Dad, and used a fork to serve. 'I've got you five fish bites. And there's a portion of chips between us.'

Margaret came alongside and removed another plate from the cupboard. 'Shall I go and call your father? He's working in the garden between showers.'

Jenkins wiped her hands on a tea towel and took her mother gently by the forearms. 'Dad isn't here. It's just you and me now.'

Margaret looked through the kitchen window, craning her neck in an attempt to get a better view of the outside. 'He was in the shed earlier. I took him a cup of tea and a biscuit.'

'He wasn't.'

'I'm telling you he was. I took him a cup of tea.'

Jenkins slammed her hand down hard on the countertop, knocking the salt cellar to the floor. 'Stop it! Please.' She crouched to pick up the broken condiment pot. 'I'm sorry about this,' she said, showing the pieces. 'You've had it a long time.'

'Since you were a little girl.' Margaret took the larger bits from her. 'Your father bought the pair of them when we were on holiday one year in Tenby.'

Jenkins fetched a pan and brush from a tall cupboard next to the back door and used them to clean up what was left of the breakage. 'Maybe we can go back to Tenby in the spring? You and me. Hunt around the shops and see if we can find a new one?'

'Your father would like that too.'

Jenkins went back to forking out the chips and didn't reply.

Chapter 48

Cory Cullinane was waiting in Interview Room 3, its door wedged open with a plastic chair. On the table in front of him were several paper coffee cups that were lined up like bowling pins. He was throwing torn balls of tissue paper at them. Reece couldn't tell if he was trying to knock them over, or land the balls inside. Either way, he was having little success.

'You didn't run away this time?' the detective said, settling into his seat. Harris had got under his skin and there was a real risk he'd take his frustration out on anyone who said or did the wrong thing.

Cullinane had a dirty towel draped across his knees, and was nibbling on the lip of one of the paper cups. 'You know how it is?'

he said, watching Reece's response. 'I don't want people thinking I'm on your payroll.'

'We're alone here.' Reece went over and closed the door. 'There's nobody eavesdropping on anything you've got to tell me.'

Cullinane checked the camera high on the wall in the far corner of the room. A small red light blinked at him. 'Except for anyone watching that.'

'It's there for your safety and mine.'

Cullinane put the cup down and balled the towel in his lap. 'Charlie reckons you're all right. Says you don't mind stirring things up when you have to. But Mali says she hasn't worked you out yet.'

'Mali?' Was she the young woman he'd met on Mermaid Quay? He could think of no one else with that name.

'She thinks you're following her. Wants to know what you're up to.'

'I'm not following her,' Reece said. 'I saw someone giving her hassle this morning and wanted to make sure she was okay.'

'She is.'

'Did she tell you who he was?'

'Nope.'

Reece knew a lie when he heard one. 'You sure about that?'

Cullinane was having obvious trouble getting comfortable. 'I thought you wanted to know about me and Dale?'

'What's wrong with you?' Reece asked. 'You've not been still since we started this.'

Mali's head scan had been reviewed and reported on by a neuro-radiologist. One of the on-call Emergency Unit doctors had then discussed the findings with her.

In layperson's terms, she'd sustained a mild concussion, but had thankfully done herself no more serious an injury than that. There was no fracture of the skull. Nor was there any obvious sign of blood collecting between the bone and soft brain tissue. No leaks, as it were.

She'd agreed with the doctor's suggestion of keeping her in hospital overnight. Not only to monitor for more seizure activity, if there was any, but also to reestablish the medication regimen she had previously been following.

It sounded like a decent enough plan. Not only that, she'd get a shower, hot meal, and a warm bed for the night. Even with the doctor's warning that finding her one might take some time, how could she have possibly said no?

'Hames's people did this to you?' Reece circled Cullinane with the critical eye of someone buying a used car. There were scratches and scuffs. Evidence of at least one heavy impact. If it had been a car he was looking at, he'd have walked away. Cullinane's flanks and lower ribs were covered in brown and yellowed bruising.

'Charlie's already told you.'

'I need to hear it from you,' Reece said. 'I can't go wading in there on the say so of someone else.'

Cullinane lowered his clothing and sat down with a muted groan. 'Charlie and Janice don't know half of what happened to me. We mostly told them about Dale. Didn't want Charlie getting into trouble for doing something he shouldn't. The centre's had more than its fair share of negative publicity recently.'

'I want descriptions of the men who did this.'

Cullinane looked towards the camera. 'I'm saying nothing in front of that.'

Reece shot to his feet and yanked the thing clean out of its plasterboard fixings. He tossed it into a corner. 'Just you and me now,' he said, clapping dust from his hands.

'It's wireless. Might still be transmitting everything I say.'

Reece scooped it up and yanked open the door to the interview room. He stood in the corridor and hurled the camera as far as it would go. 'If you're in any doubt as to what these people are capable of, I'll fill you in, shall I?' He slammed the door shut and pressed both hands onto the table top, looming over the other man. 'There's a body over in the city morgue—your mate Dale, in all likelihood—and all that's left of him are his feet and a few numbers tattooed on his back. Apologies for coming across as insensitive, but you really do need to stop fucking me about.'

Chapter 49

'Is there a telephone I can use?' Mali asked. A staff nurse was busy documenting her neuro obs for the head injury. 'I don't have one of my own and I really should let a friend know what's happened and where I am.'

The bit about not owning a phone was true enough. That was stolen not long after she'd been forced to sleep on the streets. A rookie mistake of loaning it to someone who'd then pulled a knife before running away. She'd learned her lesson the hard way and had never again been so gullible.

The reason given for wanting to make the call was a lie of sorts. She needed to know that Lisa was okay. That Tommy Hemlock hadn't harmed her. Her stomach turned over with the thought of it.

The nurse led her to the main reception desk and handed over the receiver once she had an outside line. Mali dialled a number from memory and waited while it rang. And rang. She returned the receiver to its cradle and immediately picked it up again.

'Sorry, how do I get the outside line?'

It took the receptionist what seemed like an age to look up. She was leafing through a pile of paperwork and wasn't at all pleased with the interruption. 'You're not supposed to be using that. It's for official calls only.'

'I did ask the nurse. And this was the one I was told I could use.'

'But now you want to use it for a second time. This is what always happens,' the woman said, more to herself than anyone else.

'Because I couldn't get through the first time. I need to try another number.'

'And when the other patients see you using it, they'll be asking the same.' The receptionist went back to her filing. 'I'll be having a word with Sister when she comes in.'

'You do that.' Mali walked away from the desk. 'You'd swear I'd asked her to pay for the call out of her own money,' she told the staff nurse when she found her. 'Why are they always such Little-Hitlers?'

A few minutes later, she was sitting to one side of Sister's desk, dialling a number, tapping her fingers, waiting for someone—any-one—to pick up on the other side. Her right leg refused to keep still. She rested the palm of her free hand on her lower thigh and pressed down on it. But still the leg rose and fell. She was nervous. Anxious. And had every reason to be. Where was Lisa? Why wasn't she answering her calls? She was always back at the flat by early evening. Especially during the dark winter months. Mali tried a third number that was also committed to memory. It rang twice before it was answered.

'Who is this?' a woman's voice asked.

'Candice. Thank God for that. Where's Lisa? I've tried both numbers and can't get through.'

'Mali? Is that you?'

'It's me, yeah.'

'Where are you?'

It was no longer a secret. 'I'm in Cardiff. Lisa knows – but where is she?'

'Isn't she with you?'

'Why would you think that?'

'Because no one has seen her since the day you disappeared.'

With the call completed, Mali entered panic-mode. 'I have to go,' she said, shoving donated toiletries into a patient property bag. She'd done all right there. Not a bad haul, and none of it stolen. Her own clothes had been washed and dried on the ward and were packed as spares.

'You can't do that.' The nurse said.

Mali knew she could. 'I'll sign the disclaimer. That way you won't get into any trouble for letting me go.'

The nurse refused to move out of the way. 'You could have another fit. What if you fell into the road this time? Or into a river?'

And what if she stayed put and got herself smothered with a pillow during the night? Hemlock knew where she was. Not the exact ward, maybe, but the hospital was easy enough to guess. And Bridget Payne would have contacts who owed her favours.

'Get me the disclaimer form,' Mali said, now ready to leave. 'With or without it, I'm getting out of here tonight.'

Chapter 50

THE GARAGE WAS LOCKED up for the night. Its shutters pulled down. Lights out – except for a single halogen bulb illuminating most of the front forecourt. Limping up the hill towards it was a man wearing one shoe. The other was swinging from the end of his outstretched arm. He stopped to urinate against a hedgerow, spooking a cat that was up to no good among the bins. The animal hissed at him and scarpered across the adjacent road and out of sight.

Shaun Kendle saw it all from his position beneath the overhang of a bare willow tree. He waited while the drunk walked two steps sideways for every three he managed ahead. Listened to him sing a repertoire of songs he quite obviously didn't know the words to.

A dog joined in with no more competence than the drunk. Some-one hurled abuse at them both. Someone else stood on a back doorstep calling the animal's name. A door slammed shut only moments later, and after that, all went quiet again.

Kendle marched on the spot and breathed into his gloved hands. It was freezing cold, but he'd soon have the place nicely warmed up.

He'd pleaded with the arsehole detective to keep his voice down and thought he'd got away with the impromptu police visit. But only until his employers handed him an envelope containing a couple of hundred quid and a warning to *"Sling his hook."* He'd head-butted one of them and chinned the other with a swipe of a heavy spanner.

Now he was back, and up to no good, like the tomcat before him.

There was a featureless door in the side wall of the single-storey building. Metal with a hefty padlock looped through an equally hefty ring-fastener. He knew the security camera on the external wall was for show only. As was the big yellow alarm box screwed to the garage's frontage. That one lit up with a blue light, but was no more effective in warding off would-be crooks than a cardboard shoe box would have been. His ex-employers were cheapskates. He middle-fingered their names above the door.

They'd earned what was coming.

You didn't piss off Shaun Kendle and not regret it.

Searching through a ring of master keys, he soon found one that fit the lock and let himself in. He'd fully expected them to call the police after the assault, but they'd obviously thought better of it. He had his suspicions they were peddling a lucrative business in fake MOTs and wanted no one from the local constabulary snooping around.

The side door led straight into the office, where there was a desk, a card payment machine, and an ancient-looking laptop. Alongside the telephone was a diary open to the following day's date. There were several handwritten entries and plenty of dirty smudges and fingerprints. Neither mug of tea had been finished. The milk had settled to form a white marbling effect on the surfaces of each.

A threadbare sofa was pushed against a plasterboard wall and to one side of a dartboard. A pair of darts stuck out the front of it. Kendle knew the third dart didn't exist. Hadn't since the day it was launched at a passing rat and got lost somewhere in the allotment garden next door.

He went through to the workshop and helped himself to anything that would provide a good burn. On an elevated ramp was a car with its exhaust system missing. He had no personal beef with the vehicle's owners. They were victims like he was and seemed the type of people who'd be in ownership of a robust insurance policy.

He doused most surfaces with petrol and cleaning spirits. Forced roll after roll of paper towels into a pair of bins manoeuvred into position beneath the car. The vehicle itself got a hefty spray-down where he could get at it. He wasn't going to risk lowering it to the ground. The noise the lifting mechanism made might summon unwanted attention from outside.

Pale orange street light snuck in through an arrow-slit window high in the wall. The wind rattled the corrugated roof overhead.

He was almost ready.

Any efforts to make the blaze look accidental were pointless. Even the most intellectually challenged of plods would quickly make the connection between a convicted arsonist; a sacked employee; and a devastating property fire, all at the same address. They'd be after him as soon as the fire was reported. Sending him back to prison to serve the remainder of his time, and more.

He returned to the office area of the premises, carrying a heavy jerrycan under an arm. He gave the sofa a good soaking. Then the desk and the floor – making a liquid connection between both work spaces.

It was time.

His heart raced in anticipation, thumping in his chest. He thumbed the wheel of a cheap plastic lighter and stood there staring deep into the flame. It was such a thing of beauty. Both mesmerising and innocent-looking.

But not for long.

He started with the bins, only moving away when they roared to life. Next was the sofa. He'd already shut off the water supply to the sprinkler system. The noxious smoke from the foam stuffing made him cough and cup a hand over his nose and mouth. He slung his rucksack over a shoulder and left the way he'd come in. Once clear of the garage, he sought shelter beneath the same willow tree. Watching the place burn. Waiting for the blue flashing lights and the sounds of emergency sirens.

Chapter 51

BOTH DETECTIVE AND PUPPY had slept through the night. If Reece had been a user of social media, he'd have posted details of their achievement for all to read, like, and pass comment on. As it was, he couldn't imagine there being much else in life that was so pointless and misused.

With no time available for his morning run, he got ready for work and dropped Redlar off at Yanto's farm on the way.

The news headlines had him turn up the radio and listen. A business property in Cardiff had been burned to the ground overnight. *"A blaze that tore through the building in no time,"* was how the radio presenter described it.

Reece listened for news of casualties, while wrestling his phone out of his pocket to check for missed calls or texts from members of the team.

"Given recent events in the city," the presenter continued, *"police will be working hard to establish if this is in any way related to the tragedies of earlier this week."*

Reece checked his rear-view mirror before accelerating away. 'That we will.'

He'd somehow remembered the workings of the hands-free set-up and cut back on the accelerator as soon as he learned of the fire's exact location. There were no fatalities reported and the chief suspect was already apprehended and in the cells back at the station.

Reece wanted to see the extent of the damage for himself. There was no real reason to, but he took the detour anyway. He found a spot wide enough to park among the other vehicles and crossed the road to where the most action was.

There was a modest uniformed police presence on the periphery of the marked-off area, with a small gathering of people corralled to one side. Those present in an official capacity were mostly from the Fire Investigation Department. A single appliance remained at the scene. Parked behind it were two vans belonging to the South Wales Fire and Rescue Unit.

Someone walked an investigation dog through the remains of the garage. Another took photographs of points of interest. Two men in hard hats were engaged in a lengthy conversation involving lots of pointing as they traipsed back and forth.

'Our friend Shaun Kendle,' Reece said to the nearest of them. He couldn't help but think this might have something to do with his own visit.

'Oi, you.' It was one of the men he'd seen in the garage office. Only this time, he had a black eye. 'You should have warned us of what he was capable of. My business partner is still in hospital having his jaw wired. This is all your fault.'

'You were the one who gave Kendle the job without proper references or a DB check,' Reece said, without really giving a toss. 'You're looking for someone to blame because it makes it easier that way.' They were now standing only a few feet apart. 'That someone won't be me.' He came away and let the man rant all he wanted.

'I thought Kendle was still in prison?' the firefighter said once Reece was within range again.

The detective nodded. 'He will be after this.'

Cable was waiting outside Reece's office when he got there. He swore under his breath and felt himself tense. 'Are you waiting for me?' he asked, knowing she was.

She waited for him to open the door and entered when he stepped out of the way. 'We need to talk.'

'Will it take long? I'm busy.'

'What happened to the camera in Interview Room Three?'

'If you're here, then you already know,' he said, trying to get to his side of his desk. 'I'll pay for it if you want me to. Cullinane wasn't talking. Not with the threat of anyone listening in.'

'You could be suspended. Removed from the premises and charged with criminal damage.'

He flung his coat at a peg on the back of the door. It missed and fell in a heap. 'Cullinane says Lynch had his own date of birth tattooed on his lower back. The two and the nine fit. He's going to get us something of Lynch's for a DNA check. That'll make it watertight.'

'Reece—'

'You should see the bruising on him. Hames had his thugs assault them both.'

'Reece—'

'And threatened them with far worse if they were ever again caught near the development.'

'Shut up and listen to what I have to say.'

'The net's closing in on that bastard. It looks like Jenkins was right.'

Cable spoke regardless. 'This isn't about Douglas Hames, or anyone else, for that matter.' She didn't look at him when she continued: 'ACC Harris has referred you to Professional Standards.'

Chapter 52

CARA FROST'S CAR WASN'T parked in its usual spot on the drive when Jenkins pulled up in front of their house. That in itself wasn't overly concerning. She might have been on call and out at a crime scene. But from what Jenkins could remember of recent conversations between them, Cara wasn't working again until the tail end of the week.

She took her phone and thumbed through to the shared diary app. Nothing had changed. Cara should have been off duty, and therefore, at home.

The curtains were open. Odd, it being so early in the day. There were no lights on, even though it was still dark outside.

Jenkins took the overnight bag from the boot of her car and stopped on the front path to check up and down the street. There would be no plausible reason for Cara to park elsewhere when the driveway was empty. Not unless access to the house had been somehow blocked. There was nothing obvious to suggest it had been. No new holes in the road, or mess from one that had been dug and filled in again.

She let herself in through the front door and stepped over a pile of mail and advertising flyers, calling Cara's name. The hallway was pleasantly warm, but then, the heating was on a timer during the colder months of the year.

There was no smell of toast and coffee. Bacon and bread rolls. Not in the hall, living room, or kitchen. The place smelled unlived in, even though it had been only a couple of days since Jenkins had stormed out during their row over Margaret.

'Where are you?' she whispered, sitting at the kitchen table in her coat. She pressed the icon for Cara's number. It rang three times.

'Hello,' came the groggy answer. 'Who's this?'

'Cara? Is that you?' It didn't sound like her. There was movement and a very brief exchange of hushed voices.

'Elan.'

'Cara, where are you?' The silence lasted far too long for Jenkins's liking. 'I want you out,' she said. 'Out of my house. Out of my life.'

———— ◄○► ————

'He's done what?' Reece fought the urge not to swing a clenched fist at the wall. 'Reported me to Professional Standards because someone sent me a bottle of whisky in the post? Christ Almighty. Can you believe the man?'

'Marma Creed isn't just someone,' Cable said. 'The woman is heavily linked to organised crime in this city.'

'It's not from Marma Creed.' Reece leaned on his desk, supporting himself on outstretched arms. 'Someone here at the station is stirring up trouble for me.'

Cable looked shocked. 'And who would do such a thing?'

'Plenty.' He shook his head. 'You can't think they've all been flushed out yet?'

'Do I look that naïve?'

'All they have to do in the current climate is plant a seed of suspicion. It doesn't matter it being a bottle of whisky and not a couple of grand in an envelope. Mud sticks. And it will. They've got what they wanted. I'm the one being investigated now.'

'You're not being investigated at this stage,' she told him. 'But there is a formal process to be followed. One where you will be given an opportunity to be heard.'

Reece dropped his head. 'Only a few years ago, I'd have been taken into your office and that would have been that. You'd either believe me or you wouldn't. If you did, then it was case closed and move on.'

'You're well aware that this Force is being investigated by the IOPC, over a corruption ring involving at least a dozen officers.'

'I should do, given it was me who started it,' Reece said. 'That's why they're trying to ruin my reputation. Can't you see? It's payback and so bloody predictable.'

'ACC Harris had no choice in what he did. You must know that?'

Reece did, but managed little more than a shrug in response. Ginge and Morgan's suggestion he get the package checked over before opening it, meant just about everyone in the station knew about the gift. It would have taken only one person to mention it during their interview with the IOPC and another can of worms would have had its lid blown off. Like it or not, Harris had his hands tied. 'Anyway, we'll know who sent it soon enough.'

Cable wasn't following. 'How?'

Reece sat and picked at a dry piece of skin at the corner of his bottom lip. 'I've sent the bottle and all its packaging over to Sioned Williams.'

'You're having it checked for prints? Who authorised the tests?'

Reece licked his lip and tasted blood. 'I did.'

'You?' Cable shut her eyes. 'Why, for God's sake?'

'Because whoever did this wouldn't have expected me to send it to the lab. I bet they were careless and left their dabs all over it.'

'As well as everyone else who picked it up and put it down again on the supermarket shelf,' Cable said. 'Even Maggie Kavanagh had her paws on it.'

'But only one of those people is likely to be working here in this building.'

'Didn't it arrive by post?'

Reece shook his head. 'It was packed like it should have been, but I checked – those stamps weren't franked at the post office. Meaning someone brought it in with them and delivered it straight to my desk.'

'But that would involve a high risk of getting caught in the act?'

'Not so much of a risk if the incident room is where they work,' Reece said.

Cable stared. 'Did I hear you correctly?'

'Unfortunately, I think you probably did.'

Chapter 53

With Cable gone, Reece sat at his desk, watching the incident room between the narrow slats of his window blinds. There were several detectives at work out there. Some he knew well. Others, not so much. His eye was repeatedly drawn back to the same one, but he needed to do more background work before he made his move. He'd also give Sioned Williams a ring if he heard nothing soon from the lab.

'Penny for them.' It was Ffion Morgan. She was standing in the office doorway with something held in both hands.

Reece snapped out of his trance. 'What was that?'

She entered with all the trepidation of someone about to negotiate a field of landmines. 'Is that thing with ACC Harris still playing on your mind?'

'Tell me. Do you trust your colleagues?'

It wasn't the response she'd have been expecting. She blinked rapidly. 'I'm not sure I understand you?'

Reece swept an arm from one side of the room to the other. 'That lot out there. How many of them do you reckon you can trust?'

Morgan took a look for herself. 'All of them, I'd hope.'

'Even knowing what you do of Ken Ward?' Ward had been an established and well respected member of the team. Thanks to a gambling addiction, he'd found himself in the pocket of Billy Creed, a ruthless local gangster. When it came down to it, Ward had been willing to sacrifice Jenkins's life to save his own. He'd failed and died while trying.

'What's up, boss? You're not still thinking the whisky was a plant to get you in trouble with Professional Standards?'

'You were going to tell me something?' Reece said, changing the direction of the conversation. He indicated the A4 sheet of paper clutched in her hand.

'There's been another fire overnight. Doesn't look as if it's related to ours, but I thought I'd mention it.'

Reece told her about his visit to the crime scene on his way to work that morning. 'I had a few questions, and who better to ask than someone from the fire investigation team?'

Morgan waved the report at him. 'I might as well shred this if we're not interested in Kendle.'

'I didn't say I wasn't interested. In fact, I was just about to go down there and have a word with him.'

'I don't understand? What's to be gained by that?'

'There's always something to be gained by talking to criminals,' Reece said, getting out of his chair. 'And in this case, it's getting inside the mind of a serial arsonist.'

———◦———

'There you are.' Mali had left the hospital on foot, regularly asking for directions to the city's main shopping area. It had taken a good forty-five minutes to get there and another hour of searching after that to find the *Big Issue* seller.

St David's Centre is a two-story outlet packed with the usual stores and eateries. There were several members of security around, but none were bothering Mali like Lorenzo and his team had done only a few days previously.

Aggy put her hand to the side of Mali's head. 'What happened?'

Mali told her about the seizure. 'It was all very embarrassing, to be honest, but I'm okay now.' She raised the property bag. 'And I've got enough medicines to last me for the next few days.' She'd refused to wait until the pharmacy department opened, leaving without her *Take-Home* medication. Still, what she had might just be enough until the substance misuse nurse visited the drop-in centre sometime Monday morning.

Aggy was still fussing. 'You saw a doctor?'

'I've been in hospital overnight.' She didn't mention her decision to self-discharge.

'You should still be there? You look so pale.'

'I'm always pale. Summer. Winter. It doesn't matter.'

'Even so, you don't look well.'

'Can we sit down somewhere quiet?' Mali checked she wasn't being followed. 'I need to come clean about the reason for me being here in Cardiff.'

'We go to my flat,' Aggy said. 'You stay a few nights until your head is better.'

Mali had already compromised the safety of one friend and was potentially responsible for the death of another. She had no intention of risking Aggy's wellbeing. 'I can't do that,' she said, leading the way to an empty bench seat. 'You're already a target. Just for being seen with me.'

Reece had okayed things with the officer in charge of the Shaun Kendle case. It was a professional courtesy, if nothing else.

Kendle sat opposite, slumped over the table and not showing a huge amount of interest in the detectives. When he did occasionally look up, it was to give Morgan's cleavage a quick once over.

'What happened?' Reece asked.

'*You*, is what happened. Got me sacked by shooting your mouth off the way you did.'

Reece shook his head. 'You'd never have kept the lie going. They'd have caught up with you, eventually.'

Kendle didn't disagree. 'You probably did me a favour in the long run. Crooks, that pair. You should pay them a visit once you're done with me.'

'Not my case,' Reece told him.

'Do you like prison?' Morgan asked.

Kendle raised his head and yawned. '*Like* isn't the right word, but where else would a man get a roof over his head and three meals a day – all without having to pay a penny from his own pocket?'

'Each to their own, I suppose.'

He leaned forward in his seat. 'You should try it. A pretty little thing like you would have no trouble making friends in there.'

Morgan fastened another button on her blouse. 'I'll give it a miss, if it's all the same with you.'

'Is there any point to this conversation?' Kendle asked, addressing Reece. 'Only, I had a late night last night and was catching up on my beauty sleep when *he* came to fetch me.' There was a bored-looking uniform standing next to the door. His hands were hidden behind his back. He nodded at all three of them. Only Morgan reciprocated in kind.

'What makes a person set fires?' Reece asked. 'What's the actual kick you get out of it?'

'Doesn't everyone love a good burn up?' Kendle asked.

There were few things Reece liked more than to stare into the flames of his log burner on a cold winter's evening, and he couldn't deny its primal draw on him as a human being. 'True, but most people don't torch a building in the process,' he argued. 'What makes the arsonist go that extra step is what I'm asking?'

Kendle's expression suggested he'd rarely, if ever, given the subject any thought.

Reece tried again. 'I'm trying to get into the mind of the person who killed three people in the bay this week. What would have motivated them to use fire as a weapon, as opposed to something else?'

There was little delay in the answer to that. 'For the shock value and nothing more,' Kendle said. 'Your killer isn't an arsonist. Not your everyday type, anyway. Most people are numb to knife crime these days. Maybe not gun crime in Cardiff yet. But the threat of being caught in a fire – that always gets the public's attention.'

Chapter 54

REECE OPENED THE MORNING briefing with an overview of events from the previous day. There was a lot for him to get through. 'We're now treating all three deaths as connected,' he said. 'The assumption being that someone is targeting rough-sleepers in the bay area of the city – using arson purely for its shock value.'

'Well done.' Morgan gave Jenkins a gentle nudge with her elbow. 'Looks like you were right with your *bigger purpose* theory.'

Jenkins looked like she'd been crying. 'Let's leave the high-fiving until we know for sure, shall we?'

Morgan was slow to look away. 'Okay. No problem.'

Reece played the CCTV footage of the area directly outside the restaurant. It was black and white, with an exaggerated glare from

LIAM HANSON

the street lighting. 'That's the man I saw in the altercation with the young woman we now believe to be called Mali.' He pointed at the screen. 'Dale Lynch says something to him before wandering off. And then he's followed only a minute or so later.'

'And the last person to see a victim alive is nearly always the killer,' Morgan said, more to herself than anyone else.

Reece nodded. They then watched footage of the man at the window in the café. Saw him get up and leave in a hurry. 'We've already checked the timings of this and the street camera outside, and it's definitely Mali he was interested in.' He sped the footage along. 'There. And look at her reaction when she clocks who it is.'

'She's scared of him,' Morgan said. 'I wonder why?'

Reece came back to the briefing table and sat down. 'If our theory is right, then maybe she has previous experience of what this man is capable of. We know she's a gog. She told Charlie and Cory Cullinane that she'd only been in Cardiff a matter of days. Let's get onto our colleagues in the North Wales Police and show them what we have so far. If she does know him, then it's reasonable to assume he's also local to that area.'

Ginge said he was onto it, but wanted to know what a gog was.

'It's a shortening of *gogleddwr*,' Reece said. 'Welsh-speaking southerners use it as a nickname for anyone from North Wales.'

'And they call us *Hwntw*,' Morgan added. 'Meaning something like, *the people from over there*.'

242

Chief Superintendent Cable had been visible at the far end of the briefing room for the previous five to ten minutes. With her was a woman wearing a grey trouser suit. She had a black leather document folder clasped beneath her arm.

Reece knew the reason for them being there, even before Cable did the formal introductions.

'Come to see if there was a new Mercedes on my drive when I got up this morning, did you?' He extended his arm to expose his wrist. 'Crappy little Sekonda. Not a Rolex,' he said with a wink.

'Brân.' Cable gave him a look of warning. 'Please.'

'This is bullshit.' He turned to Superintendent Piper. 'You *do* know I've been set up, don't you?'

Cable left them to it, but only after she'd issued him with clear instructions to not make things any worse than they already were.

He'd replied as expected and stormed over to his office with Piper following a few paces behind him. He let her close the door, helped himself to a seat, and waited long enough for her to take the hint and sit on the other side of the desk.

'This is just a preliminary meeting to be getting on with,' she said, getting comfortable.

'Does that mean you're coming back?'

'If I deem it necessary.'

'I'm sure you will,' he said, busy rearranging things on his desk. 'Might as well claim your pound of flesh before you realise your mistake.'

'Why so defensive, Chief Inspector?' She was staring at him.

He stared back. 'Don't be taking it as an admission of guilt.'

'What was it then?'

He ran a hand across his head. 'I go where the evidence takes me. Pissing off plenty of people along the way. Why would I shine a light on my own name if I was somehow involved in what's been going on here at the station?'

'Some might say to deflect any forthcoming attention from yourself. It's a tried and tested form of defence.'

He threw his head back and forced a laugh. 'You couldn't make this up. I'll admit to being a lot of things, but a bent copper isn't among them.'

'So tell me how you came by a gift sent by Marma Creed?'

'It turned up on my desk before I came into work that day.'

'It was there before you arrived?'

'You heard me.'

'Who put it there?'

'You tell me.'

'I'm asking the questions.'

'I *d-o-n-'t* know,' he said, forcing every letter. That wasn't strictly true. He was developing a theory, but wasn't anywhere near ready to begin sharing it with anyone else.

'Let's return to my original question regarding Marma Creed. What's your relationship with her?'

'She's a crook. I'm a cop. End of. Oh—and I'll quickly add—I spent the best part of my career trying to put her brother away. That's not really going to endear me to her, is it?'

'Unless she was looking to take over the business. Sibling rivalry and all that.'

'Meaning?'

'If you were successful in putting Billy away, then she might feel somehow indebted to you.'

'Indebted?' Reece laughed again. 'Have you ever met the woman? She's a fucking psycho, not some benevolent do-good-er.'

'You had reason to question Marma Creed recently.'

Reece nodded. 'In relation to the abduction of a young man later found stabbed and dumped in the River Taf.'

'That would be a Daniel Coombs?' Piper said, referring to her notes. 'And you subsequently released her without charge.'

'Because she played no part in his death. We proved who the killer was.'

Piper slid a sheet of paper across the table. It was the summary of a forensics report.

Reece knew what it said well enough to not have to read it. 'Coombs's DNA was found in the boot of Marma's car. She said he'd cut himself changing a punctured tyre.'

'And an officer as experienced as you believed that?'

'Not at all. But there was no evidence to prove otherwise. Nothing we could have presented to the CPS. As I've already said, we identified the killer and went all out on him.'

'And let Marma Creed walk free?'

'I know what you're trying to do here, and it won't work.'

'Didn't you give her the name of a serving police officer, implicating him in the death of her brother?'

Reece paused. Then swallowed. 'How do you know that?'

'I'm unable to share such information with you at the present time. But should this go any further, then of course you'll be given full disclosure of witness names and the accusations made against you.'

'I gave Marma limited information only,' Reece said. 'Nowhere near enough for her to ever identify the officer. And I warned Brogan. Personally. Telling him that she was closing in. It was a tactic forcing him to act and implicate himself. One that worked, I might add.'

'And not a means of providing confidential information to a known criminal in return for financial reward?'

Reece got to his feet and reached for his jacket. 'Next time you want to talk to me, make a formal appointment with my Federation rep.'

Chapter 55

'I NEED TO ASK you something?' Reece said, climbing into the Land Cruiser. He slammed the door behind him and didn't yet start the engine.

Jenkins got in and buckled up. 'Cara's having an affair,' she said, cutting him off. 'That's why I was in such a strop this morning. As if my mother wasn't enough to deal with.'

He wasn't expecting that. 'I'm sorry.' There wasn't much else to say.

'Not as sorry as *she's* going to be.' Jenkins put her hand on Reece's knee. 'Don't worry, I won't be doing anything daft. But she can pick up her shit from my driveway and sling her hook for good.'

'You threw her stuff out without talking to her first?'

'I don't need to talk to her. She can sod off back to wherever she spent last night. Anyway, what was going on in your office after the briefing this morning? It looked like something official.'

'Did you ever mention to anyone, me telling Marma Creed about Mike Brogan?'

'The conversation on his boat in the marina?'

'Yeah.'

'Ffion and Ginge knew, obviously.'

'But you spoke to no one else? This is important.'

'Not that I remember. Why? What's going on?'

Reece fastened his seat belt and started the engine. 'We have a rat on board.'

———◦O◦———

The business premises of Douglas Hames Plc were in the middle of Cardiff city centre. At the Greyfriars end of Queen Street. Getting an appointment with Hames, himself, was ordinarily next to impossible. Reece insisting that the developer's personal assistant put him straight through sped things up considerably.

They had been allocated an underground space, accessed from the rear of the building. Inside was an impressive line up of expensive cars, each nudged up to brass nameplates screwed to the brickwork. In one such space was a gun metal Aston Martin Vantage coupe, parked beneath the plate carrying the name of Douglas Hames MBE.

'And that there's the vehicle belonging to a man struggling for money,' Reece said.

Jenkins went over and stood next to it. 'My Fiat would just about fit in its boot.'

'Well over a grand for a service on those things. And a full set of tyres would cost you a fair bit more.'

'I've got a budget brand on mine,' Jenkins said. 'Forty quid each, plus the dreaded VAT.'

There was a lift that took them only as far as a plush reception area, a woman with a glued-on smile waiting there to greet them from the other side of a glass desk. On the walls behind her were a series of flat screen televisions showing looped coverage of some of the company's better known development projects.

Reece showed his warrant card and waited for Jenkins to do the same. 'We're here to see Douglas Hames.'

'Mr Hames is expecting you,' the woman said with no indication her smile would be disappearing anytime soon. 'If you'd like to take the lift to the seventh floor, then Marcia will assist you further.'

Reece thanked her and turned away from the desk.

'I'm not walking up seven floors of steps,' Jenkins told him.

'Get in,' he said once the lift arrived. When it came to a stop at its destination, the double doors opened with the quietest of chimes. Opposite was a replica of the glass reception desk downstairs, and a woman wearing the same fake smile. Douglas Hames must have ordered himself a job lot.

'DCI Reece,' Marcia said, rising from her seat. 'Would either of you like refreshments while you wait?'

Reece asked for coffee, while Jenkins settled for a bottle of still water. A buzzer sounded on the desk when Marcia was away.

'Come on. That's for us.'

'You don't know that.' Jenkins followed him over to an oak-panelled door. 'Shouldn't we wait until that woman tells us?'

Reece opened it and walked straight in. 'Morning,' he said, giving the place a quick once over. 'This is bigger than my office. I bet it's a bugger to keep warm?'

Douglas Hames was shorter than he'd imagined him to be. Television always gave a different perspective of a person's physical build. He estimated the property developer to be no more than five feet six in height, and ten and a half stones soaking wet. His suit would have cost more than a holiday abroad for a family of four. A Rolex and a tasteful gold bracelet were just two of several expensive items accessorising it. Hames returned the greeting and poked his head through the open door, checking for the whereabouts of his personal assistant.

'She's gone to get coffee,' Reece said, beating Marcia to it when she made a hasty return.

'It's okay,' Hames said, relieving her of a small round tray.

Reece took his. 'Not your cheap crap this,' he said, spooning several cubes of brown sugar into his while Hames stood there like the hired help. 'We should get some for our lot back at the station.'

Hames led them over to a meeting table next to a wall of glass separating them from the city outside. Unlike the windows in Reece's office, these were clean enough to eat your dinner off.

It was only then Reece noticed the other man in the room. He was previously hidden behind an enormous fish tank. Reece went over and dipped his finger in it. 'That's warm enough to take a bath in,' he told Jenkins. 'Have a feel.'

'Please don't,' Hames said, shepherding them both to a pair of high-backed chairs. 'You risk ruining the chemistry of the water.'

'First world problems, eh?' Reece took a seat and slurped his coffee. 'I was never much cop at chemistry.'

Hames placed the tray on the table and backed away. 'So, Detective Chief Inspector, what can I do for you?'

Chapter 56

'EXPECTING TROUBLE?' REECE ASKED Hames, as the other man in the room approached. 'This one's got the smell of a lawyer about him.' When he shook hands, it was with a firmer grip than was necessary. Immature, he knew, but he wasn't in the best of moods.

'Edward was already here on business,' Hames explained. 'I do hope you don't mind him staying for our meeting?'

Reece was slow to release Edward's hand. 'And if I do?'

'Then I'll have no alternative but to reschedule and make this a more formal affair.'

Reece nodded. 'If it's formal you're after, we can take a ride to the station. Jenkins here can play with the blue lights and siren on the way.'

Hames bristled. The lawyer likewise. Neither of them comfortable with the detective's provocative approach.

'I'm not expecting trouble, Chief Inspector. But when an officer of your rank insists on speaking with me, then I can only assume it has nothing to do with a parking ticket or speeding fine.'

'Even if it did, I'm sure Ed here could get you off,' Reece said.

'Meaning?'

'The detective ignored the question and dropped a photograph of Corey Cullinane onto the table. He pushed it across to the other side. 'Do you know this man?'

Hames barely looked at it. 'Should I?'

'You tell me.'

'Is this a game, Chief Inspector?'

Reece took the mortuary photograph of Dale Lynch—all curled up and crispy black—from a large brown envelope and tossed it towards the property developer. 'Does it look like I'm playing games?'

Both Hames and his lawyer shot to their feet. Hames sat down again, albeit slowly.

The lawyer remained standing and took a phone from a pocket concealed inside his jacket. 'I have a direct line to the Chief Constable's office.'

'Do you really?' Reece said, trying his best to look and sound impressed. He twisted to face Jenkins. 'Have you got one of those?'

She shook her head. 'Not the last time I checked.'

'That's Christmas sorted.' He turned to the front and was suddenly serious. 'I don't give a flying fuck who've you've got on

253

speed-dial. I'm here because this man is dead.' He slapped the photograph of Dale Lynch. 'And because this man claims your thugs assaulted and threatened them both.'

'Thugs?' Hames asked.

'Your security firm. Seems they're a bit overenthusiastic in their approach to keeping rough-sleepers away from your waterfront development.'

Hames shifted in his chair. 'I don't know what you're implying, Chief Inspector?'

'And you quite obviously have no proof to substantiate this wild claim,' the lawyer said.

Cory Cullinane had been in no fit state to pen a witness statement – not once Reece had informed him of Dale Lynch's murder. But he had agreed to return to the station when able.

'I'm collecting proof as we speak,' Reece said. 'My officers are checking all available CCTV footage for the night of the assaults, and it's only a matter of time before they find what I'm looking for.'

<hr>

The meeting with Douglas Hames had been prematurely ended by a text received by Jenkins. It read: *I can't get out of the bath.*

'I'll take you over there,' Reece had said without sounding like he was angry.

'Answer your phone,' Jenkins repeated, as they swerved in and out of the traffic. And for once, she didn't criticise her boss's driving. 'I told her not to go in the bath unless I was there. I bet she's fallen.'

'You don't know that.'

'She said she couldn't get out, and now she's not answering.'

'Phone an ambulance then, just in case.'

Jenkins tried Margaret again. 'I knew this would happen sooner or later.'

'What about the neighbours? Do any of them have a key?'

'They're useless. Half of them look like they're on spice.'

'So phone an ambulance.'

'Let's get over there first and see what's what.'

They could hear Margaret calling for help as soon as they approached the front door.

Reece held out his hand. 'Key.'

'You can go back in now,' Jenkins told the neighbours. 'You've probably done sod all to help.' She opened the door and led the way. 'Mam, we're coming.'

Margaret's wailing got louder as they raced up the stairs. 'I fell. I can't get up.'

'I told you not to get in when I wasn't here to help.' Jenkins pushed against the bathroom door, but it didn't budge. 'Did you lock it?'

'I can't reach the catch.'

'Why the hell did you lock it?'

'Never mind that,' Reece said. 'Margaret, move away from the door.'

'I can't.'

'Mam, get away from the door.'

'I said I can't. I'm bleeding.'

'Oh, Jesus no.' Jenkins caught hold of Reece. 'Break it down.'

'She's stuck behind it.'

'You heard her – she's bleeding. Break it down!'

Reece gave himself space. 'Margaret, move as far away as you can.' He slammed the sole of his boot against the woodwork, smashing it open. That took Margaret's screaming to a whole new level.

Jenkins crouched beside her naked mother and examined the cut on her head. 'It's superficial. It's not that bad at all.'

Reece draped his jacket over the old woman. 'I'm calling an ambulance. I don't like the look of that leg.'

Chapter 57

THE EMERGENCY UNIT AT the University Hospital was crammed to bursting with the usual array of drunks; suicide attempts; and plenty of annoying people who simply refused to go home and wait for their ailment to get better of its own accord.

Someone was shouting at a nursing assistant dressed in green scrubs. Mostly about the length of time he'd been waiting for someone to look at his "*Fucked ankle.*"

The nurse was immune to the man's ranting. She did her best to ignore him and called someone else's name from a card held in her hand. 'Take a seat,' she told the nuisance when he started up again. 'Take a seat or I'll have security remove you from the building.' The man limped towards the main exit, shouting threats of litigation against just about everyone working for the Health Board.

Reece wondered how the staff were able to work in such an under-resourced, high-pressure environment. They were clearly fighting a losing battle. He'd followed the ambulance over and was now trying to locate Jenkins and Margaret. He went to the reception area and waited for someone to appear and deal with his query. Nobody did. Not in the ten minutes he was standing there.

'I'm looking for someone,' he said to a nurse rushing past with a vomit bowl and a handful of wipes.

'Aren't we all?' she replied, but didn't stop. 'A handsome prince to whisk me away from this hellhole.'

Reece pushed on a door and went the other side. For a moment he thought someone was speaking to him, but then realised it was only a machine.

"*Shock delivered,*" it said.

Then a woman's voice—definitely not the machine's—called, "*Charging. Stand clear.*"

The robotic voice repeated its previous, "*Shock delivered.*"

"*Start chest compressions,*" he heard the woman say, and made his exit knowing he'd have been as much use to them as a chocolate teapot.

'Can I help you?'

It was a doctor. Aged somewhere between twelve and sixteen, by Reece's reckoning. He showed his warrant card and introduced himself. 'I'm looking for an old lady brought in about thirty minutes ago. Margaret Jenkins. One of my colleagues is with her.'

The doctor nodded. 'I know the one. Suspected hip fracture?'

That sounded about right. 'Can I join them? I won't get in the way and I'll soon be off.'

'Sure. Follow me,' the medic said, taking him through.

'Elan.' Reece lay his hand on Jenkins's shoulder. 'Stay where you are. How's she doing?'

Jenkins was holding her mother's hand. Margaret was, for the most part, sleeping. And mumbling incoherently. 'They've given her powerful painkillers for the hip. It's definitely broken and needs an operation to fix it. Someone's on the way to stitch below her eye where she caught it on the door handle.' Jenkins lowered her voice. 'I should never have left her alone in that house.'

Reece went closer, but wasn't sure what to do. 'It's not your fault.'

Jenkins caught Margaret's arm as it jerked upwards. 'It's me, Mam. Careful, you're going to hurt yourself.'

'Get off me.' Margaret swung her arm again.

'Shall I get someone?' Reece asked.

Jenkins told him not to. 'She's been like this since we got here. And worse in the ambulance on the way over. She'll settle again soon enough.'

Margaret went back to sleep, mumbling numbers and names that meant little to Jenkins.

A tall South Asian doctor came in from the other side of the curtains and introduced himself as the Specialist Registrar for Trauma and Orthopaedics. He explained about the fracture and its proposed treatment, going into far more detail than the Emergency Unit doctors had.

There were additional x-rays needed. A raft of bloods and other tests to be done. As well as an anaesthetic assessment. It would all take several hours to complete and required an empty slot on the busy emergency list up on the main operating theatre suite. Once he'd reeled off a list of potential complications of the operation, including death, the surgeon explained that given Margaret's current mental state, written consent for the operation would be documented by himself and a colleague.

Jenkins took no issue with that.

Reece told her he'd leave her to it. Things were about to get busy there, and she was to phone him if she needed anything.

He was on his way back to the car park when Sioned Williams phoned. 'You've got those prints for me,' he said, preempting what she was about to tell him.

'Are you in trouble?' she asked.

He rolled his eyes, even though she couldn't see him. 'Those jungle drums banging on your side of the city as well?'

'I'm deaf to them,' she said. 'I hope this helps with whatever you're up to.'

'Thanks. I owe you one.'

260

She sniffed. 'Don't think I'm not keeping track.'

'I'll get you a bottle of something nice to say thank you.'

This time, she chuckled. 'I hear there's whisky going spare.'

'Bye, Sioned.'

'Bye Brân. I'm rooting for you, as always.'

He hung up and opened the attachment. There were no surprises, although he wished there had been.

Chapter 58

REECE CAME ACROSS GINGE in the staff canteen. It was a straight-forward assumption, given that whenever the young detective wasn't working on something, he could usually be found feeding his face. 'Mind if I join you?' Reece asked, sliding onto a plastic chair.

That startled Ginge. 'Um. Yeah, be my guest, boss. Can I get you something to eat? Cup of tea, if you're not hungry?'

'You carry on with your sausage and chips. I'll fetch myself some apple tart and custard. Fancy some?'

Ginge stabbed at a chunk of sausage. 'I'm good with this, thanks.'

Reece wasn't gone long. 'Are you sure you don't want any?' he asked, balancing the bowl between his fingers. 'Hot, hot, hot,' he said, dropping it onto the table.

Ginge moved out of its way. 'If you need me back upstairs, I can leave this and get something else later.'

Reece shook his head. 'Enjoy your dinner. It'll wait for now.' He took his first spoonful of the apple pie and immediately realised that Gladys had overdone its time in the microwave. He opened his mouth and made noises. Waved his hand in front of his face and grabbed for Ginge's bottle of water. He grimaced and swilled the chilled drink around his scalded cheeks and tongue. 'Every bloody time,' he said. 'You'd think I'd have learned by now.'

Ginge told him to keep it when he offered to return the bottle.

Reece pushed the apple pie to one side. 'The other morning when that whisky turned up on my desk . . . Tell me about it.'

Ginge closed his knife and fork on his plate. 'What's to tell?'

'Who put it there? I'm still trying to get my head around that.'

Ginge looked away for a second. 'I didn't see anybody go in there with it.'

'Don't you think that strange?'

'Must have happened before I got in. I'd have seen them otherwise.'

Reece had another go at the pie, lifting its crust with the edge of his spoon. The apple-sugar mix had stopped bubbling. That made it marginally better, but not yet safe enough to eat. 'And you're still as sure as you can be that you were the first one in the incident room that morning?'

Ginge studied the ceiling while he thought about it. 'The cleaning staff were in and out, obviously. And Ffion might have been making toast.'

'I don't think so,' Reece said. 'She went straight from home to the hospital for Dale Lynch's post-mortem.'

'No.' Ginge shook his head. 'I remember now. There was a mug of half-drunk coffee on her desk. It was luke warm – like she hadn't had time to finish it before she left. I threw it out and washed the mug.'

Reece frowned. 'Ffion was there before you?'

Ginge shrugged. 'I don't know, to be honest with you. I can't remember much about it, except for the coffee mug.'

Reece ran a finger around the rim of the dessert bowl and licked custard from it. 'I want you to keep schtum about this conversation for now. Especially with everyone else upstairs. I'll tell you more when I'm able.' He pushed the unfinished apple pie to the centre of the table and tapped his junior on the shoulder as he got up. 'Let's get back to work.'

They sat at Ginge's desk, drinking takeout coffees from the staff canteen.

'Let's load it up and see what we've got,' Reece said, keen to know what their northern colleagues had sent in response to his request for assistance in the case.

There was a covering email and a separate attachment in Ginge's inbox. They began with the email.

'He's definitely on their radar,' the detective constable said.

Reece read the man's name aloud: 'Tommy Hemlock. That's trouble in itself.'

Ginge frowned. 'You know of him?'

'Hemlock is a highly toxic plant with tiny white petals,' Reece explained. 'Some people refer to it as *Devil's Bread.*'

'And you find it in this country?'

'It's just about everywhere. Hedgerows and gardens. Motorway verges and roundabouts. It belongs to the carrot family.' Reece saw the way his junior was looking at him. 'I grew up in the countryside and have a farmer as a best mate.'

'Cool.'

'It was. It is.'

They went back to the email.

'Affray. Violence with menace,' Ginge said. 'Even a couple of cautions for actual bodily harm.'

'And one for grievous bodily harm,' Reece added. 'With no charges for any of these.'

Ginge tapped his pen against his bottom teeth. 'Interesting.'

'It's more than that. He must have an expensive brief, or know someone with a decent amount of clout.'

'Someone in the Force, do you think?'

'Maybe.'

'Do you want to look at the attachment now?'

Reece nodded. The email itself had alluded to some of what it contained, but not in any great detail. The document's header carried the official stamp of the Wrexham Coroner's Court, together with a series of dates corresponding with an inquest into a fatal fall from a rock face in the Llanberis Pass. 'Look at those names.'

Ginge began reading them out: 'Johnathan Sutherland was the victim of the fall.'

Reece took over almost immediately. 'And look who he was married to. Bridget Payne, Senedd Member.' He read further on, knowing that what they had before them was the missing link. 'It says no charges were brought against Mali Ingram.'

'Hemlock and Payne were the only witnesses to what happened,' Ginge said.

'Isn't that convenient?' Reece got to his feet. 'I want you looking into the financial backgrounds of Bridget Payne and her husband. If there's any connection between them and Douglas Hames, I want it found.'

Chapter 59

Jenkins watched them scoop her mother onto a narrow theatre trolley. Margaret cried out in pain and gripped her hip. 'Careful with her leg,' Jenkins said. The look that passed between the two porters didn't go unnoticed. 'Can't she go down on the bed? It's got to be more comfortable for her.'

'We just do as we're told,' the shorter man said. 'Have a word with Sister if there's a problem.'

'I bloody well will.' Jenkins hunted up and down the ward for anyone dressed in navy blue. 'If I could only find her.'

'She's out in the car park, having a sneaky fag,' the other porter said with a throaty chuckle.

'Where are they taking me?' Margaret squealed. 'This is all your doing. You wet the floor and made me fall.'

Jenkins leaned over the side rails of the trolley and clasped her mother's hand in both of hers. 'You hurt your hip. The doctors are going to fix it. You'll be up and about in no time.'

Margaret pulled away and hit her elbow on the raised side of the trolley. 'I know what you're up to. You want my money. She's after the house!' she announced to just about everyone on the ward. 'Her and the floozy.'

'No one's up to anything,' Jenkins said, blushing. 'It's got nothing to do with money. We're all trying to get you better.'

'Right,' said the shorter porter, shooing Jenkins out of the way with the back of his hand. 'Let the dog see the rabbit.'

She glared at him, but moved all the same, not wanting to be the cause of any delay in getting Margaret more comfortable. 'How long will she be in theatre?'

'We're not allowed to answer those sorts of questions,' the porter told her. 'It's above our pay grade, love. You'll have to ask one of the nursing staff.'

Jenkins fought the urge to punch the man. 'If I could find one, I would.'

'Everything's run on a shoestring,' the porter said. 'Nobody would come anywhere near the place if they knew the truth. Too many pen pushers and not enough nurses, is what the problem is.' They started wheeling Margaret away.

'Isn't anyone going with her?' Jenkins asked.

'I am.' Someone dressed in purple scrubs appeared in the open doorway of a room marked *Sluice*. She dropped her plastic apron in a bin and gelled her hands with an antiseptic solution. 'My name's Nia. I'm a student.'

'I thought it would have been a staff nurse?'

The student guffawed. 'There's only two qualified on for the whole ward. They'll be busy now with the IV antibiotics.' She shrugged apologetically and started walking alongside the trolley. 'It's the same on every placement. We're always having to do things we shouldn't at our stage of training.'

Jenkins was trembling. Trying not to break down and cry in front of a mother who was still hurling abuse at her. 'Sister. Where is she?'

'In the office. Second door on the left. I know she wants to speak to you.'

Jenkins caught up with the moving trolley and kissed Margaret on the forehead. The porter took the opportunity to tell the housekeeper an inappropriate joke about a bishop and an actress. When the trolley got going again, Jenkins made her way over to the office door. A woman's voice was speaking on the telephone. Jenkins waited a short while before knocking.

'Come in.'

She stuck her head round the door. 'I'm Elan. Margaret's daughter.'

At first, Sister was at odds with the name. With the aid of a wipeboard on the wall opposite, she worked it out. 'Ah, got it.'

Jenkins passed on the offer of tea or coffee. 'She is going to be all right, isn't she?'

———◆———

Sister had, for the most part, reassured her and advised that she go home for a couple of hours' rest. There was nothing more she could do at the hospital until Margaret returned from theatre. On the promise of a phone call, whenever that would be, Jenkins left.

She called in at her mother's house and burst into tears as soon as she stepped through the front door. She slid down the wall in the hallway, her head in her hands, sobbing for all she was worth.

Already out of the tissues Sister had given her, she got up and went through to the kitchen. She ran the cold tap and splashed water on her face, standing there in a daze before using a hand towel to dry. Her head was banging. She felt sick. And her legs threatened to give way beneath her. Taking two paracetamol from a box in the kitchen drawer, she gulped them down.

She went around the house, making sure all the electrical appliances were turned off. That the windows and doors were shut and locked. There had been no time to do that earlier, busy as they were, attending to Margaret and her injuries. After a quick tidy up, she left for home, one decision regarding her future already made.

When Cara Frost's car pulled onto the hardstand in front of the house, Jenkins yanked the bedroom window closed and ran across the landing to the stairs. By the time she was halfway down, a key rattled in the door lock. 'Your things are on the lawn,' she shouted. 'There's no reason for you to come in.'

There wasn't enough space in the narrow hallway for the pathologist to get past. She pushed the door closed with her foot. It bounced against the lock and came open again. 'Elan, I—'

Jenkins pressed her hands to her ears. 'Save it for someone who cares.'

'Please let me speak.'

'I want you and all your stuff out of my life.'

'You don't mean that.'

'I needed you, Cara. I was at my wit's end doing the best I could for my mother. How could you do what you did?'

'Can we talk?'

Jenkins pointed at the door. 'Don't make me hit you.'

'You wouldn't. I know you wouldn't.'

'Are you not getting this? I want you out of my house.'

'It's our house. Our home.'

Jenkins shook her head. 'My name on the deeds. You were only ever a tenant.'

Frost's eyes widened. 'My place is rented for the next six months.'

'Do I look like I give a fuck?'

'You're as much to blame for this as I am,' Frost said, fighting back the tears.

'And how do you come to that conclusion?'

'I've been lonely.' The pathologist reached an arm. 'We've spent next to no time together recently, and—'

Jenkins slapped the arm down. 'I don't believe this. Are you really blaming me for what you've done?' She dragged her fingernails across her scalp. 'I'm going to the kitchen to fetch a knife. If you're still here when I get back, there's going to be one hell of a mess for the CSIs to busy themselves with.'

Chapter 60

REECE HAD BEEN SUMMONED to Chief Superintendent Cable's office. It came as no surprise, but irked him nonetheless. 'I went to see Douglas Hames because that's where the evidence took me.' He straightened his tie. 'Cory Cullinane and Dale Lynch were threatened and beaten up by Hames's security staff. Did you expect me to ignore that, in light of what's been going on?'

'Of course not,' Cable said. 'But you only have Cullinane's side of the story.'

'I saw the bruising. You didn't.'

'Anyone could have done that to him.'

'Why would he lie?'

'I'm not saying he is.'

'Sounds to me like you are.'

Cable paused. 'Let's say you're right.'

'I am.'

'Let's say you're right,' she repeated. 'What was to be gained by the approach you took?'

'I did it to wind him up and show I didn't give a shit how much money he's got.'

'And what did you gain from such an approach?'

Reece had to concede they'd learned very little. 'We got called away before I had a chance to get properly stuck in.' He outlined Margaret's fall and their urgent trip to the hospital. 'Hames is hiding something and I'm getting closer to knowing what that is.' He handed over a printed version of the email and attachment from the North Wales Police. 'Read that.' When he decided she'd had long enough, he continued: 'Bridget Payne's husband died in a climbing accident three years ago. Mali Ingram—an instructor at the centre—was initially blamed for the fall.' He made reference to the medical reports that had subsequently exonerated her. 'Ingram claimed that Tommy Hemlock was paired up with Jonathan Sutherland. That Hemlock deliberately caused Sutherland to fall to his death. Something he and Bridget Payne denied at the coroner's inquest.'

Cable handed back the paperwork. 'And you don't believe them?'

Reece left it on the desk. 'What was a Senedd Member doing in the company of a man with Hemlock's reputation and history? And what are he and Mali Ingram doing in Cardiff three years later?'

Cable pulled a face. 'I really am struggling to piece this together and see the same picture as you.'

Reece took a deep breath and counted five back to zero in his head. It helped offset his mounting frustration, but only just. 'I'm looking into a connection between Hames and the others. It could be financial. Could be something else.'

'And you'll recognise it when you find it? *If* you find it?' Cable quickly corrected.

Another count from five back to zero. 'Payne, Hemlock, and Ingram were all together when Jonathan Sutherland died,' Reece said. 'That's a fact. Agreed?'

'Yes.'

'But the details of the fall were disputed among the group. Payne and Hemlock claiming one version of events. Ingram another. Agreed?'

Cable had read the report for herself and nodded.

'Now all three are in Cardiff—their paths crossing—with only Payne being a resident of the area.' Reece leaned back in his chair. 'What would have brought the other two here at the same time? They're clearly not friends. And both were at the house fire crime scene, which in itself is suspicious.'

'True.'

'Ingram is a rough-sleeper. As are the victims of these crimes,' Reece continued. 'Payne just happens to be making an announcement about the future of the drop-in centre, and Hames has his thugs assaulting the very people who use the place. Believe me, there's a connection between all of this. It could be financial, blackmail, or . . .' Reece paused.

'Or what?' Cable pushed.

'Or Ingram is here for her pound of flesh and everything else we've seen is collateral damage. I've asked Maggie Kavanagh for everything she has on Payne and Hemlock. She'll be discreet.'

'In return for what?'

'She'll get the story before anyone else.'

The long silence between them was broken by Cable. 'Okay. What's your next move?'

'Do you really want to ask me that?'

'Probably not. Tread carefully.'

'That's not my style.'

'Make it your style. I'm being serious, Reece. I want you on best behaviour while you're at the Senedd.'

Chapter 61

REECE SAT DOWN AGAIN when Cable told him to. 'I thought we were all done?'

'Superintendent Piper tells me you walked out of your meeting with her and refused to discuss anything else without the presence of a Federation rep.'

'It was either walk out or say something she could sack me for.'

'Why are you doing this?'

He stared over her left shoulder and got lost in the dark cloud formations outside the window. It brought back unwanted memories of the lumbering whale he used to see in them. He dragged his gaze away. 'I could ask you lot the very same question.'

'*You lot?*'

'You know what I mean. Everyone pushing my buttons, only to have a go when I react to it.'

'That's not what's happening here. We've already discussed the reasons for ACC Harris's disclosure to the IOPC. You even said you understood.'

'I did. I do.'

'So what's the problem?' Cable asked. 'Go through the motions. Behave and answer their questions without being a dick.'

'*This* is the problem,' Reece said, sliding his phone across the table. He'd opened the email from Sioned Williams. The attachment took him three attempts, but he got it in the end.

Cable read the results of the fingerprint analysis. 'This only proves they handled it at some point. They were all there with you in your office.'

'Jenkins wasn't, and I'd trust her with my life. Only Morgan and Ginge were there at the time, and as you can see from that, only one of them had their grubby paws on it. Look who the other identified print belongs to.'

Cable read the name to herself. 'I'm so disappointed.'

'I'm way beyond that,' Reece said. 'And after all I've done for them.'

Cable rested her elbows on the table. 'How do you intend to play this?'

Reece got up. 'Like I play cards. Close to my chest for now.'

———◄○►———

Jenkins had left Cara Frost to collect her things, telling her to close the front door behind her when she left. Upset and with nowhere else to go while her mother was being operated on, she called into work to wind down time. Worried at having heard nothing from the hospital, she lay her phone on the surface of her desk and almost immediately picked it up again to check for missed calls. 'Come on,' she muttered. 'What's keeping you?'

Morgan looked up from her computer screen. 'What was that?'

Jenkins made another check of her phone. 'Nothing.'

'I'm trawling through the latest MISPER list,' Morgan said. 'It's more for my own education, really. Do you have any idea how many people go missing each year in the UK alone?'

'No.'

'Nearly three hundred and fifty thousand. Can you believe that?'

'No.'

'Thankfully, seventy-nine percent of them are found safe and well within twenty-four hours.'

'Good.'

Morgan swivelled slowly on her chair. 'The rest are whisked away by little green men in flying saucers. For all sorts of experiments.'

'Sounds about right,' Jenkins said, staring at the wall. 'They're the ones sent back to Earth to work as hospital porters and pathologists.'

'Huh?'

'Don't worry. Not your problem.'

'What's wrong?' Morgan dragged her chair across the gap between them and sat down again. 'And don't you dare say it's nothing. We're mates, remember?'

Jenkins let out a long sigh. Then a few tears. She clasped her hands together and wedged them between her knees. 'Mam fell this morning. When I was at Douglas Hames's office with the boss.'

'He didn't say anything when he was in here earlier. Hasn't said much to me at all, to be honest. I told you there was something weird going on with him. How's your mum?'

'We had to leave in a hurry. Reece was brilliant about it. Now Mam's in hospital having an operation. And to cap it all off, I've just thrown Cara out.'

'Wait.' Morgan raised her hand. 'What? Margaret's having an operation and you're here at work?'

'There was nothing else for me to do. Cara's collecting her things, so I don't want to be there for that. It's peeing with rain, on and off, and I want to be contactable when the hospital rings.'

'Bloody hell. You've had it rough lately.'

Jenkins drew the back of a hand across her nose and sniffed loudly. 'Tell me about it.'

Morgan reached for her hand. 'But you shouldn't be at work.'

'It'll take my mind off things. I know how the boss used to feel now.'

'Can I ask what happened with Cara? You two were like the perfect couple.'

'Looks can be deceiving.'

'Don't want to talk about it?'

'Not really. I don't see how it will help.'

'Fair enough. Want me to tell you what's been going on with the boss?'

Jenkins blew her nose in a handful of tissues. 'Go on then. You might as well.'

Chapter 62

REECE WAS ON HIS way to see Douglas Hames's security team at the waterfront development. He'd twice called Jenkins to ask how Margaret was getting on, but gave up when he got no answer. He swung the Land Cruiser off the road and through the makeshift gates of the building site, emptying puddles as he went. The vehicle was designed for negotiating thick mud and deep potholes, and got those thrown at it in spadefuls. He pulled to a halt at the barrier and watched as one of two security guards lumbered towards him. The man didn't look like much of a fighter or bully, but you never could tell. Plenty of would-be Rambos had been ceremoniously put on their arses by the skinny guy in the local pub. He showed his warrant card.

'Mr Hames isn't on site.' Security told him. 'Have you tried his office?'

Reece hung his head out of the window. 'It's you pair I've come to see. Where do I park?' Once he'd been shown, he zigzagged over to their hut and scraped mud off his boots using a rock that stuck out of the ground like a wonky tooth.

One of them offered him coffee. The other waved an opened packet of biscuits from an outstretched arm.

He passed on both and took Cory Cullinane's photograph from an envelope in his jacket pocket. 'Do either of you recognise this man?'

'Should we?' Biscuitman asked, taking it from him. He passed it to his colleague before it made its way back to the detective.

'The man in that photograph says he was assaulted near here the other night. And that he was warned things would get far more serious if he ever came back.'

Security were staring at one another and shaking their heads like a holiday camp double act.

'Only, his mate did come back and got himself killed in the process,' Reece said.

'Whoa.' Biscuitman reversed a few steps with his lower jaw hanging open. 'That's got nothing to do with me. Us,' he promptly corrected.

'Nothing at all,' the other one said.

'So you pair didn't give them a kicking?'

'Why would we?'

'Because Douglas Hames told you to. He's pissed off with rough-sleepers lowering the tone of the neighbourhood.'

Biscuitman shook his head. 'Mister Hames was angry because of the incident with the tower crane. He made it clear what would happen to our jobs if there was a repeat.'

'He never mentioned using violence,' the other man explained. 'Only that we had to keep people out of here.'

That took some of the sting out of Reece's tail. 'What incident?'

'A few of the employees were a bit lax with the keys to the machinery, leaving them in the ignition overnight. Someone got into one of the tower cranes and started it up, causing thousands of pounds of damage when he whacked the boom against the side of the building. The thing was out of service for weeks, knocking the schedule way back. All the keys are kept in that now,' he said, pointing at a grey box on the wall.

Biscuitman helped himself to one from the packet and nibbled at its edge. 'It doesn't always work, though. Only yesterday we chased a woman out of here. She'd spent the night in the cab of one of the bulldozers.'

'Tuesday night?' Reece asked.

The man nodded. 'Tuesday night into Wednesday morning.'

'What did she look like?'

'Twenties. Maybe a bit older. Short dark hair and a sleeping bag. I didn't get a good look at her myself, but one of the guys said she climbed that fence like a cat with a boot up its arse.'

Mali Ingram. 'Can I take a closer look at those cranes?' Reece asked.

'You'll need a hard hat and hi-viz jacket.'

Reece put them on and followed Biscuitman outside, while his colleague remained at his post. They trudged through mud and water, leaving him wishing he'd worn his boots. Even from a fair distance away, the tower cranes looked enormous. 'How tall are those things?' he asked, shouting to make himself heard over the noise of the busy building site.

'Just over two-hundred and sixty feet.'

Reece felt sick. Like a land lubber weathering a storm at sea. 'And someone has to climb a ladder to get all the way up there?'

'They have to be pretty fit.'

'Pretty stupid, more like. Why would anyone in their right mind want to do a day's work all the way up there?' he asked.

'For peace and quiet. That and good money.'

Reece had seen enough. 'Not even if you put a gun to my head.'

Chapter 63

JENKINS HEARD THE COMMOTION long before she arrived on the hospital ward. It was a sharp-tongued and foul-mouthed outburst that was all her mother's doing. She went running past the front desk, following her ears.

'You can't go onto the ward until they're ready for you,' the receptionist called after her.

'That's my mother,' Jenkins answered without slowing.

The cubicle door flew open to reveal a red-faced nurse. 'She bit me!' the nurse claimed in a high-pitched whine, and held out her arm as evidence of the fact. She recognised Jenkins and lowered her arm, said no more, and marched off towards Sister's office.

'Get off me. Help. *Help!*'

Jenkins pushed on the door and forced her way in. 'It's okay, Mam. You're safe.'

'You can't go in there,' the receptionist insisted, but didn't follow her inside. 'I've already explained,' she told the staff nurse, 'but she's not listening to a word I say.'

Jenkins spun to face her. 'Look, lady. Get security if you feel there's a need to. This is my mother, and right now, she sounds like she needs me.' The receptionist went racing off. To where, Jenkins couldn't care less. 'Mam, what are you doing?' She pressed her hand to her mother's shoulder. 'You can't get out of bed yet. You've only just had your operation.'

'They're trying to kill me,' Margaret snarled. 'Fetch my slippers. I'm going home.'

'Everyone's here to help you get better.'

'You're in on it as well.' Margaret swung an arm, catching Jenkins full on the cheek. 'Fuck off!'

'Stop swearing.' Jenkins put her hand to her face. It was hot but not bleeding as far as she could tell.

'Let me go.'

'Listen to me.'

'I'll call the police.'

'I *am* the police.'

'You're a lying bitch!'

Jenkins wasn't fast enough to fully avoid the contents of the water jug when it was hurled at her. 'Stop it,' she pleaded. 'You're being silly.'

Margaret thrashed in the bed. 'Help. Help. *Help!*'

Jenkins sat in Sister's office with a mug of coffee held in both hands. She was trembling and had no control over it. 'I can't believe this is happening. She's so much worse than she has been.'

'We see it all the time in the elderly,' Sister told her. 'Not *all* the time,' she corrected. 'But you know what I mean? It's a combination of many things. Pain. The drugs we give. Sleep deprivation, as well as disorientation from being taken out of their home environment. In your mother's case, it's also compounded by the dementia.'

Jenkins flinched at the mention of the term. It wasn't incorrect in any way, but that didn't make it any less palatable to hear. 'Mam used to be so switched on. As sharp as a tack. Isn't that what they say?' She drew her gaze from the brown bits floating on the surface of her coffee. 'When do you think the specialist will be here to see her?'

'After their rounds today, hopefully. We'll chase them up if they're not. It's important we get a package of care in place, and this ward isn't the right one for Margaret.'

'You won't move her so soon after surgery, surely?'

'She'll stay with us until the wound heals and the physio and occupational therapy teams are happy.' Sister put her empty mug on the desk and rested an elbow on either side of it. 'Have you given any thought to what you're going to do when Margaret's ready to go home?'

Jenkins frowned. Something she'd caught herself doing frequently of late. 'What do you mean?' she asked, delaying the need for a proper answer.

'You work full time, don't you? And I can't imagine you're doing regular hours as a police detective?'

'Yes. I mean *yes* to the working full-time bit. And no, I don't work regular hours. Especially when we're winding up a big case like we are now.'

'You do understand this is only going to get worse? That Margaret will need full time, specialist care that's well beyond what someone like yourself is capable of providing?'

'So everyone keeps telling me.'

'What does your husband do for a living?'

'I'm not married.'

'Do you have a partner or sibling to help you?'

Jenkins put the coffee down and left without answering.

Reece marched into the drop-in centre and went straight over to Cory Cullinane. 'I want a word with you.'

Cullinane made eyes at him. 'Not here, remember?'

'Sod that,' Reece said, taking a seat. Two other men at the same table got up and left without finishing their meals. 'Why did you lie to me?'

'Lie?'

'Don't mess me about, or I'll come round there and dig you in the ribs myself.'

'Is this about the other night?'

Reece nodded. 'You told me it was Douglas Hames's men who beat you up.'

'It was.'

Reece shot to his feet and shoved the table away from him.

Cullinane curled up. 'Okay. Okay. It might not have been them. Probably wasn't, now I've had more time to think about it.'

'There was no *them*.' Reece hadn't yet sat down again. 'This was one man's doing?'

'It was dark.'

The detective cracked his knuckles. 'Last chance to tell the truth.'

'I'd already told you I wasn't a grass. You sounded interested in Hames, so I let you think it was him.'

'You made me look like a mug.'

'I'm sorry.'

'It's too late for that now. Who beat you up?' Reece already knew, but needed confirmation.

'I've never seen him before.'

'Talk, Cory. You tell me everything you know about him and the girl.'

Chapter 64

REECE PARKED NEXT TO the Norwegian Church and took a moment to compose himself. 'I'll be seeing you soon,' he whispered, and blew a kiss.

He locked the car door and made the short walk over to the Senedd building. Once inside, he was shown to Bridget Payne's office and wasn't left to wait long.

'Chief Inspector.' Payne extended a slim arm with a gold Tank Francaise watch at the wrist and shook his hand. He accepted without gripping her fingers like he was trying to grind her bones to dust. That greeting he kept mainly for lawyers and ACC Harris. 'What can I do for you?'

There was no one else present in the room. No one he could see, anyway. He took a seat when invited and gratefully accepted a coffee. 'Thank you for accommodating me at such short notice.' He'd promised Chief Superintendent Cable he'd be on best behaviour during the visit and was making a decent attempt of it. 'I wanted to start by asking you about the drop-in centre and why you'd be wanting to relocate it after all these years?'

'It isn't my doing,' Payne said calmly. 'As a government, we've been debating whether it could be better placed elsewhere in the city.'

'Local businesses think it could. Or should I say, one businessman in particular?'

The pause in reply was almost imperceptible. 'You mean Douglas Hames?'

'I do. Didn't he approach you personally?'

'Only because of my responsibilities for local housing. There is a formal process to be followed, you understand?'

Reece stirred his coffee, for no other reason than to create tension using silence.

'What are you not asking?' Payne said, before Reece's spoon was back on its saucer.

'The waterfront development is in financial difficulty. Am I right?'

'I really wouldn't know, Chief Inspector. That's not something their legal team would have shared with us.'

'Those apartments aren't being sold quickly enough to fund the rest of the build.'

'Again, Chief Inspector, it's not me you should be asking those questions of.'

'You haven't invested in the project?'

'That would amount to a clear conflict of interest.'

'You're damn right it would.'

Payne placed her cup and saucer on a low table and sat up straight in her chair. 'Chief Inspector, I—'

'Your husband's death three years ago. Please forgive me for asking, but what's your recollection of what happened that day?'

Payne had clearly spent time manicuring her eyebrows, but still they morphed into a single strawberry-blonde line. 'I thought you came here to speak about the drop-in centre?'

'I did. You'll soon see where I'm going with this. The day of the fall – what happened?'

Payne took a moment to compose herself. 'Jonathan died in a climbing accident in North Wales a little over three years ago. At first it was thought his fall was the result of negligence on the part of the instructor. We suspected she was intoxicated at the time.'

'But that wasn't the case. No drugs or alcohol were found in any of the tox screens run by the investigating team.'

'If you already know this, Chief Inspector, then why are you asking me to recount something that is quite obviously distressing?'

'Apologies again. Please continue.'

'The instructor was found to have a medical condition that incapacitated her during a crucial phase of the climb.'

'Absence seizures.'

Payne nodded. 'She wasn't to blame.'

'And you were happy for the case to close at that point, with no further investigation required.'

'*Happy* isn't the term I'd use.'

'But you agreed not to pursue the matter any further?'

'I didn't think it appropriate, given the medical reports.'

'You were paired up with Tommy Hemlock?'

'Yes. And Jonathan with the instructor. Being the weaker climber, we all thought it best.'

'But the instructor claimed at the coroner's inquest that you were paired up with her?'

Payne's eyebrows chanced another kiss. 'I really don't think the girl knew what was happening that day.'

'How long have you known Tommy Hemlock? Sorry, let me rephrase that. How long had you known him before the day of the climb?'

'We'd never previously met.'

'Are you sure about that?'

Payne got to her feet, but didn't walk away. 'Absolutely.'

'The instructor got the impression you knew one another. And that the two of you were in conversation together whenever your husband wasn't present.'

'Jonathan never made an issue of me talking to other men. He wasn't one of those knuckle-dragging Neanderthals.'

'So why did you choose to speak to Hemlock in private and behind a toilet-block Portakabin?'

Payne paced. Reece watched her. 'I never did. The girl got that wrong. Another absence seizure, perhaps?'

'Did your husband have any financial dealings with Douglas Hames? Was he investing in the waterfront development here in the bay?'

'Not to my knowledge.'

'You don't know?' Reece thought that odd.

'Jonathan and I owned several businesses each, but rarely discussed the finances of any of them in detail.'

'So you wouldn't know if he'd ploughed money into Hames's project or not?'

'Correct.'

'And are you invested in the development?'

Payne stopped pacing to look at him. 'What is it you're after? You're obviously here under false pretences.'

Reece was getting a nibble and knew it was time to let out more line. 'Are you aware that both Tommy Hemlock and Mali Ingram are here in Cardiff right now?'

Payne folded her arms and looked like she might be trying to comfort herself. 'How could I possibly?'

'You've not heard from either of them?'

'Absolutely not.'

Years of sitting opposite suspects in stuffy interview rooms had fine-tuned the detective's senses to most of the mannerisms accompanying bare-faced lies. 'Here's what's troubling me most . . .' he said, readying himself to strike.

Chapter 65

IT WAS LATE WHEN Reece got back to the station. Once finished with Bridget Payne, he'd gone over to the Norwegian Church and sat for a while in its Arts Centre. The café there was closed. Hungry, he'd picked up a Chinese takeaway on the way back to the station—enough for a few others to join in—but sat alone at his desk to eat it.

Morgan and Ginge had already packed up and gone home. He sat there thinking about the two of them, and how one had so badly let him down. That person's days on the team would be over by the end of the week. Their time as a serving police officer, soon after that.

Jenkins had returned his calls, stating that Margaret was back on the ward, and despite *"a stormy couple of hours,"* had since settled and was doing well. So much so that she had insisted on coming into work the following day. Something he hadn't been able to change her mind about.

He turned on his computer and practised his mediocre chopsticks skills while he waited for the machine to boot up. The pork was in a lemon and ginger sauce – his favourite. The noodles were done to perfection. The phone rang. It was a call he'd been expecting. 'Maggie. Tell me you've found something.'

There was a brief period of coughing, followed by the sounds of the reporter clearing her phlegmy chest. 'Would I let my boy down? I've sent some stuff that might help.'

Reece opened his mail and skim-read. 'Thanks for that. I've got confirmation from the lab as well. Now I know how you managed to be waiting in my office that day.'

'I couldn't drop the poor sod in it, now could I?'

He pushed the carton of unfinished food to one side. 'You don't feel sorry for them after all the trouble they've caused me?'

'Not really. But you'll see from what I've sent you, they probably didn't have much of a choice.'

Reece was making notes. 'There's always a choice.'

'I'm also forwarding everything I have on Bridget Payne. The size of the photo files is going to slow the transfer, but they should be with you in a bit.'

'I'm opening the first one now.' He almost punched the air in triumph when he saw it. 'Maggie, this is dynamite.'

Chapter 66

'How's Margaret?' Reece asked. 'Did she get a decent night's rest?'

Jenkins nodded. 'The agitation is loads better this morning. I called in quickly on my way here. She'd been asking for a few bits and pieces – like my dad's wristwatch.'

'I told you yesterday not to come in. We'll manage.'

'It's easier to deal with if I keep myself busy. You understand that, don't you?'

He did. And more than most people. 'Your call. But if you change your mind . . .'

'She's needing a bit more oxygen than they'd like,' Jenkins explained. 'But they aren't overly worried at this stage. That's what they said, anyway.'

'She's in good hands, I'm sure.'

Another nod. 'Did you go to the Senedd yesterday, like you said you were going to?'

Reece brought her up to speed with his meeting with Bridget Payne, as well as everything Maggie Kavanagh had sent him. There was also the forensic stuff from the whisky bottle and its packaging, together with prints lifted from a pen he'd sent for comparison.

Jenkins was visibly shocked at the revelation and put her hand to her mouth. 'I'd never have guessed it. Not in a million years. And after all the support you've given them. You must be really pissed off?'

'There's no time for any of that now.' He got up and put the photographs of Bridget Payne in a large envelope. 'Fancy joining me on a short trip to the Senedd?'

Mali had searched the streets looking for Aggy. Checked all the usual places without success. At first, she was frustrated. Now, deeply worried. It wasn't like the *Big Issue* seller not to be out and about on her rounds. It was her main source of steady income.

She stopped to ask a couple of men stood next to a tent pitched on the flagstones of the main shopping thoroughfare. One of them was tuning an acoustic guitar that was missing two of its strings. The other was just getting going on a plastic harmonica. They both knew who she meant—most people in the homeless community were familiar with Aggy—but neither of them could claim to have seen her that day.

Worry was fast turning into panic. Surely Tommy Hemlock hadn't caught sight of them together and gone after Aggy? Mali couldn't believe how stupid she'd been. There was only one place left to check, and that was Aggy's flat. Not knowing where that might be, she decided it was time to find Cory Cullinane.

———◦———

Bridget Payne was in a meeting when they got there. Not that Reece cared. He gave her secretary two options, the second of which involved him walking straight in and *"telling it like it is."* That had resulted in a brief telephone conversation between the secretary and someone Reece couldn't see. After which, a string of people left the room, each of them carrying notepads and drinks.

Bridget Payne stood in the doorway. 'Chief Inspector, this had better be important.'

Reece shook the envelope at her. 'Believe me when I say it is.'

They sat around a large wooden table. Reece helped himself to a bottle of water and offered one to Jenkins, who was preoccupied with her phone.

'Missed call,' she said, sharing sight of the screen with him.

'Do you need to answer it?'

'It can wait,' she said, putting it away.

'You said this was important,' Payne interrupted. 'Shall we get on with it?'

Reece checked with Jenkins before opening the envelope. He removed its contents and dropped the first photograph onto the table. 'You told me you'd never met Tommy Hemlock before the day of your husband's death?'

'I did. Yes.'

Reece straightened the photograph. 'What do you see here? What and who?'

Payne picked it up off the table and studied it. 'A formal function. Several people in evening dress. Most of them enjoying a glass of something.' She lowered the photograph. 'Chief Inspector—'

'Don't forget the *who*.'

Payne went through a laboured routine of checking for a second time. 'That's quite obviously me in the foreground.'

Reece nodded. 'And what about the man in the background? The one staring at you?'

'Good heavens.'

'And you still maintain you never saw him before that day in North Wales?'

'Do you know how many functions I attend every month as a Senedd Member? Not to mention the charity dinners and other social events connected to the businesses I own and run?'

'Quite a few, I'd imagine.'

'Exactly. So please forgive me for not remembering them all.'

Reece prepared the second photograph in much the same way he had the first. Then he sat back and folded his arms. '*Who,* not what, do you see in this press shot?'

'Chief Inspector, I meet and speak to so many people at these things. I couldn't possibly remember them all.'

'That's you and Tommy Hemlock, deep in conversation.'

'Yes, but as I've already said—'

'You're shying away from the camera, looking like you don't want to be seen in public with him.' Reece dropped several other photographs onto the table. Taken at numerous social events. 'And yet, in each of these, you're flashing those pearly whites like someone in a Colgate advert.'

The heavy office door closed behind them. 'You'd better answer that missed call,' Reece said. 'It could be important.'

'You don't mind?' Jenkins asked. 'It shouldn't take long.' She wandered over to one of the windows and kept her back to him while she dialled the number for the hospital ward.

Reece tried not to pry. It wasn't easy. Hospitals didn't usually telephone family members with good news. He waited, deep in thought until Jenkins returned. 'Everything okay?'

'I think so. They said I didn't need to go racing over there, but . .
.'

'But what? What's wrong?'

'They're taking Mam for a scan of her lungs. To rule out a blood clot being the reason for her needing so much oxygen.'

Chapter 67

IT WAS WELL INTO the afternoon when Mali found Cory Cullinane playing dominoes at a table in the drop-in centre. 'Where have you been?' she asked, taking the chair next to him. 'I've been looking all over the place for you.'

'I was here,' he said, as though that should have been obvious. 'What's wrong? You look worried.'

'Aggy's disappeared. I've hunted everywhere except her flat. And asked around. No one's seen her since yesterday.'

'Maybe she's got a bug and needs to stay close to the loo.'

Mali worried it was more serious than that. 'I'm going to need your help.'

One of the dominoes players smacked his lips. 'You don't want to be asking this one for help. It was only yesterday he shopped you to the police.'

'Shut up,' Cullinane said. 'You don't know what you're talking about.'

'Cat's out of the bag now. You're in trouble,' the man cackled.

Cullinane glared at him. 'I'm warning you.'

'What does he mean?' Mali asked, looking from one to the other of them.

'Bullshit as usual. Don't listen to him. He's been drinking.'

'Saw it with my own eyes. And heard it with my own ears,' the man said with a toothless grin. 'That sharp-dressed detective – I thought he was going to give Cory here a right good smack before he fessed up everything he knew about you.'

Mali got up and leaned over Cullinane with her fist cocked. 'What did he want to know? What did you tell him, Cory? What did you say?'

'You're a prick,' Mali shouted over her shoulder as she exited the drop-in centre. 'A prize effing prick.'

Cullinane rushed after her, his ribs making it more difficult than it should have been. 'He made me tell him. There wasn't much he didn't already know.'

'I trusted you. Only you and Aggy know why I'm here. You broke that trust. You let me down.'

Cullinane came to a stop and looked like he might cry. 'They murdered Dale. And those people in the house fire. The detective told me. This isn't a game. It's some serious shit you've got yourself into.'

Mali walked slowly towards him. 'I'm sorry about your friend. Honestly, I am. But this *shit* you're talking about is mine, not yours. You shouldn't be shooting your mouth off about it.'

He shook his head. 'It's not just you now. If Hemlock's got Aggy, like you think he has, you've put her in danger as well.'

It was impossible to deny. Rhydian might have died because of her. There was still no word of Lisa back home. And now Aggy. Things couldn't get much worse. 'I didn't do it on purpose,' she said defensively.

'I'm not saying you did.'

'So what are you saying?'

'That you should hand this over to the police. You can't deal with something as big as this on your own.'

They were almost within touching distance. She didn't go any closer. 'Only once have I ever left things to the police, and that led me to where I am today.'

<hr>

Jenkins had gone outside to make a phone call to the hospital. 'I'm her daughter,' she told the nurse. 'What do I know so far? *Um*, Mam needed more oxygen than she should have done overnight. You sent her for a scan this morning, which showed a clot on her lung, and now she's on a blood-thinning drip. That's about it, I think.'

The nurse confirmed that her understanding was correct.

'Has she got any worse during the day?' Jenkins asked. 'I'll be coming in later. Unless you need me there now?'

The nurse told her that there was a possibility of a move to the High Dependency Unit annexed with the ICU. But that wasn't definite, as yet.

'That doesn't sound good. She is going to be all right, isn't she?'

It was for a higher level of monitoring, the nurse explained. And so that frequent blood samples could be drawn to measure the amounts of oxygen and carbon dioxide in Margaret's system. The nurse also told her that no move to the High Dependency Unit would be possible without a review by a Critical Care Consultant. They were still waiting for that. The unit downstairs was busy, and it was likely to take a while longer.

'You've got my number?' Jenkins checked. She knew they did, but wanted to hear them confirm it. 'And if she gets any worse, you will let me know?'

The nurse promised they would.

'And I can call for another update before I leave work?' She checked the time on her phone. 'I shouldn't be too much longer.'

Again, the nurse reassured her.

Jenkins climbed the steps to the entrance of the police station with a sense of dread descending upon her.

Chapter 68

BRIDGET PAYNE WAS ON the ninth floor of the waterfront development, waiting for Douglas Hames's arrival. He was on his way. She'd received his call telling her as much.

The place smelled of recently poured concrete. There were long lengths of electrical wires hanging from the ceiling. Bare pipework snaking up the walls. Drapes of transparent plastic sheeting flapping in a draft caused by several holes not yet fitted with windows.

The detective was worryingly close to discovering what was going on. There were too many people involved. Things had got messy. It was time for some overdue pruning.

'Douglas,' she said, on first sight of him. 'Better late than never.'

Hames didn't quite manage a smile. He looked as though he'd tried but fallen short in his attempt. 'Why the cloak and dagger approach?' he asked, standing there in an expensive suit and long black coat. He stamped his feet and rubbed his gloved hands together. 'My office would have been a lot more comfortable than this.'

Payne was heavily made up and wore a full-length fur coat. 'This particular conversation requires the utmost privacy. We can't risk anyone knowing it took place.'

Hames checked over his shoulder as though he'd heard something on the floor beneath them.

'Just the wind,' Payne told him. 'Don't look so nervous. Nobody's listening in.'

Hames ran a hand from front to back across his head. 'I'm under so much pressure to get this development finished,' he said. 'And as if that wasn't enough, now the police are sniffing around. They've been to my office. Here too, asking all sorts of questions.'

'What did you tell them?'

'Nothing.' Again, his smile failed him. 'They're making connections between this place and those rough sleepers you did away with. It's only a matter of time before the truth gets out.'

'*You* did away with them, too. It was a mutual venture.'

'I told my men to warn them off. Nothing more. It was your maniac who went well beyond what we'd agreed.'

If Payne was ruffled, she didn't let it show. 'We're in this together, Douglas. You and I. Everything from what happened to Jonathan when he threatened to pull his money out of this build, right through to the collateral damage we've experienced along the way.'

'You're talking about people's lives as though they don't matter,' Hames said. 'I never would have got involved in any of this had I known how far you'd take it.'

'Really? Wasn't it you who suggested the climbing accident? We both know it was.'

'That was different, and directly related to the build. Without Jonathan's money, I'd have gone bankrupt, and you'd have lost your cut.'

'I need you to remain calm,' Payne told him. 'The police have no proof of any impropriety on our part. What they do have is circumstantial and gathered from people existing in the city's gutters.'

'I'm getting out while I can,' Hames said.

'That won't be possible. You're already in way too deep.'

Hames turned side-on to her. 'That's where you're wrong. Come with me. There's something I want to show you, a couple of floors below us.'

It was well after dark when they got to Aggy's place – a four bedroom terraced house divided into separate flats.

'Is this it?' Mali asked?

Cullinane rechecked his bearings. 'I've only been here once before, but I'm pretty sure it is.'

'There's only one way to find out.' She approached the front door and gave it a push. 'Locked.'

'Try the buzzer.'

'The buttons don't have the tenants' names, only flat numbers.'

'I didn't go in last time.' Cullinane reached past her and pressed the button labelled *Flat 1*. 'We'll have to work our way through them.'

There was no reply.

'Do you think that was Aggy's?' Mali asked, chomping on her worn fingernails.

Cullinane shrugged, reached again, and pressed the button for *Flat 2*.

'Hello.'

'Hello back,' Mali said, giving him a thumbs-up. 'We're friends of Aggy. Could you let us inside, please?'

'No.'

'I said we're Aggy's friends.' There was silence. 'Hello. Did you hear me?'

'Yes.'

'Can you open the front door, then?'

'No.'

Mali aimed a boot at it but didn't deliver. 'Have you seen Aggy at all today? Hello. *Hello.*' She turned to face Cullinane. 'Stupid cow's gone.'

'Two to go,' he said, already stretching for the button for *Flat 3*.

Mali knocked his hand out of the way. 'Let me have a go. You're nothing but bad luck.' She skipped a button and went straight for *Flat 4* instead. 'Hello, we're Aggy's friends. We've popped round to see her, but she's not answering.'

There was a beep before the front door clicked open.

'We're in,' Mali said, leading the way.

'But we still don't know which flat is hers.'

Mali stared at him. 'There are only two choices when we get there. How difficult can it be?'

Chapter 69

MAKING THE CORRECT CHOICE wasn't at all difficult. *Flat 1*'s door was ajar. There was no light sneaking around it. 'I reckon it's this one,' Mali said, poised to enter.

Cullinane tugged her shoulder. 'Don't go in there. Hemlock could be waiting for you?'

'If he is, and he's hurt Aggy, then I deserve everything that comes my way.' She took him by the hand. 'I shouldn't have involved either of you in this. It isn't your fight.'

He stared deep into her eyes. 'I've been running away from things all my life. Trying to pretend they never happened. You've taught me that wasn't the right thing to do. I'm staying with you on this, whether you like it or not.'

Mali pushed the door. There was no resistance from the other side. 'Aggy, it's Mali and Cory. The police are on their way,' she added as a bluff. 'They'll be here any minute now.' She tried the light switch and was relieved when the bulb illuminated above them.

There was no mistaking the fact that a struggle had recently taken place in the room. The bedding was untidy. Pillows and quilt dragged onto the floor. A table lamp lay on its side with its fabric shade dented. A chair rested on its back. But there was no sign of Aggy.

Cullinane went over to the table and picked up a folded sheet of paper. 'It's got your name on it,' he said, looking ever more worried.

Mali held out her hand. 'Give it to me.'

'What does it say?'

'They've got her. They've got Aggy.'

Cullinane took the note and read it for himself. 'You can't. Promise me you won't.' He followed her out of the flat and downstairs to the hallway. 'Don't go there. It's a trap.'

Mali was already jogging along the pavement. 'You read what it says. If I don't go there, they're going to kill her.'

<hr>

'What is it you want to show me?' Payne said, unable to hide her mounting irritation.

'We're almost there,' Hames replied, sweeping back a length of plastic sheeting that hung from the ceiling to the floor. He clapped his hands, wiping cement dust from his gloves. 'I've had a couple of my men prepare the perfect solution to all our problems.'

Payne stared at several large containers. 'What are they?'

Hames stood next to them like a proud father introducing his children. 'We're going to burn the place down. Burn it down and collect on the insurance.'

'Have you gone mad?'

'We're financially ruined,' he told her, placing a cigar lighter on top of a stack of bagged cement. 'This place is finished. *We'll* be finished. It's the only way,' he said, dragging one of the containers over to the steps. 'Everything below this level has had its final fix and fit. There's plenty that'll burn down there.' He pushed the container over and stepped aside when its lid broke off, spilling its pungent contents into the dark void below.

'How could you be so stupid?' Payne asked through gritted teeth. 'Do you think they won't realise what you've done?'

'Doesn't matter,' he said, going for another container. 'That's the genius of this. Who's going to question arson in light of everything that's happened lately? This is our get out of jail card.'

'You fucking fool.' She swung an arm and slapped him across the face. 'You're a liability.'

He grabbed a handful of her fur coat and shoved her against the wall. 'In that case, there's only one way this is going to end. Too bad you won't be there to witness it.' He drew his arm back, the other hand gripping her throat. Preoccupied, he didn't hear the plastic sheeting shift until it was already too late.

Chapter 70

CULLINANE RACED THROUGH THE streets, headed for the drop-in centre. His ribs hurt and his cough did all it could to slow him down, but it was now a case of mind over matter. He had to be mentally strong and do all he could to help Mali. 'And Dale,' he told himself, pushing through the pain and fatigue.

By the time he got to the centre, he was wheezing and coughing like a forty a day smoker. He hung over one of the concrete bollards, spitting brownish-red phlegm. He vomited. Not much, as he hadn't eaten since first thing that morning. He straightened and tried to catch his breath. He was dizzy and used the bollard for support until he felt strong enough to walk the short distance to the door.

He pulled an edge of the towel from around his neck and used it to wipe his face and hair.

Charlie came straight over. 'Have they been at it again?' he asked, taking him by the shoulders. He let go and looked like he was readying himself to leave and sort out Hames's men.

'It's nothing like that,' Cullinane told him. 'Mali's in trouble. And Aggy.' He spent the next couple of minutes explaining the events of earlier that evening, briefly outlining what he knew of Tommy Hemlock, Bridget Payne, and her husband's death in North Wales. 'They'll kill her,' he kept saying. 'You've got to phone that detective and tell him to get across to the development site.'

Mali was already on the muddy side of the perimeter boarding, scared and wondering what might happen next. Were security in on it? If she ran across the quagmire to the building itself, would they give chase, or turn a blind eye, as they'd been told?

There was only one way to find out.

Into the glare of the lights, she stepped. Like a scene from a Colditz movie, waiting to be machine-gunned down by a soldier in the watchtower. She ran, slipping and sliding, losing her balance, then regaining it again. She snaked in and out of the excavators and wasn't far from the giant tarpaulins that hung from all sides of the building like an ill-fitting overcoat.

No one challenged her. She knew that wasn't necessarily a good thing. There was no obvious way in that she could see. She went round the other side wondering what point there was of telling her to get over there, only to deny her entry.

She needn't have worried. There was a padlock on the floor and a makeshift door wedged open. This was it. She was going in, not knowing if she would ever get out again.

———◆◇◆———

'Have you not gone home yet?' Reece asked. 'Come on, get out of here. Go see your mother.'

Jenkins raised a hand to shut him up and swivelled her chair to face the other way. 'Okay, thanks for that, Charlie. We'll be straight over. You and Cory stay put. You got me? I mean it Charlie. You leave things to us.'

'What did he want?'

She got to her feet and stuck an arm through the sleeve of her jacket. 'It's all kicking off on Hames's building site.'

Morgan and Ginge came over to listen.

What's up?' Morgan asked.

Jenkins fastened the bomber jacket's zipper. 'Longish story cut short: we need to get our arses in gear. I'll explain on the way.'

Reece stopped Morgan when she reached for her coat. 'Not you. You stay here.'

'But I thought—'

Reece turned away before she could finish. 'Ginge, you're with us. Sharpish.'

'Right you are, boss,' he said, catching his foot on the chair leg as he got up.

Reece grinned at him. 'More speed, less haste.'

'What shall I do?' Morgan called after them.

Reece stopped in the doorway to the landing. 'Chief Superintendent Cable wants to see you in her office.'

'The chief super? What for?'

'Make sure you go straight up.' Reece said no more and walked away.

Chapter 71

THEY WERE BACK ON the ninth floor where they'd started, Hames looking the worse for wear following his violent encounter with Tommy Hemlock. His long coat and suit jacket were lying on the cold concrete beside him.

Payne was busy issuing commands to Hemlock as he tossed a length of electrical cable over a piece of steel spanning the width of the room. He knotted a makeshift noose at the end of it and told her it was ready for use.

'Bridget. What the hell are you doing?' Hames gripped a shirt that was blood stained and missing several of its buttons. It gaped open in places, revealing areas of broken skin on his chest and neck.

Payne stepped out of his reach. 'You still haven't figured it out? You disappoint me. What did Jonathan ever see in you?'

'Bridget—'

She left him to his grovelling and pulled a sheet from what looked to be another pile of bagged cement or plaster. There was movement from the object. Not building materials, then. Aggy stared wide-eyed, unable to utter anything more than a moan from behind two layers of duct tape. She pressed her back against the upright of the seat in an attempt to get as far away as she possibly could.

'It goes like this,' Payne began, alternating her attention between Hames and Aggy. 'Douglas here was unable to complete his waterfront development and faced financial ruin and public humiliation.' She turned to Aggy. 'Enter you and your sort. *Rats!*' she shrieked, adding an exaggerated laugh. 'And what does one do with an infestation of vermin?' She paused for Aggy to answer, knowing fully well she couldn't. 'Fire. It works every time.'

Hemlock caught hold of Hames's kicking feet and dragged him over to the waiting noose.

'Bridget. *Bridget!*'

'Douglas, do stop whining like a child. I expected more of you.'

Hemlock looped the noose over Hames's head and pulled it tight at the neck until the property developer was forced to support himself on the tips of his toes.

Payne stood behind Aggy and rested her hands on her shoulders. 'Let's get back to our story, shall we?' She tapped Aggy's head. 'You were the first to realise what Douglas was up to and were going to the police before deciding you'd use him as a cash cow instead.' Payne came round the front to stoop and stare into Aggy's eyes. 'You were here tonight to negotiate the payment required to keep you quiet.'

Aggy shook her head and mumbled behind the tape.

Payne caught her by the chin and forced her head straight. 'This is my version of events, not yours.' She flashed a perfect smile. 'But Douglas couldn't have that. He could pay you tens of thousands and still risk the threat of you shooting your mouth off whenever you wanted more.'

Aggy rocked back and forth on the chair, mumbling and thrashing her head side-to-side.

Payne crossed the room and returned carrying a clear plastic bag. She dragged it over Aggy's head and used more duct tape to seal it at her neck. 'And so Douglas silenced you. Permanently.' Payne gave Hemlock the command to raise Hames's body and secure the cable so that he was held a few inches off the ground. 'Then, in a moment of deep remorse, he took his own life.'

Aggy sucked at the plastic bag, desperate for oxygen-rich air.

Hames rotated on the end of the cable, kicking and bucking with his face turning darker shades of purple.

That's when Mali Ingram stepped out of the shadows. 'There's just one problem with the ending,' she said. 'I'm here to spoil it.'

Chapter 72

MALI HAD SECONDS TO take in the environment and evaluate the danger it presented to her. At one end of the room was an almost-dead Douglas Hames, guarded by Tommy Hemlock. At the other were Aggy and Bridget Payne. Mali made her decision and ran at the politician, knocking her over and onto the concrete floor. She pulled at the bag on Aggy's head, but it wouldn't budge.

Hemlock was coming for her with a fearful look of menace about him.

She picked at the tape, but there wasn't enough time to undo it. She forced her fingertips into the bag, breaking through it in places. It was the best she could do under the circumstances.

Hemlock reached for her.

Mali ducked behind Aggy, and went running towards the wide steps leading up through the building. The last things she saw over her shoulder were Hames going still and Bridget Payne making her way towards the exit. 'I'll be back for you,' Mali called, disappearing into the dark stairwell.

⸻

Bridget Payne was taking no chances. There were sirens wailing in the distance, and she instinctively knew where they'd be headed. It was while she was passing the sixth floor and inhaling the noxious fumes from the spilled containers that an idea struck her. 'Good old Douglas,' she said, turning to go back up to the seventh. 'Perhaps you did have your uses after all.'

Most of the fluid had seeped into the concrete. Some of it had already evaporated. There were several other containers remaining, and none of them looked to be too heavy for her to overturn. If Hames was right, then the first six floors should burn well enough to leave no trace of anyone upstairs.

She repeated what Hames had done – loosened the lids and toppled them over. The cigar lighter was on the floor. Knocked there during the struggle with Tommy Hemlock. There were the echoes of shouting above her. Outside, the sirens were getting louder. She squatted and ignited the lighter's flame, quickly moving from one puddle to another when they roared to life with searing levels of heat.

Then she went down a floor, dragging one of the smaller containers with her. She poured fluid under the doors of several completed apartments, set it alight, and made her escape.

Mali's escape was nowhere near as simple. She was making her way up through the building with Tommy Hemlock in close pursuit. There was also the issue of Aggy having been left behind. Hames was a lost cause and had himself to blame for the fate that had befallen him.

Mali could see, smell, and feel the effects of a fire starting somewhere below the level she was on.

Hemlock might have been giving her fifteen to twenty years in age, but the man was fit, and closing on her. If she kept to her current strategy, she'd be done for.

She considered her strengths. It didn't take her long. Climbing was the sum total of them. Hemlock was no slouch in that regard. She remembered how easily he'd scaled the quarry face. But she remained the better of them and that might be enough to swing things in her favour.

She broke away from the stairwell. Went left and along a drafty and unfinished landing, swiping at cables, leaping over buckets and stored building materials. She had to get outside and climb down to Aggy's level. Once there, she had no clue what she'd do, given that the lower half of the building was ablaze and spewing copious amounts of black smoke and ash into the night air.

Chapter 73

Reece's Land Cruiser would have smashed through the barrier next to the security hut, had it been in the lowered position. It wasn't, and he passed straight through unhindered. The flames spewing from the waterfront development were clearly visible from where they were. 'Call it in,' he said. 'We're going to need every fire appliance in the city, as well as the *eye in the sky*. By that, he meant the Force helicopter.

Two security guards flagged them down. 'There's people inside,' one of them said once Reece's identity was known.

'Who and how many?' the detective asked.

'Douglas Hames and Bridget Payne.'

'Anyone else?'

The men stared at one another, the taller of the two looking like he wanted to break the silence.

Reece slammed the Land Cruiser's door. 'If there is and you don't tell me, then I'll be doing you both for manslaughter.'

'Another woman,' the taller man said. 'A rough-sleeper. Bridget had us let her in when she got here.'

'Nobody else?'

'No.'

'Are you sure about that?'

'As sure as I can be.'

'And what about you?' Reece asked the shorter of them. 'You don't agree with your colleague?'

'There was another man,' he blurted. 'Tall, with a beard. The type that looks like they shouldn't be messed with.'

'What the . . .' Jenkins said, pointing to an area just above the inferno. 'Someone's climbing out of a window.'

Mali estimated the drop to be just short of two hundred feet. She'd climbed higher structures in the past. Negotiated challenging overhangs and loose rock. But on every occasion, she'd been connected to someone else, via a safety line. And never once had there been hot flame licking at her arse.

It was beginning to rain. That wouldn't make her grip any easier. Her boots—not climbing shoes—were already having a tough time on the narrow ledge.

She was on the twelfth floor. It was easy enough to have worked that out. There was an information notice showing an - **8** - on the wall of the floor below Aggy's. Mali had counted three flights of steps, three times, before breaking off along the corridor to climb out of a window. The problem with that was, it had taken her around to the side of the building.

Hemlock hung out of the same window, swiping for her. He disappeared momentarily, only to return with an armful of makeshift missiles that he threw in her direction.

Mali moved further along the narrow ledge, but was not yet fully out of reach. Something caught her left shoulder and bounced into the air above her. Now it was falling towards her head—a sharp-pointed trowel—that missed by inches only.

The angle was making things difficult for Hemlock. He had to reach well out of the window, rotate his body, and then fling whatever it was he had in his hand. This time, it was a screwdriver that impacted the wall next to Mali's fingers, skidding off the surface to fall to the ground below.

There were blue lights beneath her. Lots of them. Partially obscured by smoke and flame. The roar of the fire was thunderous. The heat almost too much to bear. When she next looked, Hemlock was gone. Initially, she thought it was to rearm himself. When he didn't return, she knew it was in order to save his own neck.

331

⸺◈⸺

Reece waited while Jenkins answered her phone. There was a problem. That much was clear from her reaction.

'They want me at the hospital,' she said. Even in the darkness, the look of worry on her face was clear to see. 'Mam's taken a proper turn for the worse.'

Reece glanced at the burning building. 'Go. You need to be there.' He called a uniform over to where they were. 'Take DS Jenkins to the hospital. Sharpish.'

'Are you sure about me leaving?' she asked.

'Ginge is here with me. And there's plenty more help on the way,' he said over the noise of arriving sirens.

Jenkins left in what would have been a sprint were it not for the awful ground conditions.

Ginge stood in awe of the spectacle above them. 'There's no way she's getting down from where she is.'

'Fire and Rescue should be here anytime soon,' security said. 'We called them just before you got here.'

'They'll be too late,' Reece said. There was no way up that he could see from where he was. They needed ladders. Or something similar. He looked to his right—towards the nearest tower crane—and walked towards it. 'Does that long bit poking out of the front reach over here?'

'That's what it's there for.'

'Yes or no?'

'Yes.'

'And the keys are in that hut of yours?'

'That's right.'

'Go fetch them.'

Both men looked unsure. The taller one spoke: 'But Mister Hames will—'

Reece finished the sentence for him. 'Be dead in a few minutes' time. That's if he isn't already.'

The man went running off.

'What are you going to do?' Ginge asked.

'Take a crash course in crane driving,' Reece said, instantly regretting his chosen terminology.

Chapter 74

Jenkins rushed through the hospital corridors, her phone signal lost and found depending on where she was. 'It's Mam,' she told Cara Frost. 'I think this is it. I need someone with me when it . . .' She couldn't finish the sentence and ended the call prematurely. When the lift pinged on her floor, she was poised to run.

There was a huddle of people stood outside a cubicle on the ward.

'I'm Margaret's daughter,' Jenkins said, pushing her way between them. 'I came as soon as I could.'

A flustered staff nurse tried to usher her away.

A middle-aged man with greying hair and spectacles stopped her from doing so. 'I'm Doctor Gibson,' he said with a reassuring smile. 'I'm one of the Intensive Care doctors.'

'The consultant?' Jenkins asked.

'That's right.' He turned to the nursing staff. 'Is there an office I can use to speak with the family?'

'I'm all the family she has,' Jenkins said. 'My partner's on the way. She's a doctor too—in the mortuary—so nothing like this. I'm hoping she'll be able to explain everything you tell us.'

The consultant checked his watch. 'I really do have to go see another patient in a minute. If there's anything you don't understand, let the nursing staff know, and either myself or a colleague will pop up again when we can.'

<hr/>

Security was back with the key. Before Reece took it from him, he asked: 'I don't suppose you can work that thing?'

'I can't drive a car,' the man said. 'I use the bus.'

'What about you?' he asked the other one.

'There's no way you'd get me up there.'

'I'll have a go,' Ginge volunteered. 'I know you don't like heights.'

Reece's fear went well beyond a mere dislike. Abject terror better described it. He'd got himself stuck when climbing a rock face as a child and had to be talked down by several men from his village. He'd since regularly suffered with nightmares relating to the event. 'This is something I have to do,' he said, unlocking the entry door to the steps of the tower crane. He looked up and into the tunnel of steps rising above him. 'Come on, Reece,' he coached. 'You can do this.'

———•◦•———

Jenkins had never felt so frightened in all her life. Not even that time in Billy Creed's basement. She was trying to listen to what the consultant was saying, but simultaneously, not wanting to hear a word of what she was being told.

Margaret was dying. Because of a large pulmonary embolus blocking much of the blood flow to both of her lungs. With hindered forward flow, the blood was welling in the right side of her heart—creating a huge strain on it—putting it at risk of failing any time soon. Other organs of the body were showing signs of shutting down because of the massive insult. She'd been catheterised, but hadn't passed adequate volumes of urine for several hours.

'What would normally be the options?' Jenkins asked, just about holding it together.

'Clot busting drugs,' the consultant said. 'But we're unfortunately past that stage. Despite blood thinning medicines, the clot has rapidly progressed in size, and the clotting screens we've run are showing very abnormal results.'

'Could you do an operation?'

'The likelihood of Margaret surviving such an extensive procedure is extremely low. Even if we got her through the surgery, her stay in the ICU would be another huge battle for her to overcome. I don't believe it would be in her best interests to put her through something like that.'

'No,' Jenkins agreed, in a daze that was broken by a shrill and rapid-sounding alarm.

There was a knock on the door only moments later. A young Filipino nurse standing behind it when it opened. 'Doctor, they need you in the cubicle. The patient has gone into cardiac arrest.'

Chapter 75

MALI SWUNG HER LEGS and missed the metalwork of a fire escape bolted to the side of the building. It was of limited use to her. Even a few floors further down, the flames and smoke were now so thick, she'd have no chance of surviving them. She could, however, get to Aggy. But she needed to be quick.

The rain was falling heavier. The lights of the city—beautiful under different circumstances—little more than a kaleidoscopic blur.

She swung her legs again and managed to get one of them over the other side of the fire escape railing. She wrapped her ankles around it. 'Shit or bust,' she grunted, letting go of the handholds and forcing all her bodyweight over to her left. She slammed into the metalwork, winded. When she slipped backwards, she grabbed again, hanging one-handed with the best part of one-hundred and eighty feet of nothing between her and the ground.

The sharp edges cut into her hands.

The cold wind bit at them.

And the rain crept between her fingers, threatening what little grip she had.

Mali Ingram was on the verge of falling to her death.

―――――◄○►―――――

'Oh, shit! What was I thinking?' Reece said, ascending the rungs of the ladder. His eyes were closed. He was doing it by touch alone. The rain lashed down, and the wind made the structure sway. There were creaking noises. The sound of metal scraping against metal. So frightened was he that letting go and ending it all was an option worthy of consideration.

What would it be like when he got all the way to the top?

Then his mind started playing tricks on him. Had the weather forecasters said anything about lightning in the area? He was soaking wet and clinging onto a metal structure that was far taller than anything else in the area. 'If I survive this, I promise I'll start believing in God.'

He opened one eye to check the state of the building. It was worse than anything he could have imagined. He looked down and regretted it instantly. He forced himself to look again and saw some-

LIAM HANSON

one come running out the front of it. Even from where he was, he recognised the puffball of fur as Bridget Payne.

He wrestled his phone from his pocket and leaned into the structure, gripping it one-handed for all he was worth. He thumbed his PIN and scrolled his contacts. 'Ginge,' he said, when his junior answered. 'Arrest Payne. Don't take any of her bullshit. Arrest her and put her in a cell until I get there.' He hung up, and was knocked sideways by another gust of wind, his phone falling from his hand.

He looked up. The platform to the crane's cab was still another fifty or more feet away.

———◦———

There was a chaotic scene playing out in Margaret's cubicle when they got there. Someone was kneeling on the bed, counting aloud while they performed chest compressions. Someone else held a breathing mask to Margaret's face, squeezing one-hundred percent oxygen from a clear bag. Another was connecting Margaret to something Jenkins recognised as a defibrillator. She'd had basic training on one during a first aid course she'd attended sometime in the past.

Someone tried to get her out of there.

'I'm staying,' she said. That wasn't up for negotiation.

'Stop a moment,' the consultant told them. 'I want to see what rhythm we have.' He went round the front of the defibrillator to take a better look. Then reached under Margaret's nightdress to feel

340

for the femoral artery in her groin. 'It's a PEA,' he said, voicing each individual letter in turn. 'Pulseless Electrical Activity,' he repeated for anyone who didn't understand.'

More people were arriving in the cubicle, including an anaesthetist, who took over from the nurse with the breathing mask and bag.

'Margaret's heart isn't beating, despite it having electrical activity,' the consultant told Jenkins. 'I'm very sorry, but there's nothing else we can do.' He turned to the team and spoke loud and clear: 'This lady's cardiac arrest is due to an unsurvivable pulmonary embolism. Any further resuscitation attempt would, therefore, be both futile and not in her best interests. Unless anyone present disagrees, I'm calling it.'

No one did disagree. The nurse stopped compressing the chest and got off the bed.

The anaesthetist turned off the oxygen supply and hung the bag and mask on the wall.

'Time of death is eight twenty-three,' the consultant said, checking his watch. 'May you rest in peace, Margaret.'

The room went deathly quiet.

But only until Jenkins started screaming.

Chapter 76

MALI DIDN'T WANT TO die. Not when she was so close to getting even with Bridget Payne. Aggy was still inside the burning building, bound to a chair, and with a plastic bag stuck over her head. She couldn't be sure how effective the holes she'd torn in the front of it might be. If not effective at all, then the *Big Issue* seller was already as dead as Douglas Hames.

Mali grabbed for the railing with the other hand and knew she had only one chance at this. Bending her knees, she drew her legs up under her, bringing her rate of breathing under control. She took herself back to the days on the rock faces of home. Somewhere familiar. 'You can do this,' she said, pulling herself up and towards the horizontal surface of the fire escape. She dragged herself onto it and lay there on her belly.

There was no time to waste. Rest would come later. Once they were both safe. She got to her feet, unsteady and exhausted, coughing and spitting in the billowing smoke. The surrounding heat had intensified. She found the window she'd escaped from and counted down to where she knew Aggy was. The flames were now only a single floor below that. She descended the steps of the fire escape and pulled on the door leading back into the building. It refused to budge. For reasons of security, it could only be opened from inside. 'I don't believe this,' she said, having no option other than to once again shimmy along the narrow ledge.

<hr />

Reece opened the cab door and swore so loudly they might have heard him on the ground well below. He didn't know what he'd been expecting to find up there, but it certainly wasn't this. The cab was full of levers, and buttons, and small television-type monitors. It looked to him as though he'd ventured onto the flight deck of a holiday jet.

There was only one place the key would fit. Small mercies and all that. He sat down in the operator's seat, inserted and rotated the key. Everything in the cab came to life. Lights. Monitors. The whole damn lot.

The crane moved. By a few inches only. But even that was enough to unnerve him. 'Jesus, what's happening?' he said, gripping the first thing he could get his hands on. He screwed his eyes closed and swallowed sour bile. He opened them again. One at a time. 'They don't pay me enough for this shit.'

The building was over his left shoulder. He could see it only if he forced himself. To get there meant swinging the long bit of the crane—he still didn't know its proper name—by about one hundred and seventy degrees from where he currently was.

Two short control sticks stood proud in front of him. One by his left knee, the other next to his right. One of them would command all horizontal movement of the *long bit*. The purpose of the other, he hadn't yet worked out.

On the basis that right-handed people outnumber their left-handed counterparts, he began with the right stick. There was a whirring sound, but no movement of the cab. A wheel rotated on the other side of the glass, spooling out a long length of cable and whatever was fastened to it. Wrong one. He pulled the same stick towards him, winding in some of the cable.

'Okay,' he said, feeling like he might be getting the hang of things. 'If that one operates the winch, then this one here must move me about my axis.' He caught hold of the left stick and angled it away from him.

Chapter 77

MALI HADN'T FALLEN FROM the ledge. She'd made it back inside, unscathed. The heat coming through the concrete floor could be felt through the thick soles of her boots. It was cracking in places—like tarmac baking during a balmy summer—and making worrying noises. She knew the Twin Towers in New York had collapsed during the burn, and wondered for how much longer the waterfront development might hold out.

She had to crouch to keep her head lower than the smoke creeping along the ceiling above her. 'Aggy, I'm coming for you.' She knew Hemlock was in there somewhere. Waiting in the shadows. Poised to pounce. There was no way he could have got out of the building. Not with the fire raging like it was.

Aggy was moving. Strapped to the chair still, but alive and breathing. Mali snatched a trowel from a dirty bucket and used its thin edge to saw through the plastic ties at Aggy's wrists and ankles. She pulled her to her feet, but the *Big Issue* seller's legs were too unsteady and she fell onto her knees and then over on her side again. Mali stooped to help her up. Caught her under the armpit and heaved. Next, she peeled at the duct tape.

Aggy's eyes bulged. She licked her lips, wetting them enough to speak. 'He's behind you!' she croaked.

<hr>

Reece had seen someone skirt the outside of the building and then re-enter it via a missing window. It had to be Mali Ingram. There would be few other people in the area with the skills required to undertake such a dangerous climbing manoeuvre. She must have gone back in to rescue someone. Either that, or she intended to get onto the roof to be rescued.

Reece checked what he could of the sky outside. Where the hell was that helicopter? He tapped his pockets and remembered his phone taking a tumble. It would be in bits and completely useless if ever found.

The crane was taller than the building was high. Believing Mali to be heading for the top floor, he swung the long end to his left. When the cab turned side-on to the wind, it was caught in its full buffeting effect. Terrified the whole tower crane was about to topple over and crash to the floor, he took his hands off the controls and withdrew into his seat. He couldn't move. Couldn't speak. He was alone, incapacitated, and very much out of the game.

———◦———

Mali ducked, swivelled, and swept at the air behind her with everything she had. The trowel sliced easily through the front of Tommy Hemlock's neck, spraying her face and hand with his warm blood.

He grabbed for the gaping wound, not her, hopelessly trying to stem the flow from the pulsing red jet. He staggered backwards, his clothing already soaked, uttering something that didn't come out right. His knees buckled. One arm pointed at her, accusingly. Then he slumped forward and faceplanted onto the cracked concrete.

Aggy was screaming. And far louder than she had been.

Mali tried to calm her down, but with little success. 'We need to go,' she said, shaking her by the shoulders. 'We have to get onto the roof. It's our only chance.' She was about to leave when she heard something outside. She put a hand over Aggy's mouth to silence her. They went to the window and waved madly at the arriving helicopter. 'We're going to get out of this alive. I promise you,' she said, steering Aggy towards the smoking stairwell.

The noise the building was making was a warning of its imminent collapse. Mali didn't need the opinion of a structural engineer to realise that. She forced Aggy up the stairs until they came to a door blocking their way. 'No, no, no,' she said, pressing her full weight against the horizontal bar. The door clicked open and swung outward, exposing them to the rain, and powerful downdraft from the aircraft's rotors. A bright spotlight followed them across the flat roof.

Mali could no longer hear anything the building said; its voice drowned out by the deafening noise coming from only a few metres above. Someone spoke through a public address system, instructing them to lie down where they were.

Aggy wasn't listening. She was in a state of shock. Mali pulled her face-down in a puddle.

They were soaked.

Exposed.

And not yet completely safe.

Chapter 78

IT TOOK TWO FIREFIGHTERS and the best part of forty minutes to get Reece down from the cab of the tower crane. An almost carbon copy of his experience as a child, and no doubt, the subject of many a bad dream to come. He was embarrassed and considered himself a joke and a failure.

The general topography of the development site had prevented fire crews from getting their appliances close enough to use ladders. The threat of the building collapsing on them had also played a factor in the helicopter quickly becoming the only possible means of escape.

'You did well to get up there in the first place,' Ginge said. 'Don't be so hard on yourself.'

Reece couldn't disagree more. 'You arrested Payne, like I told you to?'

Ginge said he had. 'She claimed Tommy Hemlock had kidnapped her. That he and the girl had killed her husband and now wanted her dead as well.'

'She can save it for the judge and jury,' Reece said. 'Have you heard anything from Jenkins? I lost my phone up there.'

Ginge checked his. 'Nothing,' he said, closing the screen.

The blanket around Reece's shoulders came free and slipped to the floor. He picked it up and gave it to someone sitting in the back of a waiting ambulance. 'I'm all right now,' he told them. To Ginge, he said: 'Where did the helicopter go?' It was nowhere to be seen.

'They took both survivors straight across to the hospital,' Ginge told him. 'Simpler that way than trying to find a place to land here and then take them by road.'

'I'll pop over there and see what's what,' Reece said.

'Bridget Payne?' the young detective called after him. 'What do you want to do with her?'

'She can wait in the cells till morning.'

'And me?'

'You can go home and enjoy what's left of the evening. I'll see you in the morning.' Reece started the Land Cruiser and pulled away.

At the hospital, he first checked on the status of Mali and Aggy. Neither of them was fit to give a statement as yet. Even Mali was overwhelmed with shock now that she'd had time to reflect on the harrowing incident. He left a couple of uniformed officers with them and promised to return as soon as they felt ready to speak.

He found Jenkins in the relative's room on the ward. She was alone with a cup of tea, and a box of paper tissues on her lap. He held his arms wide open. 'Elan, I'm so sorry.' He was crying, and now he'd started, he couldn't stop.

She accepted his embrace and rested her head on his chest. 'There was nothing else they could do for her in the end.'

He wiped his nose on the back of his hand and rubbed his eyes. 'It happened so quickly.'

She broke away to offer him a box of tissues. 'Take some of these.'

He helped himself to a handful. 'Look at me,' he said, blowing his nose. 'I'm supposed to be here to support you.'

'You are,' she said. 'And more than you'll ever know.'

He doubted that.

Cara Frost appeared in the open doorway. 'I came as soon as I got your message. How is Margaret?'

'Read the room,' Jenkins told her. 'You're too late. I shouldn't have called you in any case. It was a moment of weakness on my part.'

'I should go,' Reece said. 'And leave the two of you to talk.'

'You stay.' Jenkins moved around him and stood in front of Cara Frost. 'I never want to see you again. Get out of here.'

Frost turned and left with no further argument.

'What happens now?' Reece asked.

Jenkins puffed her cheeks. 'I meant every word of what I said. That woman had better stay out of my way.'

'With your mother?'

'Oh, sorry.' Jenkins went back to her seat. 'They're giving her a freshen-up wash. I can go back in as soon as they're done.'

'Would you like me to go in with you?' Reece asked.

She stared at him. 'You'd do that?'

He fought back more tears. 'There's no way I'd let you go through this alone.'

Chapter 79

IT WAS FIRST THING Saturday morning and Reece had called the team into work. Everyone except Jenkins. There were a few loose ends to tie up. A couple of matters still to be dealt with.

Bridget Payne was one such loose end.

'You couldn't help yourself,' Reece said. 'Like all your type, you craved more, and took it at the expense of others.'

'You have no proof of any involvement on my part, Chief Inspector. I'm as much a victim in all of this as my poor husband was.'

'Don't give me that.'

'And had that awful creature survived to be interviewed,' Payne continued, 'then I'm sure the truth would out.'

Reece got up and went over to the door of the interview room. He opened it and let Mali Ingram show herself from the corridor outside. 'She looks good for a corpse, don't you think?'

Payne's lower jaw fell open. 'It'll be my word against hers,' she blurted. 'And we all know which way that will go.'

'There was another survivor,' Reece said. He hadn't brought Aggy with him. She remained too traumatised for that. 'Someone who'll testify to you having Tommy Hemlock murder Douglas Hames. And to you, personally, trying to kill her.'

'I don't know what these vagrants claim to have happened, Chief Inspector, but—'

Reece raised a hand and cut in. 'Your bank records have been released to a team of forensic accounting specialists. I'm expecting them to find plenty of evidence supporting abuse of position for your own financial gain. We've also been in contact with the CPS regarding the deaths of your husband and a Rhydian Bale in North Wales. New investigations will commence for both cases.'

Payne sat in silence.

'I can also tell you that Lisa Jones has been found alive and has an interesting tale to tell about your accomplice, Tommy Hemlock. It's also my best guess the forensic team will uncover evidence of arrogant complacency on your part, showing payments to Hemlock for services rendered.' Reece leaned on the table. 'With all due respect – you're fucked!'

When he got back upstairs, there were more people present than he'd expected there to be. 'What's going on?' he asked Chief Superintendent Cable. He nodded towards Superintendent Piper. 'And what's she doing here?'

'I know you wanted to deal with this your way,' Cable said. 'But Ginge presented himself this morning and has admitted everything.'

'Where is he?' Reece asked.

'In your office.'

'I want to see him.'

Cable nodded. 'He wants to see you, too.'

Reece made his way across, not sure of what he was going to say. He hadn't expected it to end like this and had nothing prepared. Ginge stood on first sight of him. Reece closed the door. It was just the two of them. 'Why?'

'I had no choice.'

'There's always a choice,' Reece told him. 'Some might be more difficult than others, but they're there all the same.'

Ginge shook his head. 'Not in my family. You're either in or you're out.'

'Your uncle put you up to this, didn't he? Heaped pressure on you and made you throw away your career to get back at me.'

'I can't talk about that.'

'Can't or won't? If he's threatened you, I can help.'

'It's over, boss. I'm done.'

'It doesn't have to be,' Reece said. 'We can sort something out. You're a good copper.'

Ginge stopped him. 'The irony in all of this is, I never wanted to be one in the first place. I was made to join the Force. Used as a pair of eyes and ears on the inside. I'm not proud of what I've done and I'm genuinely sorry for all the trouble I caused you.' He opened the office door and called to Superintendent Piper. 'I'm ready.' And with that, he left without looking back.

Reece swung a kick at his bin, sending it crashing against the opposite wall. 'What a bloody waste.'

By the time Jenkins wandered in, everything was back to normal again in the incident room. She went over to Morgan—who was busy typing—and put a hand on her shoulder. 'Morning.'

'What are *you* doing here?' Morgan got up and gave her a big hug. 'I'm so sorry to hear about Margaret.'

They let go of one another. Jenkins put a fist to her mouth and composed herself. 'Maybe it was the best outcome in the end. At least Mam had most of her dignity left.'

'I don't know what to say. It must be awful for you. Can I get you a cuppa?'

Jenkins declined the offer. 'It's only a fleeting visit,' she said, opening her desk drawer and reaching for the white envelope. 'There's something I have to tell the boss.'

Chapter 80

Reece hadn't slept at all well. There was far too much on his mind. Even Redlar was restless; no doubt picking up on his master's vibes. Admitting defeat, they'd gone for their morning run an hour earlier than usual.

He was ready when Yanto arrived some time later, and had been for a good while. 'At least it's dry for it,' Reece said, taking the dog inside the cottage before locking up.

Yanto put their rucksacks and other belongings in the back of his Land Rover Defender. 'It had to stop sometime.' He slammed the door shut. 'Are you okay?'

Reece wasn't, but nodded. 'Bearing up,' he said. There were mixed emotions flooding his system. Today was a stark reminder of mortality – of those the Reaper saw fit to take and the ones it left behind. But the Reaper caught up with everyone in the end. Reece knew that for sure.

The area outside the Storey Arms in Brecon was packed with the usual weekend warriors. Ants trailing their way from the car park to the summit of Pen y Fan – stopping along the way to snap photographs like a bus-load of Japanese tourists.

'Let's get in front of this lot,' Reece said, quickening the pace.

The route took them past the Tommy Jones memorial: an obelisk erected by the people of Brecon in 1902, in memory of the missing five-year-old later found dead on the mountain. They stopped to read the inscription, as they always did, with their woolly caps held at waist level.

Reece was already tearful.

Yanto lay a hand on his shoulder but said nothing.

Onward they went.

Mostly in silence and constantly buffeted by the wind.

And then they were there. On the summit itself.

Yanto found a place to sit, leaving Reece to his private thoughts and rituals.

'There's so much to tell you this time,' Reece said, getting up off his knees. People stared in his direction, but he didn't give a damn what they thought. He dried his eyes and took a deep breath, standing on the exact spot he'd scattered Anwen and Idris's ashes.

He told Idris about Ginge's uncle and the hold he had over the young detective constable and his family. 'They've thrown the book at him,' Reece said. 'I asked Cable if we could help him in some way. But as she pointed out, no one would ever trust him again. Shame that. He'd have gone places in the Force.'

He rescued a stray flower and lay a small rock across the stems to better weigh them down. 'I brought your favourite colours,' he told Anwen. 'Yellows and purples.'

'Jenkins's mother died on Friday. Of complications following hip surgery.' He looked over at Yanto, who nodded and raised his coffee.

'Good news about the drop-in centre,' Reece said. 'Not only is it staying put, but the Welsh Assembly Government has pledged to refurbish it. As well as make a donation in the memory of Dale Lynch, Abeeku Quaye, and his girlfriend. We're still trying to get a name and family details for her.'

He felt better now and managed a smile. 'Mali Ingram is on her way back to North Wales with Cory Cullinane in tow.'

Yanto approached when beckoned and paid his own private respects before the pair of them left for home.

They were already halfway down the mountain when Reece realised he hadn't told Anwen and Idris about the contents of Jenkins's envelope. 'Oh, well,' he said, continuing along the well-trod path. 'Maybe there's still time to make her see sense.'

About the Author

Liam Hanson is the crime and thriller pen name of author Andy Roberts. Andy lives in a small rural village in South Wales and is married with two grown-up children. Now the proud owners of a camper van nicknamed 'Griff', Andy and his wife spend most days on the road, searching for new locations to walk Walter, their New Zealand Huntaway.

If you enjoy Andy's work and would like to support him, then please leave a review in the usual places.

To learn of new releases and special offers, you can sign up for his no-spam newsletter, found on his Facebook page:

https://www.facebook.com/liamhansonauthor

Printed in Great Britain
by Amazon